When danger hides in plain sight.

When Danny turned to Moira in the kitchen after dinner, and she bounced off his chest, this time, he caught her. The heat flying between them had been nearing an inferno. They'd talked and laughed like normal people having dinner, but the looks they'd shared had been so hot, the flames engulfed them.

He'd known cleaning up the dishes—few as there were since they'd had takeout—would be a good excuse to get close to her, to touch her hand when handing off dishes to dry. And he knew that bumping into her could also be an option. Case in point.

He held her arms tightly against him. He heard, rather than felt, the hitch in her breathing. It fed his desire to take her to bed. And it was damn time he did that with her.

"If you don't want this," he said in a hoarse voice, "now is the time to speak up."

With her adorable Irish accent, she said, "Aye, I want this."

Titles by Sheila Kell

H I S SERIES

His Desire

His Choice

His Return

His Chance

His Destiny

His Family

His Heart

His Fantasy

A Hamilton Christmas

AGENTS OF H I S

Evening Shadows

Midnight Escape

MIDNIGHT ESCAPE

AN AGENTS OF HIS NOVEL

SHEILA KELL

Cunningham Publishing

MIDNIGHT ESCAPE

PUBLISHER: CUNNINGHAM PUBLISHING

EDITOR: HOT TREE EDITING

COVER AND INTERIOR DESIGN: RMGRAPHX

ISBN 9780999249697 (Electronic copy)

ISBN 9780578637938 (Paperback copy)

Printed in the United States of America

To

Jamie McDowell Reinhardt—AJ's biggest fan

You're the first reader to have a tattoo of my book.

I'll always remember that.

Acknowledgments

I had some unique help while writing *Midnight Escape.* First, I had to learn how to handle a helicopter emergency. Not personally, but how to describe it for my readers. Thankfully, Wayne Breeden, Chief Pilot at Helicopters, Inc., in Memphis, Tennessee, came to my rescue. His experiences drove my decision on the type of emergency for Danny to handle.

Second, I had to learn all things Irish. Well, enough for an Irish character in the U.S. Again, someone came to my rescue. Actually, two people. Both Natasha Maher and Maria McHugh helped me understand Irish slang and sayings. Oh, and a bit of Irish Gaelic also. I hope I was able to explain all Irish terms or phrases within the scenes.

Next is the best cover designer ever. RMGraphX took my ideas and, once again, put together a cover that made me say "Wow." The cover is Danny's story in one picture.

As always, my work cannot be complete without Becky Johnson and her team at Hot Tree Editing. I enjoy the interactions with my post-beta readers: Crystal Earl, Franci Neill, Kim Deister, and Robert Holland. Their commentary and suggestions have me laughing most of the time. Every now and then they give me a thumbs down on something I wrote that I thought was extraordinary. All in all, they are the best next to last step.

The last step before RMGraphX formatted *Midnight Escape*, Rebecca of Rebecca's Fairest Reviews gave the manuscript a tight proofread. She's a great addition to my group.

Finally, and several steps above, I have four ladies whom I adore and have done their best to help make sure this is a brilliant story. My pre-beta readers—Linda Dossett, Helen McNabb, Lily Greer, and Jessica Neuhart are amazing. I don't envy them as they read my story before I send it to the editor. I wouldn't have made it forward without their input. My deepest appreciation.

Chapter One

BALTIMORE, MARYLAND

Danny Franks's calm shattered at an audible pitch that signaled the helicopter rotors slowing while in midair. The Q and A between him and his FAA examiner ended abruptly as Danny's check ride took a deadly turn.

Allowing Wayne Singleton, his examiner, to plummet four hundred feet and die in a fiery crash would guarantee a failure of his private pilot license test. Not that he'd need it at that point either.

As a former DEA agent and current HIS agent—an elite security organization—he'd faced death on more than one occasion, but he'd always had wits and access to a weapon to protect himself, whether it be a rifle, a handgun, a knife, or whatever he could find close at hand—and there was always something or a teammate near. Now, however, he only had his wits and instincts to safely land the 1676-pound aircraft on the outskirts of Baltimore, allowing them to both walk away unscathed.

Even though hardened to danger, fear jolted his system, his gut clenched, and his heart pounded painfully and with frightening speed, setting his nerves on edge, ensuring he was indeed still alive. He'd been trained to control the impulses in his body and mind enough to act with calm and precision. At the moment, he couldn't harness that control. With the sick feeling washing through him, he fought the internal battle to clear his mind and hone his senses to the current challenge.

Slowing rotors was enough trouble, but he knew other trouble could exist. Wayne surely expected him to handle this and would only assume control if Danny was headed toward death, instead of a safe landing. A nervous *Can you really land?* slipped into his mind as his conscience rightfully questioned his ability. As a bead of sweat formed on his temple, his first instinct of *What the hell did I get myself into?* gave way to a *Hell, yes, I could land this baby,* in his mind's response.

With crystal clear focus, Danny immediately recognized the nature of the emergency. Ironically enough, he and Wayne were on their way to the airfield to simulate the autorotation and power failure problems they faced. Whereas, he'd have simulated the power loss and conducted a power recovery at three feet above ground level, without actually landing and not having the engine truly fail, he had to put the bird on the ground and in a hurry.

"There's no RTB. Can you handle it?" Wayne asked without any inflection in his voice. Although his need to state the obvious that they couldn't "return to base" annoyed Danny. Yet he wasn't a licensed pilot. Wasn't the man worried? They were awfully close to the ground, with no room for error. Any wrong action meant their death. *No pressure.*

The craziness that had immediately happened inside him steadied. Firmly and without hesitation, he responded with "Roger." The determined side of him vowed he would land this helicopter, without the examiner assuming control.

In an instant, every action necessary for recovering the aircraft breezed through Danny's mind. First and foremost, he had to avoid a full rotor stall since there would be no chance of recovering control of the helicopter. He had the training to prevent that deadly situation, and, while he'd never hoped to have the problem outside of simulation, he could manage it. Experience had taught him the next few seconds would move swiftly but feel like a lifetime.

With the power slowing in the engine—it no longer controlled the rotors—he faced another major challenge. He'd lost all torque. Losing the force that produced, or tended to produce, rotation, reinforced the danger to them.

After long hours of studying, hours of flights in a

simulator and then with an instructor, a grueling oral exam, and required hours of solo time, he knew he could manage this emergency. Heart pumping with adrenaline and a bit of fear, he vowed dying wasn't in his plans for the day.

Comfort with the Erstrom 480B allowed him to tackle the task at hand with expert actions. They had probably seven seconds before they would impact with the ground. With no airport in the vicinity, and no tower control, he quickly scanned the area for a safe place to land. They were over a fucking forest. There had to be something, or he may as well just let them drop like a rock as it'd have the same end result.

From his training manual, the words on the page on this situation flashed in front of him as if he'd had the paper there. *"In all cases, correct glide angle has the effect of producing an upward flow or air to spin the main rotor at some optimal rpm—storing kinetic energy in the blades—and slow descent using the stored up kinetic energy in the rotors—if done perfectly, the landing will be quite gentle by executing a flare, pitching the nose up at the right moment.... This will also have the effect of transferring some of that energy from the forward momentum into the main rotor, making it spin faster, which will allow for a smooth landing."*

All that gibberish had once meant nothing to him, and he knew that to most non-aviation individuals, it probably still did, but after a while, he'd understood, and the knowledge had been ingrained in him, so he would automatically react to save the aircraft and passengers. He had to keep the nose down—enough to keep air flowing to optimize the rotation speed so they'd have a chance to land—but not too much, so he couldn't recover enough to land on the skids. Softly.

Okay, he told himself. *Time to get this show on the road.* Registering the winds about ten knots, he didn't overly worry about their impact on landing. His white-knuckle grip on the cyclic pitch control, or joystick to video game advocates, that in layman's terms was his steering stick, gave the appearance his life depended on it. Who was he kidding? It did. With his left hand grasping the collective pitch control, similar to the old emergency brakes where the handle pulled up to lock, he got down to business working the two controls, so the revolutions per minute of the rotors remained fast enough to avoid the deadly stall, plus gave them enough time to land. *Softly*, he reminded himself. He'd have scoffed if had a second to do so.

He continued to assess the area, hoping for a clear spot to land. With a shot of relief, he caught sight of a clear area nearby. Mostly clear. Enough that they could land this bird. If he could make it that far.

The dive he held dropped their altitude rapidly, which limited the distance they could travel. It'd be tough, but he wouldn't give up. The alternative was to crash into the forest, which dramatically reduced their chances of survival.

With confidence—and knowing it to be their only option to survive—he moved the cyclic to the right, ultimately turning the helicopter to the right to clear the forest and make for the level ground. His destination would be in the middle of someone's field, but he didn't care. With the power continuing to decelerate to nearly nothing, he had no other option than to nose the aircraft down a bit more to slow their glide speed.

While the ground closed in faster, a bead of sweat slipped down his temple as they approached the landing spot. To his dismay, the power continued to bleed out of the helicopter. He still had the ability to control it, but….

When his evaluator said, "You're doing great. Check your glide speed," Danny nearly jumped out of his harness.

He'd been so focused he'd forgotten he had a passenger. His mind couldn't register the fact Wayne not only praised him but hadn't taken control of the situation. Although, in his peripheral, Danny caught his examiner's hands hovering over his controls. He did, however, do as Wayne had said. Satisfied things were as they should be—with the exception of the necessary power and full rotor speed—he took a hasty glance at the control panel. They'd just passed below two hundred feet, and he couldn't fight the pounding of his heart in his chest.

When a wind gust hit them, giving the aircraft a slight push, an all-encompassing fear nearly took over as he knew he hadn't calculated for a change in the winds this close to the ground. If the wind kept gusting, it'd impact his split-second landing because he wouldn't level out in time.

Refusing to fail himself and his goal, he pushed the fear away and kept his hold on being calmly controlled. He had less than a few seconds before they met the ground. *Damn.* So little time.

With an acute sense of survival, he murmured, "Time to land this bird." The flare-out he needed to execute had to be somewhat dramatic. By bringing the nose up—not just level, but up—it put an immediate halt to his rapid descent before landing. The tricky part—extremely tricky—was making sure the rear of the helicopter didn't hit the ground before he leveled the helo to land. He'd successfully completed the maneuver several times in training, but he'd always had the knowledge that the power failure was not real and could be increased at any time to prevent a crash.

With a surprisingly steady hand that had led him this far, he pulled back on the cyclic and held his breath as he performed the flare-out maneuver. His heart lurched, attempting its jailbreak from his chest, that he had the rear of the helicopter closing in on the ground faster than the front. On purpose.

He half-expected Wayne to grab control from him, but he didn't. Danny suspected he had the reaction that many did when riding in a car with someone when they are catching up to a car too fast and automatically push on the passenger side floorboard as if engaging the brake. Self-preservation existed in everyone.

Almost wanting to close his eyes to concentrate even more on the hair's breadth of altitude left, his mind registered there wasn't enough clear land surrounding the field, so they'd land in the crop, but there was no other option. Slowly—yet rapidly, time wise—he leveled the aircraft and in what seemed like milliseconds, eased it down—foot by agonizing foot—until—with immense relief—the skids safely touched the ground with a small jolt.

Danny couldn't relax and expel that breath of relief yet as it wasn't over. "Go," he said to Wayne. "I've got this." Unclasping his seat harness with one hand, he fumbled with the controls with the other one, automatically shutting down the powerless engine.

As he shoved the belts, trapping in his shoulders, aside, he yanked off his headset, noted their location, and took a quick glance to ensure his passenger was exiting the aircraft. Of course, Wayne stayed to watch him perform the proper emergency shutdown procedures. At least he'd already rid himself of the harness. However, as the pilot-in-command, it was Danny's responsibility to see to his passenger's safety.

"Go," he demanded, as he grasped the door handle and pushed it open with a force that almost sent it crashing back into him. Although probably unnecessary, Danny wanted Wayne to evacuate in case their problem was more severe than thought to be and the bird caught fire.

He and Wayne hastily exited the aircraft, and meeting a safe distance away, eyed the front of the helo.

After confirming Wayne didn't require medical

attention, Danny continued following procedure, knowing not only that Wayne still evaluated him, but because his responsibility hadn't ended. After pulling his phone from his flight-suit pocket, he removed his flight gloves and called base operations. In a few moments, he'd relayed the nature of their emergency, souls on board, and their location via lat/long. After a confirmation of their response, he ended the call and expelled a breath of relief.

As the tense muscles in his shoulders eased, tremors overtook his body, and he didn't care what Wayne thought of it. He fought it, but he couldn't control the delayed terrifying reaction within him. He could've died. Strange how he'd never reacted this way when he'd been nearly killed in action with his employer Hamilton Investigation and Security, better known as HIS.

He hoped he'd be checked off on this procedure and not have to redo the actions in simulation. He never wanted to be a part of this nightmare again with the trapped feeling, knowing life or death settled with him, but he couldn't fight his way out. There'd been too little time while having too much time to think about life. While his mind had focused on landing the bird safely, in the back of his thoughts was what was important to him. He'd regret not having a family.

"Ten seconds."

Danny's mind had a tough time wrapping itself around Wayne's words. Ten seconds from the initial sound signaling a problem to setting them down on the ground? Impossible. Although he hadn't kept count, it had to have been longer. Or had it? Maybe that was just how it'd felt since so much rushed through his brain at mind-warping speed. If he was right—and the FAA examiner was always right—it'd been the longest ten seconds of Danny's life.

"You expertly handled the situation. And a nearly soft landing to boot. I never felt the need to take control."

Danny didn't know how the nearly soft landing happened—although that'd been his hope. The need to land before more trouble occurred had been his only requirement.

Thinking back, Danny's heart fell at his failure in his emergency procedures. "The transponder," he croaked. "I didn't—" He hadn't changed his transponder to the emergency code of 7700, so the tower would see them on radar and be prepared for an emergency landing. Even without being under tower control, their aircraft—a small blip on the screen—would flash to notify the controller. Although at their low altitude, it'd be iffy if the radar picked them up. Of course, he also didn't reach out to them via radio on VHF Guard, or 121.5 MHz, to declare an emergency and receive priority control.

Shit! He wanted to shout. After the sweat and terror—yes, inside suppressed terror had churned—he'd fail the examination anyway for not doing either.

"You didn't have time for either. If you had, we wouldn't have landed safely." Wayne paused. "Or, at all."

"But—" He knew Wayne was right, but he'd not

completed the proper procedures.

"Even I didn't have time. My focus had to be on whether I had to jump in before it was too late. I couldn't break away either or it might've been too late to react." Wayne shrugged. "Besides, as low as we were, they probably wouldn't have seen us on radar."

Well, they were on the ground. No need for the FAA to send out a search party. He'd notified base operations, so that should count as a point in his favor on the exam.

They'd survived. He couldn't think it enough. Like in the movies, he'd almost touched all over his body to ensure he remained in one piece. Sanity prevailed on that one since they hadn't wrecked.

Standing and staring blankly at the helicopter, Danny answered Wayne's questions about his actions and inactions during the flight. Why he took them? Why he didn't?

Neither had grabbed their flight bags, but Wayne had recorded their pre- and post-flight conversations to transcribe later. He assured Danny it'd be easier for the interviews and paperwork that'd have to be completed. Danny hated paperwork. Hated it with a passion.

We survived! broke into all thoughts again, bringing his mind back to the moment. Even wearing his aviators, the glint of the sun off the windshield of the bird that he'd landed without power, made him thankful the weather had been in their favor.

While he'd glanced at the crop, it hadn't registered, so he checked again to see what he'd have to replace. He nearly laughed. Being former DEA, he should've noticed immediately the type of plant. Then his body went on alert. *Shit.* "Wayne?" He slowly drew out the name and didn't really regard it as a question.

"I see."

Circling around, Danny ensured the field was clear around them with no visible structure or person in sight. "You call the sheriff. I've got another call to make."

Not arguing that Wayne should've been giving the orders, they both turned to their phones. Wayne dialed 911 while Danny hit speed dial.

Stone—Alpha team's new computer support—answered Danny's call before the first ring ended. "I was just about to check on you. Your name popped up on an aircraft landing."

Danny chuckled, despite the seriousness of his situation. A HIS program captured an agent's name when it popped into any emergency, hospital, or police report. At first, Danny hated the thought of being tracked, but now he appreciated it. If he hadn't been in a position to phone in, someone would've arrived to check on him. Family.

"I landed safely. My problem is we landed in the middle of a pot field and"—he squinted at spots afar, and his gut clenched— "I see a welcoming party coming our way."

Chapter Two

"Number?" Stone quickly responded.

Danny squinted harder to make out the number of dots in the distance as his mind raced on how to keep himself and Wayne safe, if this party turned into a threat. "One"—a ding sounded in his ear— "maybe two." Pulling the phone away, he glanced quickly at the screen and breathed a short sigh of relief that someone from the teams would respond to the emergency alert that Stone had just sent. Not knowing anyone's ETA, he had to plan to survive and protect his examiner. *Maybe*, his mind hoped, *they aren't armed.* He silently scoffed at that idea.

"Are you carrying?" Stone asked.

"Only my backup weapon in my ankle holster."

"Standby."

Danny wanted to reach out and choke Stone for that. He needed help now. Before the dot—which he expected was at least one ATV with the owner of this field aboard—reached them. And he believed the rider, or riders, would be armed. He focused on options of how he'd protect Wayne without cover. Except for something with a large gas tank on it.

"The sheriff's ETA is twelve minutes. Boss and Sugar's ETA is five, maybe four."

While Boss—Ken Patrick, HIS Alpha team leader—and Sugar—Samantha Patrick, former team sniper—were perfect backup, five minutes—even four—might be too late. He held confidence in his abilities as an agent, but this situation might test him.

"Armed?" Danny asked, meaning his boss and former teammate.

Stone snorted. "What a stupid question."

He'd realized that as soon as the words had left his mouth. Those two were always prepared. Especially after all they'd dealt with as agents.

Leaving the call open, Danny dropped his phone in his left pocket. The bird was the only possible shelter, but a stray shot to the gas tank concerned the hell out of him. Hoping the possible threat didn't carry rocket launchers—aware of the damage one would do—they had to take the chance and use the helo as cover. At least on the step with the doors open as protection. Their calves would be exposed, but it'd have to be a risk he'd take.

"You don't think that's a nice welcoming party?" Wayne's hopeful voice held a tinge of strength, which

Danny should've expected since the man had been a Navy pilot.

"Doubtful." Reaching down, Danny removed his weapon and checked the load. It shocked and pleased him when Wayne pulled a weapon from an ankle holster. He wanted to ask why his examiner carried a weapon on an examination, but he'd probably be asked the same question in return and wasn't prepared to answer.

"The bird's our only option," Wayne calculated. "It's not a good one."

"Agreed. Landing in this open field seemed like a good idea at the time."

"Hmph. No other choice existed." Wayne snapped his clip back into his weapon and pulled back the rack to load the chamber. "That is, if you wanted us to survive."

True, but he may've put them in a situation that reversed that outcome.

Engines revving drew closer and the two ATVs put distance between the vehicles, as if to surround them as only two threats could do. He and Wayne couldn't play stupid like they had no clue where they'd landed, but Danny had to try something. They couldn't run; they couldn't hide for long, and he didn't have a second clip.

"Use the bird for cover. I'm going to welcome our guests." Danny's firm voice made no difference to the former naval officer.

"I don't think so," Wayne argued.

"I need you taking pictures of who's approaching and shoot the pics off to the sheriff's department before we engage."

"I'd rather you went in the bird since I'm responsible for you."

"But, we're on the ground now. My agency is on the way and can handle what we can't. Now, take the damn pictures."

The reality must've penetrated Wayne's mind. "You know they might kill you before I can get what we need."

Danny didn't have to be told that. Still, one of them had to do it and standing here wouldn't provide enough time if a shootout or other unfortunate incident occurred. And, he'd be damned if he'd allow these men to get away with breaking the law and possibly murder. That shouldn't be his first thought, but it bled into his bones as the threat approached.

Lethal determination wove up his spine as he could make out the figures of three men—two on one vehicle and one on the other. Time would tell how this interaction played out. He needed Boss and Sugar now.

"Go," Danny ordered and tucked his weapon in his right flight suit pocket. Greeting the men with a weapon in his hand would surely bring trouble. More trouble than he wanted or needed.

"I still don't like it, but I agree we need to do it." Wayne shifted. "I'll still be backing you up and will be back out here once I've sent the pics off." His flight examiner hurried out of sight.

Narrowing his eyes, Danny made out the features of the men and their pissed expressions. His heart raced, and he took slow, calming breaths to keep control of his actions.

"I'm so glad you arrived." Danny shouted over the noise of the four-wheelers with fake relief in his voice. He waved his left hand in a hello gesture, keeping his right hand on his pocket, so he could quickly retrieve his weapon if needed. "I'm sorry I landed in your field, but my helicopter died. I sure could use a ride back to civilization." He hoped they hadn't made out Wayne, so the two trespassers would have an advantage.

With no answer, Danny swallowed, itching to draw his weapon, and tried again. "We called base ops, and they're on their way." The men tensed when he'd told them someone knew where they were. "I'm sorry if I landed here. I'll compensate for the crops I killed."

The riders disembarked, throwing their legs across the seats. Still on alert, Danny couldn't get a good look at the man on the back of one vehicle, but the hairs on the back of his neck stood at attention. When the man stepped in view with a shotgun held low at the man's side, Danny nearly drew his weapon. Only patience and training held him back, hoping to resolve the situation without gunfire.

The man didn't hold the weapon threateningly, so Danny remained still, somehow knowing Wayne had his back. Damn, he couldn't see all the men straight up unless he took his focus off the weapon.

Silence remained between his greeting party, and the tension from the three men held strong. The man with the shotgun never took his eyes off Danny, but through his peripheral vision, the other men scanned the area as if they expected someone to jump out and interfere. As one began to move toward the helo, Danny knew as soon as they tagged Wayne, their welcome would change.

Within moments of the man moving out of his sight, the click of the door opening sounded loudly in the still air. The man began yelling in Spanish that we'd reported them to the authorities. How he knew that, Danny had no clue, but he didn't have time to ponder it.

Adrenaline snapped into his veins as the man lifted the shotgun and, with what appeared to be menace, cocked the weapon, dropping the shell into the chamber. Without thought, Danny launched -himself sideways. He ignored the painful impact of his left shoulder and the ground, pulled his weapon and fired as a shotgun blast boomed in the air.

Chapter Three

Immediately, the other man in front of Danny drew a weapon from the back of his waistband, racing to the ATV, firing behind him as he retreated. Danny fired and missed—an oddity for him—and quickly rolled on his back after hearing two shots. That turn was in case Wayne needed him or if the asshole attempted to shoot him in the back.

Seeing Wayne drop out of the seat, using the door as the only protection it provided, his examiner fired three quick rounds. Rolling back over and flattening himself on the ground, Danny ignored the unmistakable odor of the pot plants. Frustration wrenched him as he watched the third man race away on an ATV. With the drop in the man's shoulder, one of them landed a shot.

"Did you get his pic off?" Danny's question came out more breathy than usual in a combat situation. Of course, a close-range shotgun, with no cover, hadn't occurred before today.

"Yeah."

Danny jumped to his feet, keeping his weapon trained on the man who'd held the shotgun. Seeing the weapon had dropped from the man's hand, Danny closed in, kicking the weapon out of the way.

"Mine's alive but needs an ambulance," Danny heard from behind him.

"Mine too." Stepping back from the man's possible reach, he scanned the area, watching the other man get away. He'd left his phone line open with HIS headquarters, but with it lodged in his left pocket, he had no idea if they'd heard anything—surely the shotgun blast—or if he'd broken it during his dive.

The corners of his lips lifted when he saw a truck racing through the field and cut off the retreating ATV. Backup had arrived. Then he heard a thump. Turning, expecting the other threat to be back in the ballgame, but seeing Wayne on his back mixed in with the crop sent a jolt to his system. Quickly reaching Wayne, Danny gulped at the redness of his examiner's hand that clutched to the side of his lower abdomen.

With a steely resolve, Danny took the chance no other threat was imminent and replaced his weapon in his pocket. Down on his knees, he jerked the phone from his pocket. A quick visual assessment screamed the urgent need of medical attention. With his phone to his ear, lodged between his shoulder and cheek, he demanded, "I need Life Flight and two ambulances."

"Copy. Life flight. Two buses. Standby" was the response he received.

Dropping the phone, so he could use both hands to staunch the blood flow, he urged Wayne, "Tell me."

The pain blazing on Wayne's face reinforced Danny's request for Life Flight. "One bullet. I don't feel the pain in my back, so maybe lodged." His examiner groaned and took a few deep breaths that seemed to help calm him. As calm as the man could be with a bullet in his abdomen.

Seeing the blood flowing around his hands, Danny didn't need to see the wound. He couldn't do anything about it anyway, so he did the one thing that could help. He kept his hands over Wayne's to staunch the flow of blood.

Wayne hissed. "Fuck, it hurts."

"I expect it does." Danny visually examined Wayne's body for any other injuries. He'd first thought of the two shots between Wayne and the third man but remembered the man who got away wildly shooting behind him. The metallic tinge of blood floated from Wayne. "Are you injured anywhere else?"

Gritting his teeth, Wayne's voice began to waver. "Isn't this enough?" His eyes fluttered and his consciousness began to slip.

"Stay with me, Wayne."

The blood flow from Wayne began to slow, but it hadn't stopped, which worried the hell out of Danny. He'd been the one to land them here. He'd been the one who'd decided to greet the men with fake pleasantries instead of standing their ground from the beginning. Losing Wayne would weigh heavily on him. But, most importantly, Wayne's family would suffer a great loss.

Shifting those thoughts aside, he jerked his head around at the roar of an engine. Relaxing a notch, he turned to see Wayne struggling to keep his eyes open as Danny's gut wrenched at the pain Wayne suffered.

Hoping to give Wayne a smile, he asked, "So, did I pass?"

A quick grin appeared on his examiner's face before it turned to a painful grimace. "You did good, kid."

Good? He'd gotten his examiner shot. Who does that and passes their licensing exam?

Danny heard fast movement through the plants approaching. A quick turn confirmed Boss and Sugar behind him. "Life Flight ETA two mikes," Boss informed him. Those two minutes passed agonizingly slow.

Blessed relief slid through his system at the echo of the Life Flight. The approaching sirens actually shifted into an angry mood. He understood the sheriff's department had a large area to cover, but their slow response helped not one iota.

"He's out," Sugar stated.

"This one too," Boss responded.

Without a need to glance up, Danny knew they stood guard over the two threats. That released one focus of his mind. "Did you get the other guy?" Danny didn't want someone trying to return with backup.

"He's in the truck," Boss answered. "How is he?"

Assuming he meant Wayne, Danny answered, "Not good."

"Tell them we're friendly," Boss stated on his phone, over what Danny expected to be the HIS emergency line. The last thing his group needed was the deputies to pull their weapons on armed agents of HIS.

In no time, everything turned into a controlled chaos as the emergency teams from both Life Flight and the ambulances jumped into action and the deputies directed the scene. Reluctantly, Danny lifted his hands to a paramedic who—with another paramedic—quickly assessed Wayne and hurried him to the waiting helicopter.

After finding out where they would take Wayne, Danny nodded and turned back to what he knew would be twenty questions and a grueling interrogation from law enforcement.

He gave a quick statement on the scene, then was asked to go to the station and provide a more complete one.

Hours later—after questions upon questions, and then "Sit and wait, while I check out your story"—Danny hitched a ride with Boss and Sugar for the airfield to pick up his truck. He'd wanted to see Wayne but had been told to wait until tomorrow. While he was stable and would recover, they had him sedated.

As Boss dropped him off, Danny couldn't help but laugh when Sugar told him, "This is no reason to cancel tonight."

With an easy laugh, he admitted to forgetting about his evening plans. Only Sugar wouldn't consider nearly dying in a crash or being killed by stupid marijuana farmers an excuse to back out of something.

Well, he thought about the blind date, *today can't get much worse.* Then another whisper hit him, *You both survived.* *Yeah,* he nearly snorted out loud, *although my instructor was shot.*

After returning home, he prepped for the date Sugar had set up for him. Once she'd fallen in love with Boss, she'd made it her mission to help Danny find the right woman. Being that this was Sugar, he'd promised to meet the women she thought he might enjoy getting to know. It'd been a risky promise, but she'd been their teammate and he respected her.

After showering, he took extra time fixing his hair. While not vain, there was little he could do with it. With it being a bit too long, it curled uncontrollably up in the back. He shrugged. It was what it was.

For some reason, choosing his attire became a challenge. He remembered his female cousins, while preparing for a date, had nearly everything in their closets spread across their beds and tried on damn near everything, before choosing something to wear. He laughed at the memories and how he'd learned they typically ended up in the first outfit they'd tried on. At the time, he'd thought their actions ridiculous. Now, not so much.

Since the date was at the coffee shop, he decided

on casual. Jeans instead of slacks made the cut. Giving up the stupid worry about how she'd see him, he picked out a baby blue button-down and rolled the sleeves about a quarter up his arms. He'd be warm wearing it, but he couldn't bring himself to wear a T-shirt on this first date.

Clasping on the Invicta Aviator watch his father had purchased for him for his twenty-first birthday, he exited the bathroom. The watch had been through a great deal, but he'd never wear any other watch. It'd been emulating his father that started him wearing the aviator sunglasses in high school. They'd become branded to him.

Nearing his front door, he halted and tossed his head back in frustration. "Cologne." Turning back to the bathroom for something he rarely used, he reminded himself of what to expect tonight. Sugar described her as tall for a woman. At five foot eleven inches, he wasn't overly tall for a man. But he could deal with that. Her being a brunette added a checkmark in her favor.

He stared at himself in the vanity mirror. Did he get her name? Racking his brain, he couldn't recall it.

After adding his smell-good stuff—not the official name of the liquid, but what he'd dubbed it—he made a quick call to Sugar to get the woman's name. All he recalled was she'd be wearing a baby-blue sundress.

"That little scheming matchmaker," he muttered when Sugar didn't answer his call. He hoped that meant nothing was wrong with her family, but something told him she refused his call, so he wouldn't cancel. She should know that he'd never leave the woman waiting by herself.

Damn. He hated going in unprepared.

After checking to ensure he had cash and his credit cards in his wallet, he shoved the billfold in his right back pocket. He snatched up the keys and tossed them before catching them with a jangle. He wouldn't allow something as simple as not knowing her name to stop what could be a good evening.

Even though the coffee shop was within a few blocks, he drove and braved snagging a parking spot, so he didn't sweat to death on the walk. He'd prefer not to arrive with a sweaty stench and rings under his armpits.

With frustration at finding a parking spot and rethinking of his plan to drive, he'd been around the block twice before someone emptied a space near his destination. Checking his watch, he cursed as he hadn't been as early as he'd planned. He wanted to be the first to arrive.

Forgetting her name, waiting to park, and arriving later than planned. The "*three strikes, you're out*" sentiment yanked at his positivity for the evening. At least he had the comfort of his ankle holster. It was a different backup weapon, as the sheriff's department still held his, but he'd never leave home without one.

Not one to leave a lady waiting, he turned off the ignition in his truck and whipped open the door to exit. Jaywalking, he approached the coffee shop and stiffened in surprise, then a damn burst and hatred flooded him. He knew the woman in the blue sundress approaching him.

Damn. He'd taken forever to get rid of her to include finally giving her the impression he'd moved out of state. Not one of his best moves to lie like that, but this woman clung like no other. She'd been a nuisance of biblical proportion.

"Danny," Barbie—her shortening of Barbara, because no one would naturally acquaint her to a Barbie doll—whined. "It is you. I so hoped it was."

Danny vowed the next time he saw Sugar, he'd wring her skinny neck for this and fire her as his dating service. Of course, she couldn't have known. It wasn't like he gave her a no-go list of women.

Wrestling with the demons inside of the torture of once having this woman in his life, he did something he shouldn't be proud of, but he didn't care at the moment. Without a word, he spun on his heels and walked away.

When she chased after him, calling out his name, he finally stopped and whirled to meet her. The smile that had once entranced him made him sick to his stomach. The woman was beyond psycho, and now she knew he still lived in the area. "I've said it before, Barbara—"

"Barbie, darling. Don't you remember?" she purred and arched her back to push her breasts higher. Her rather large breasts.

Unfortunately, he did remember. But, all together, the move and voice did nothing but make him loathe her more. "Barbara," he emphasized, "I've told you before to stay the fuck away from me. I haven't changed my mind about that."

At the stunned expression on her face, Danny turned and walked away without a backward glance.

That's it, he told himself. *I'm done dating.* As he slammed his truck door, he knew that unless the right woman just fell into his lap, he'd remain off the market, and his dream of a family of his own would surely die.

Chapter Four

DUBLIN, IRELAND

An unladylike snort slipped from Moira Gallagher, and she quickly looked around to see who might've overheard. Thankfully, only her best friend, Cassie Connor, stood within hearing distance.

"What's so funny this time?" Cassie asked, as her eyes remained fixed on her phone and, most likely, social media. Whereas Moira would rather read a romance novel on her cellphone.

"Listen to this." She read out loud, "*He swooped her into his arms and took the steps three at a time.*" Moira stopped and looked up at Cassie. "Now"—she emphasized the word— "she just went into labor. I don't know about you, but three steps at a time? I mean, come on. She couldn't be light at nine months pregnant. What man can actually do that?"

Cassie sighed, as if Moira were a child being told the same thing for the hundredth time. "It's fiction, Moira."

"Aw, sure look it—" After dropping into slang, she sighed, knowing the truth in Cassie's statement. "—it just makes mortal men fall short of these expectations." She bookmarked the page on her Kindle reading app, the hunky Highland laird forgotten. "Speaking of impressive men, is Quinn working today?"

Although he came from old money and didn't need to work, Quinn Murphy—Cassie's fiancé—held the position of Junior Minister to Elizabeth Donnelly, Minister for Justice and Equality. It was part of the reason she and Cassie were working today, instead of enjoying the beautiful sunshine.

"No. Minister Donnelly has him doing last minute errands, so she can be fresh for the dinner tonight."

The way Quinn had told it, the minister couldn't function without him by her side. Moira had known it was to make himself seem more important than he was, but she let it go for her friend. "I'd have thought you'd accompany him to the dinner."

Cassie shrugged her indifference. "He said he'd be busy networking for his boss, and, frankly, I didn't want to go, so we agreed I wouldn't." A secretive smile touched her lips. "He's so considerate."

Moira was happy for her friend. She was. Really. Okay, maybe a bit jealous. Moira only wanted the best for her. Quinn Murphy made Cassie happy. He tended to make everyone around him happy. His charisma was to die for.

It never took long for him to turn a frown into a smile, and even a laugh. Moira envied that bit of personality in him.

Of course, his money didn't hurt Cassie's happiness. Not that her friend wanted Quinn for his money, but it did allow Cassie to pursue her love of creating jewelry.

Moira reached her hand up and rubbed the amber pendant, in a unique Celtic setting, between her fingers. Cassie told her that it resembled Moira's life—deceptively unique. She'd bristled when Cassie had used the term *deceptively*, but she'd allowed an explanation.

"It's not that you try to deceive people, but you never let people see the uniqueness inside you. The woman who hurts along with the laughs and smiles you easily bestow." Cassie's expression had changed to one of concern. "You deserve to be this happy inside, Moira. Don't hide behind the free-living woman and pass up the best thing that ever happened to you. You avoid things that might upset you, and getting hurt is one of those things. But, you have to let a man see"—she'd pointed her finger at Moira— "inside you. To the real you."

Why did all happily-in-love people want that same joy for everyone else? Casual relationships worked perfect for Moira. As an *ealaíontóir*—artist—when her muse struck, the world outside ceased to exist. Most of the men she dated—even her friends for that matter, Cassie excluded—didn't understand that. So, when Moira would disappear for days at a time with her phone and social media off, she'd lose whatever ground she'd gained in a new relationship. Which she appreciated, as it told her the man's priorities up front. If he could wait it out, he might be a keeper.

None had waited it out.

As for long-term relationships, she guessed if she had that deep love for a man that Cassie had for Quinn, she might… *might*, consider something more. But only if he didn't make her pick between him and her *ealaín*—her art. She'd never lose that part of herself.

"What are you girls doing?" The sharp female voice startled her, and Moira almost dropped her phone. Obviously, their break on this temp job had ended.

The strong scent of garlic burned her nostrils, and she scrunched her nose to fight off the heavy odor. The *báire tí* was the worst housekeeper taskmaster, and no matter how much effort Moira or Cassie put into shining, dusting, or cleaning, they had to redo the work as their efforts never passed muster. It was a brutal job.

Yet, they'd stayed to clean this house. Nay, not house. Mansion, or *teach*. Mostly because Cassie wanted the place to look great for Quinn's working dinner.

With a heavy accent, the mean woman—Moira hadn't cared to remember the woman's name—nearly growled, "What are those?" She reached out a beefy arm and Moira automatically took a small step back. Why had the woman asked if she obviously knew what she and Cassie held? "Hand them here. You know they aren't allowed."

Anger rose within Moira. Under her breath, she cursed the woman with the best Irish Gaelic her grandmother had taught her. Sure, the employers of the temp agency had stated mobile phones weren't allowed on the job, especially in the minister's home, but she'd be damned if she'd surrender it, especially to this woman. The phone held her life. Losing it would be devastating. Heck, she didn't even remember her brother's phone number. She hoped she never got arrested and had her phone taken away. She'd be in a world of hurt trying to find people's phone numbers or remembering the password to her cloud account where they'd be stored.

Moira's gaze slid to Cassie in an effort to gauge her friend's reaction. Moira had only taken this gig because Cassie had asked her to work with her. If only her friend's jewelry making business would take off, Cassie wouldn't need this job. But Moira knew that Cassie had no idea how to manage the money flow. So, her friend always ended up taking odd jobs to supplement the lifestyle she lived. One that Moira didn't crave as she believed in living within her budget.

Moira made a decent living as an artist, but she squirreled most of it away like her parents had taught her. "For an unknown emergency" her mam had always said with a tone that made Moira think her parents had experienced at least one emergency. She'd also taught Moira that people were fickle and her art could be hot one day and hard to sell the next. Over the years, the pain in her heart at the loss of her parents had lessened, but she didn't imagine it would ever go away.

If only Cassie and her hot-and-heavy fiancé would

marry already. When Quinn gazed at Cassie, the love radiating from his eyes warmed even Moira's heart.

Moira was disappointed Cassie didn't say, "Screw this. Let's go," to the *báire tí*. The pay would be nice but not necessary this month.

"Fine." Cassie handed her phone to the mean woman, although her voice held disdain that went ignored by its intended recipient. She looked at Moira as if pleading with her to behave.

Incredulous and still smarting at Cassie's caving, Moira almost walked away, but wouldn't do that to her friend since Cassie had recommended her. With a huff that she didn't care could be overheard, she stretched out her arm and reluctantly dropped her phone into the housekeeper's large hand. Now wasn't the time to kick herself for never resetting the password from the factory setting.

After pocketing the phones in her pristine white apron, the *báire tí* pointed at Cassie. "You, dust the shelves and artwork in the front entry." Her eyes squinted as if giving the evil eye, which only made Moira want to laugh since she looked like a pig snorting instead. "Don't break anything."

"You,"—she hadn't needed to point at Moira as it'd been obvious in her tone who the woman spoke to—"upstairs. Help the real maid change the sheets in the guests' rooms." The housekeeper turned, and Moira felt like giving her a salute and then the finger. She hadn't done that since… well, she couldn't remember when, but this woman brought out this behavior.

As the housekeeper hurried away, she mumbled under her breath. Moira caught the words "*falsa*" and "*míbhuíoch*" in her grating tone.

Standing in place, Cassie asked, "Did she just call us lazy?"

Nodding, Moira took a step toward the large mahogany staircase. "Not only lazy but ungrateful."

"She's such a wagon."

Although always trying to find the good in people, Moira wholeheartedly agreed, but, in this case, she'd straight up say bitch versus wagon. On many occasions, she had been dubbed a happy-go-lucky person. Or a "free spirit." Since the labels fit, she'd never argued. Today tested even her bright side.

After two hours of making beds and straightening rooms, Moira decided she'd find Cassie and see if they could leave. Muscles that hadn't worked this hard in a long time ached with overuse. It didn't matter if she spent all the earnings from the hours they worked on a much-needed massage, or two. A pleasure-filled groan slipped from her lips at the thought of her favorite masseur, Ryan's, magical hands rubbing her body down. If she'd had her phone, she'd have scheduled herself for his next available appointment.

Damn and double damn the woman. Stopping at the top of the staircase, she mentally told herself, *Think happy thoughts*. She took a deep breath and held it until her chest burned. Slowly, she released the air from her lungs and relaxation slid down her body from her the top of her head to the tips of her toes. Okay, her feet still hurt. If only she'd been allowed to wear her tennis shoes….

Glancing downstairs, she didn't see Cassie. Taking the steps slowly—as if her godawful mule shoes would make noise—she searched for the *báire tí*, then her friend. Although, her goal was to find Cassie and avoid the *báire tí*.

Passing through the dining room, she stopped and gawked for a moment. Elizabeth Donnelly—the Minister of Justice and Equality—had pulled out all the stops for the dinner party. Crystal and silver glistened on the table that sat—she counted chairs—thirty. Decorated with Easter lilies, which weren't in season, touched off the elegance of the room with their semblance of peace and hope for the future. A plain white tablecloth and white covers over the chairs didn't detract from the overall appearance. The only exception to the classiness of the table was the scattering of shamrocks along the center of the table that screamed "this is Ireland." To her, they were technically the only classy thing on the table. The rest was just dressing.

She'd learned this event had something to do with a zero-tolerance program the *gardai, Ireland's police force,* and the minister planned to roll out. The Assistant Commissioner of the Dublin Region of the *gardai* would attend, so it seemed a done deal. The police and the politician. Even Moira, who didn't keep up with politics, knew Minister Donnelly was positioning herself for the role of President, which would become vacant in one year. Moira had no idea if she'd vote for the woman or not.

If the minister could achieve the set goal on drugs—which Moira highly doubted since "zero" prefixed it—she'd definitely consider voting for the minister. But Moira didn't have her hopes up, so when it came down to right before voting, Moira would listen and read, then ask her brother. Only once had she abstained from voting. She couldn't decide which candidate was less of an idiot.

Shrugging, she continued on her search for Cassie. The size of the *teach* had created a challenge, as she and Cassie got lost at the get-go. Turning a corner, she almost smacked into her friend. Before Cassie could speak, Moira rushed out, "I know you want this to look good for Quinn, but do you really need this job?"

Cassie looked relieved. "No. I thought you might."

They each chuckled at how they'd, once again, looked out for the other. "Good." Moira snagged Cassie's hand, nearly tugging her along. "Let's head out before Miss Smellsalot returns.

"Smellsalot?" Cassie asked, then wrinkled her nose and chuckled. "She does, doesn't she?"

"After this, let's grab something to eat. My stomach's growling." As if to emphasize the point, a noise rumbled up from her belly.

Before they could depart, Minister Donnelly neared them. They kept their heads down and swiftly used the dusters they'd been issued and dusted whatever was in reach. To Moira's relief, the politician didn't stop as she strode to her office.

Whew. Time to hand over this apron and get on her way to her flat. "Our phones," she mourned.

"I'm on it. Meet you at Liam's Tavern." Before Moira could respond, Cassie slipped away. At least Moira didn't have to deal with the housekeeper.

Assistant Commissioner Shawn Fitzgerald walked past her into Donnelly's office. Probably prepping for this evening's dinner with the minister's hope to bring people on board with her plan. Her brother told her the *gardai* was running in circles trying to catch the distributors and needed more support from lawmakers.

With both high-level leaders inside the room, Moira turned to escape. Unfortunately, the only way out—that she knew—led her past the minister's open office door.

With no wish to be noticed, she tiptoed like a child but stopped in her tracks at the next person to pass her line of sight. *Hen's teeth.* Was that really the Boyle fella? The drug king or something like that? It couldn't be. She shook her head and then realized she'd look like a twit if he'd seen her, she turned her back to him and, once again, pretended to dust. Only, she ran into a wall. Perfect.

Squeezing her eyes shut, she counted to five in hopes that Boyle passed her and she could get the hell out of there. Of course, it hadn't worked. He might not have noticed her, but the minister had, and issued an order. "Go to the kitchen and ask for a tray and bring it here."

The compulsion to turn and act confused saying,

"Me?" rode high. However, her professionalism stopped her from the childish act. She almost laughed out loud. Her professionalism wasn't stopping her from walking out on this gig.

With a new plan, she'd have the chef prepare the order and be gone before it was ready, so someone else would be required to carry it to the office. Aye, that sounded perfect.

Of course, her luck kept getting worse. The chef had anticipated his boss's request. "It's ready for you to deliver," the man in a pristine white shirt stated. How did these people keep their clothing so clean and white?

Oh crap. Moira swiveled her head around, hoping to find someone—anyone—to cart the rather large tray to the minister's office. After stints with Cassie at temp serving gigs, Moira knew she could tote it, but she had no desire to do so.

The chef passed her a sympathetic gaze. "They're making beds upstairs. You'll have to take it yourself."

"But I just made the beds." The cook didn't deserve the indignation she'd inserted into her voice.

"Remaking."

Moira closed her eyes, took a deep breath, then slowly let it out. She'd taken those relaxing breaths one too many times today. Remaking beds. Another task gone arseways. Although, after today's disaster, and Cassie abandoning her, her friend would have to work to regain her position as BFF. Once she caught up with Cassie....

She should just leave without this last task. Run away

and not look back. Not even ask for her pay. But, her professionalism—that kept returning—and a curiosity, that'd typically gotten her in a jam over what type of conversation was occurring in the office, kept her there. Government leaders and a known criminal?

Maybe the leaders had a sting in process for Boyle. Wouldn't that be cool to witness? That arrest would be worth the hellish day she'd spent cleaning. A slight eagerness crept into her that she knew she should ignore, but she didn't always listen to reason—even from herself.

Before she turned away, the chef reached across the kitchen island and pulled something from an oddly out of place decorative box. "Here."

Moira wanted to kiss him. Their phones. Although Cassie would be searching, she wouldn't allow them to remain until her friend found them. Just in case. After accepting them, she dropped both mobiles in her apron pocket. "Thank you."

"Before I could give them to your friend, she got caught by—"

"Let me guess," Moira interrupted. "Miss Smellsalot." She nearly slapped her hand over her mouth for the slip. These people worked together. Who knew? They could even be married or something.

The chef chuckled and nodded. "That's a good one. Cassie rushed out of here without the phones."

"Right." With a brief nod to the chef as he turned away, Moira left the chef lover's kitchen, wondering if Cassie planned to return for the phones or abandon them. That'd be the first thing she'd ask her when they met up for their late lunch. She hefted the tray and hoped this trip would be worth something more than a few minutes pay.

Close to her destination, Moira slowed her steps, her heart thudding loudly in her chest, and while excited something big might happen, fear drizzled down her spine. That made no sense to her. It was only delivering a tray of tea and light snacks. Sure, there were powerful people in the room, but that shouldn't drive her emotions back and forth. Then it hit her. She worried about being caught earwigging. Well, she'd just have to be sneaky about it.

The office door stood open a crack, and she didn't want to push her way through without permission. Plus, they'd probably quit talking when she entered.

Not willing to juggle a large tray full of afternoon tea on one arm so she could knock with the other, she lowered the tray to the carpet.

Knowing earwigging was terrible, she couldn't help herself. An opportunity like this didn't happen often. After a couple of minutes and disappointed she couldn't make out the words, she raised her hand to knock. Time to just get out of here. She could always tell Cassie, who had been in the room, and see what Quinn had to say about it. He'd probably be more in the know working as a junior minister under Donnelly.

Wait! She nearly snapped her fingers.

Dropping her hand, she reached into her apron for

her phone. Maybe it would pick up the conversation and she could listen to it later at a higher volume. If it worked, she'd have some nugget of information for her brother. If she caught the sting, or whatever happened, it would put a smile on Declan's face. He needed something to lift his spirit. He'd been blue lately, and while he argued to the contrary, she saw it in his eyes, forced smiles, and voice.

She could already hear him accusing, "You were *earwigging* again. Aye?"

Finding the recording app, she stepped over the tray and moved the phone closer to the sliver of open doorway. While itching to open the door more, she wouldn't dare and potentially be caught.

At the few words she'd made out clearly, she glanced nervously up and down the hall. She had to move because she didn't want to be standing here if one of the three—or all—exited the room and saw her. They'd know she'd heard them. She couldn't even imagine if they knew she recorded their conversation.

Bored and disappointed that she couldn't understand more, she decided her departure was well overdue. She'd knock and get this done. If the recorder picked up any words, she wouldn't have wasted her time.

"You said you knew who the fuck is sleeping with my daughter." She couldn't make out the raging voice. It had to be Boyle or Fitzgerald, as she'd heard Donnelly on television often enough, plus the voice had definitely been masculine.

Although it sounded like juicy gossip, a knot inside her belly told her to get the heck out of there. It had been the tone of the voice. Menacing. Angry. Accusing.

Listening to that warning, she dropped her phone back into her pocket and decided to leave the tray where she'd placed it near the door and depart. Screw professionalism. She'd left it in the kitchen when she'd decided to play snoop.

A name she recognized was growled inside the room. With a jump, fear lodged in her throat. It hadn't been loud, but it'd been clear to her. Or had it? Maybe she'd misunderstood. Really, what were the chances these three would speak of her brother?

"I'll kill Declan Gallagher and my pregnant whore of a daughter!"

Her limbs froze. *Jeanie Mac!* She didn't care she'd jumped back to slang. Murder and her brother's name spoken in one sentence was too much.

While her thoughts could be thick sometimes, she couldn't help the fear that shot through the muscles she'd recently relaxed. She didn't wait around to find out more. Something told her that her instinct had been right on board to leave. If these men found out who she was, would they kill her to keep her silent?

Spinning around with haste, she tripped over the tray, spilling the silver teapot with a clatter that sounded like a bomb exploding in her ears.

Legging it down the hallway, she didn't look back. Declan had taught her that could lose valuable time if someone followed her. Where was her overprotective brother now when she needed him? A sob nearly lodged in her throat. Could she get to him in time? *Please let them be speaking of another Declan Gallagher.* While she didn't wish death on anyone, she loved and needed her brother.

As she passed through the door near the kitchen, she ignored the chef's call out to her.

Her pulse pounded so loudly in her ears, she wouldn't have been able to hear if footsteps pounded the pavement behind her. She just had to make it to her car and escape.

If only she hadn't knocked over the tray, no one would've known she'd been outside the door. Then again, maybe they hadn't heard it like she hadn't heard them.

Moira raced straight to the door leading to her car, past the gaping taskmaster, and exited, not caring about returning the damn apron she still wore. Let them charge her for it.

Her breath shortening and shaking like a leaf, she fumbled with her car door handle, thankful she'd felt safe enough to not only leave her door unlocked but keep the key fob in her glove box. She fumbled in her purse—spilling most of the contents—then finding what she'd sought, brought her inhaler to her mouth, and gave it two quick puffs. After a moment to resettle, she drove off with haste, ignoring the blasted beeping reminding her to latch her seat belt.

Tapping her fingers nervously on the steering wheel, she kept glancing out her rearview mirror to see if someone followed. After several minutes, she blew out a solid breath. No one followed.

What now? Her heart sank. What would happen to her if they found out she'd overheard? She could be called into court as a witness, or—she gulped past the hard lump lodged in her throat—she could be taken out as a witness.

Not knowing her next step—whether reporting it to the *gardai* or hiding out—she drove on autopilot to her brother's home. Using a voice command through her car's Bluetooth, she phoned him. When he answered, her wavering voice announced, "Someone wants to murder you." Just saying that sent tears welling in her eyes and the aftershock rocked her system. The weight of what she'd heard terrified her.

Fighting back against the wash of emotion threatening to send her into a near breakdown, she swallowed back and wiped her eyes. It only helped a bit, but that bit would get her where she needed to go.

"What?" Declan's alert voice settled her a bit more. He'd fix it. He'd always done so when she needed him.

"He wants to kill you. And, I think Diana, too." She could be taking it all out of context, but she wouldn't take the chance. Not until her brother helped her decipher everything and make a plan.

When her brother didn't speak right away, her heart lurched and tears streamed down her face unchecked. What if he wouldn't help her since his big boss had been involved?

"How do you know?" he asked again.

"I overheard it"—her words broke, admitting the truth— "at the minister's house." She sniffled loudly. "Boyle was there."

"Feck. Get over here ASAP."

Her heart sank, turning her stomach sour. Shushing her mind to the futility of the questions as to what he'd do to help her, she drove, feeling safer.

Chapter Five

On the drive to Declan's home, the events of the afternoon had shifted and grown in Moira's mind until paranoia had rooted its ugly self in her senses. She'd lost all track of the fact she'd only overheard something—probably out of context.

By the time she'd parked, that paranoia—which had her constantly checking the rearview mirror for a tail—had morphed into anger and outrage at the audacity of the threat. Nay, fear remained for her brother, but the thought of Boyle made her blood boil. Boyle and boil. Ha. If only she could actually laugh at it.

Her brother opened her car door before she could, and she launched herself out of the vehicle and at his chest. She allowed him to take control of everything. To her horror, a sob escaped when she secured herself in his arms. How could she be crying when she was so angry?

In a low, loving voice, he murmured, "Shh, my *deirfiúr.*

I've got you."

Declan calling her "sister" in Gaelic brought back all the times he'd been her protector growing up. Whether it had been a skinned knee or, apparently, a death threat against him, his arms always held the key to holding her together. This situation wasn't fair.

Time passed slowly before she collected herself enough to function. Stifling the flow of tears, she searched his eyes through her watery ones and whispered on a broken note, "I don't want you to die."

Always prepared, he handed her a tissue, before leading her into his home. The place where the two of them had grown up in a loving family. The home that now held two additional people in it.

Moira had met Diana Boyle more than a year ago when Justin Franks—her and Declan's American friend since childhood—had introduced them. Justin had stated he worked for her dad, but the two had been tight-lipped about who that man was or what exactly Justin did for him. Although rich and secretive, Moira hadn't wanted to believe the amazingly nice woman was the daughter of a known drug lord.

She'd also not wanted to believe Justin worked for a criminal. From as early as she could remember, Justin and his family visited hers for nearly a month every summer. Their parents had a close relationship. But, for some reason or other, her family never visited the Frankses in the US. More than once, she'd asked to visit, but her parents always said it wasn't possible. In her young mind, she'd equated that to mean they didn't have enough money. They'd never been poor, but they'd never been described as well off.

During those younger days, Justin and her brother had been close. Danny, Justin's younger brother by four years, hung out with them, but as a girl three years younger than Danny, she'd been banned from their antics. Not that she'd wanted to do some of the stuff the boys did at those ages.

Always kind, and probably feeling sorry for her, Danny made it a point to spend time with her during each visit. They'd walk, play, and she'd give him tours of areas that she'd later learned he'd visited many times. Danny never excluded her or made her feel like she hadn't belonged. Justin hadn't really either, but when the two oldest boys were together, she was treated as if she had the plague. As a child, it'd broken her heart when her brother had ignored her, but after the Frankses left, Declan became the attentive and loving brother he'd been before their visits.

She hadn't seen or spoken with Danny since the family's last visit when she was sixteen. From her brother, she'd later learned that their father had died on a DEA op. That's when she'd found out that the sons had followed in their father's footsteps and were both DEA. Scratch that, had been DEA. They'd left after their father's death. Although she didn't know the particulars, she'd understood the brothers hadn't parted on the best of terms.

Justin, however, appeared two years ago, claiming to have moved to Ireland for work. From the beginning, Justin had described his boss as nothing more than an Irish businessman who dabbled in many things. When he'd just shrugged off telling her the name, she hadn't pursued it. Truly, it hadn't been her business. Though, she'd noticed tension between him and her brother that she couldn't define.

When Justin introduced Diana, he'd informed Moira that escorting her was sometimes a perk of his job. Justin had winked at Diana when he'd said that, but Moira had only noticed the playfulness in it. Nothing felt sexual between the two. Like when you can't stand to be near two people because the electricity is zipping back and forth.

Like when Diana and her brother were near each other.

That's when she'd learned who Justin worked for and why the underlying tension existed between the two men. If it hadn't been for Declan's draw to Diana, she'd worried he might arrest Justin on the spot. However, the two men must've come to some agreement because the four of them spent time together.

When she'd told her brother about her discomfort befriending Diana because of her father, Declan convinced her to not hold that against the woman. Given that her brother was a guard and hated criminals, that'd surprised the hell out of her. But he'd been right. She enjoyed the times she spent with Diana.

In the house, Justin turned to her and nodded as he walked away, speaking quietly on his mobile phone. His unusual tight-lipped smile shot her ball of fear to a new level. If he—someone who worked for the criminal who'd spoken in that office—was concerned, then she hadn't heard wrong.

With red-rimmed eyes and a tissue in hand, Diana waited on her brother's khaki couch that had seen better days. The spots of black dog hair that clung to the woman's peach-colored blouse made Moira notice the absence of said dog. Normally, Moira would've been bowled over by the beast before she made it through the entryway.

She turned back to her brother, who'd closed the front door behind them, sliding the dead bolt. "Where's Bella?" Really? Those were the first words out of her mouth? Where was the dog? She'd heard someone wanted to kill her brother and Diana, and she asked about the dog. Great. Avoiding serious situations had been one of the things Cassie had told her she had to stop doing. Moira would consider this fitting right into that realm.

When he ignored her, she walked over and plopped on the sofa beside a pale Diana. Hadn't Boyle said she was pregnant? Once again avoiding the main issue, she repeated, "Where's Bella?"

Declan dropped into the chair opposite the couch. He looked ten years older than yesterday, and her heart clenched at his obvious pain. This couldn't be easy for him. She'd be freaking out worse if the threat had been against herself. Maybe it was the cop thing that helped him remain calm. "The neighbor has her. Don't try to stray. Tell me what happened. Then we'll make some decisions."

"I'm here." Justin returned and stood near the front window. After he peeked through the curtains that she'd just realized were closed on this beautiful day, he gave the room a nod. "Tell us."

With a sudden fierceness, she wanted to rail at Justin. It'd hit her hard that he worked for the man who wanted her brother dead. And, how could he? The Frankses had been good people. While Justin appeared to be a good man, his choice of profession stymied her. He'd been deadly serious in his response of "No" when she'd once asked him if he was a cop working undercover to catch Boyle's criminal activities.

Before she dug into her recitation, she allowed part of her anger to spring forward. Turning her gaze from Justin, she pleaded with her brother, "How can you trust him? He works for the man who wants to kill you? He could be here to kill you now."

Before she realized it, her hand slapped over her mouth. She'd said all that out loud—in front of Justin. Good grief, why not give him a chance to kill them all now? This was the time a person's loyalties would be tested. It scared her to know that she had no idea where Justin's lay. How could her brother have allowed him inside knowing of the threat? Heck, he'd even brought Diana with him. Kill two birds with one stone. Now three since she'd opened her big mouth.

Justin laughed, and she tossed him a venomous gaze. Why hadn't her brother tied him up or something?

"If I planned to kill you, I'd have already done it and been long gone."

She bristled. Okay, his lethal tone and the fact his statement was probably true nearly put her in her place. Nearly. Declan had always told her she didn't know when to stop, so she opened her big mouth, once again. "Well, what are you going to do then? Take us some place and do away with us, so no one can find the bodies?"

Leaning back, with his feet crossed, against the wall beside the window, Justin assumed a relaxed pose with his arms draped over his chest. Under eyelids that seemed to droop, he slowly stated, "It depends on what you have to say."

As her heart pounded at his threat, her gaze raced back and forth between her brother and the man she no longer knew if she could trust. If Declan wasn't jumping up to fight Justin, he must trust him. Although, his tenseness when looking at their friend didn't go unnoticed.

Diana bolted up and rushed into Declan's lap. "I can't believe it. I knew he was upset when he found out I was pregnant and wouldn't tell him who the father was, but this?"

Closing his eyes, her brother pulled Diana into his arms and rubbed his hand up and down her back. Her brother's loving, soothing touch appeared to calm Diana, somewhat, but she remained glued to him. "We knew things wouldn't go well if he found out about us. We'll figure this out." Looking pleadingly at Moira, he demanded she tell them everything.

Pushing aside her jealousy for the attention her brother bestowed on Diana and not her, she spent the next fifteen minutes speaking. It should have taken less time, but Moira halted every time Diana wailed for Declan to calm her. Justin only broke in for clarification.

In wonder, she observed the closeness of the couple. Their love for each other glowed in their gazes, even with the fear in Diana's and the combination of fear and anger in Declan's. As she thought back, she remembered all the sensual looks, light touches, and whispers between the two when the group had connected. She'd not put it together more than that, and it made her feel like such a fool for being blind to her brother's happiness.

While it'd become glaringly obvious Justin had known of the relationship—actually helping push it along—her irritation at him swelled. Although, she should've wondered why the four of them hung out more often. When Justin had started offering to take her to her flat, she'd thought maybe he'd been doing it for time alone with her. He'd been friendly but never crossed a line. She'd found that odd but hadn't questioned it. Long hugs and kisses on the cheek or forehead always seemed sisterly to her.

Now she knew that he'd been giving Declan and Diana time alone without her father knowing. Of course, Declan had wanted Diana. Heck, the woman was beautiful and elegant. But Declan was a policeman and her father was a criminal. How did he ever think that'd work out?

Shaking her head, she reminded herself that sometimes love was blind. Which was why she hoped it'd never happen to her.

"You said you tried to record them?"

It took her a moment to realize Justin had circled around to the beginning of her earlier activities. She cleared her mind of the stupidity of love and returned to the present conversation. Given everything else—like the threat of murder, a blank recording didn't seem important. She reached into her pocket for her phone, then stretched her arm out to him. "Here. There's nothing there."

Justin's face tightened with what she thought was worry. He moved forward and accepted the phone, his eyes never leaving hers. "Christ, Moira, were you trying to get yourself killed? If it's the three people you say—"

Ignoring the irony of his words versus the threat hanging over them from his boss, she nodded firmly and interrupted him. "It is." They'd breezed over Fitzgerald and Donnelly being in attendance. Her curiosity about why the meeting occurred had been flushed down the toilet at the murder threat.

"Passcode?" he asked.

Instead of telling him her stupidity in never changing the code from the factory setting, she jumped from the couch, snatched the phone from his hand, entered her pin, then opened the recording.

Pulling the phone close to his ear, Justin closed his eyes as he listened to what was low tones.

Even now, she didn't hear anything but unrecognizable mumbling. "See, nothing." She couldn't help the sarcasm. Her hackles were still on alert at Justin's being there while they discussed everything. It seemed so… wrong. Yet, observing how he was handling everything made her feel like he was on their side. No matter his boss. But the scales hadn't fully tilted completely in his favor. As long as he didn't pull a gun, that she knew he hid under his jacket, all would be fine. At least she told herself that.

At her snide remark, Justin narrowed his eyes at her in what she expected to be a "shut up" directive, but she ignored the threat. Abruptly, he tapped keys on her phone, presumably, deleting the recording to protect his boss, then he removed the sim card. When he slid the phone into his pocket, she opened her mouth to object.

As if expecting her retort, he held up a hand to stall her and withdrew his mobile from the front pocket of his jeans that had just dinged. Holding her tongue, she waited while he did something on his phone. Heck, he could've been ordering dinner for all she knew. Nay, she knew better.

When she couldn't hold her tongue any longer, he held up his phone and restarted the conversation. Although some words were more garbled than the others, the conversation could be heard. Whatever app Justin had used, he'd amplified their voices somehow.

"What's in this for me? Sounds like you've turned, hanging me out to dry." Although she'd not heard Boyle's voice until today, his threat stuck with her, so she recognized those as his words.

"Boyle, I'm not doing anything of the sort. We'll remain partners," Minister Donnelly said in a soft, easy politician voice that seemed insincere to her ears. Being the only female, she'd been easy to identify.

"*Partners?*" she mouthed to Justin, who only raised an eyebrow. This made no sense to her.

"You'll allow Fitzgerald to make a few busts, and you'll operate more secretly," Minister Donnelly explained.

Boyle's angry voice rose. *"What? Let you take people, product, and money from me?"* he demanded.

Fitzgerald—she thought by process of elimination—cleared his throat. *"We already do that. What we're talking about is targeted, so we're on the same page. We'll discuss when and how. As far as personnel, if you have any people you're done with, have them work the location of the planned bust with a quantity we can afford to lose."*

We? She couldn't be hearing this right. The three of them together? Having Boyle visit during daylight seemed awfully bold to her if they wanted their "partnership" kept confidential.

"Other than that," Minister Donnelly stated, *"we'll have the gardai go light on daily drug arrests."*

"Yeah." Boyle sounded frustrated. *"Ten percent to each of you is too much. I take all the risks and only have these verbal promises that won't do me shit if something seems to put a smudge*

on your career."

Eyes wide, Moira was glad she'd not understood this when she'd been standing there. Those were huge accusations.

Thank God she hadn't actually heard this conversation. Maybe they didn't know about her. But then there was the noise she'd made. And her name was on the list of employees. Much as she tried to convince herself she might not be in trouble, she mentally fell flat on her face accepting the truth.

A bit more mumbling happened before the explosive words she'd heard while standing in the hallway outside Donnelly's office. Boyle wanted to kill her brother and Diana.

"Why can't we just leave earlier than planned?" Diana asked.

Stunned, Moira's attention turned and sharpened on her brother. "What does she mean?" A feeling of betrayal bit into her gut.

Clearing his throat nervously, Declan stilled his hand on his pregnant girlfriend. "Since we know Diana and I can't be together here, we were planning to leave Ireland. To disappear." He said the last part staring lovingly into Diana's eyes.

Selfishly, Moira asked, "What about me?" Her mind couldn't grapple on how her brother would leave her—forever—for someone he'd only known a year or so.

"You're leaving the country as well." Declan's matter-of-fact statement took her aback.

"What do you mean I'm leaving Ireland?" Moira shouted. It seemed extreme to her. Moving from Dublin might be acceptable, but the country itself? Ireland was her home. Cassie was her best friend and she lived here. Moira hadn't done anything wrong. *Okay, maybe,* she silently accepted, *I did overhear them threaten the two people sitting before me.* But how did Boyle know for sure she'd overheard? And he surely had no idea about the recording. Her eyes narrowed on Justin. Unless he snitched.

"Listen to me—" Declan began in his attempt to explain or pacify her. She didn't care which one. This wouldn't happen.

"No." She jabbed her finger at him. "I am not leaving Ireland. In case you didn't understand, I said nay. N A Y."

Declan released an aggrieved sigh, which, knowing him as she did, he didn't like what he was about to say and that had her squirming in her seat. "I think you need to get far away from here. Out of Ireland and their reach."

Panic set in and her heart pounding erratically. "What? Why? This is where I grew up… where I live." She shook her head, hoping to dislodge her unease. "They didn't know I was listening."

"Maybe, maybe not."

Declan slid the hand that'd been rubbing Diana's back only a moment ago over his face, as if to wipe away the weariness that permeated his mood.

"Why do I need to leave?" she persisted like a petulant child. Moira allowed her gaze to slide back to Justin again, who appeared bored with the conversation. He was the wildcard. If he was on their side, she'd be fine. But, if not, this conversation was a waste of their time.

"Be realistic. Don't you think if they are looking for me that they'd come to you to find me? And, if they want to kill me, what extreme do you think they'd go to find out what you knew?"

Justin stepped forward. "Okay, here's my plan."

His plan? His plan? her mind screamed. He should be the last person who knew what they would do to save themselves.

However, she listened. Mostly because her brother told her to keep an open mind. Worse, he told her he trusted Justin to keep them safe.

Justin's phone rang, and they all froze, conversation ceased. She just knew it was his boss. Just knew it. Somehow, they'd figured out she was there and overheard. Something inside her screamed that her brother's trust in the man was grossly misplaced. Her mind began to think of avenues of escape. Only, she wouldn't run and leave her brother and his pregnant girlfriend to their death.

"Franks." His gaze bore into Moira and became darker as he listened to the caller.

She swallowed hard. It was his boss. No doubt in her mind. Her thoughts scrambled on what to do.

"Are you sure you want all three dead?"

Oh God, they'd waited too late.

Before her, Justin transformed into what she'd expect a cold-blooded killer to look like. His lack of voice inflection in the call scared her. Those scales had just tipped back to not trusting Justin. He'd just been humoring them until now to see what they knew. And she'd given him the recording. The only evidence they had.

"You can count on me to take care of it."

After he ended the call, it appeared the other room occupants held a collective breath.

The menace in Justin's voice grew as he continued, "Time's up." He turned to Diana, and his eyes appeared pained to Moira. Not lethal like they were seconds ago. Maybe he had more feelings for Diana than he'd expressed. "I'm sorry, Diana."

Diana burst into tears and turned back into Declan's chest.

Justin straightened and a terrifying transformation overcame him. "My orders are to kill all three of you."

If the blood in Moira's veins had grown any colder, she'd have frozen to death at the next few words as they'd contradicted his earlier plan.

"There's no time like the present."

Chapter Six

When Moira, Declan, and Diana remained frozen, Justin continued. To Moira's everlasting relief, he relaxed and spoke authoritatively, but not threatening. "If you want a life, you have to leave now. With me." He checked his watch. "We don't have much time, grab only what's important, and let's get out of here."

As if expecting them to jump into action at his command, he punched a finger on his phone, then put it to his ear. "It's time. I need wheels up ASAP." He paused. "I'll text you the specifics for the flight plan. Expect long enough that it'll take two pilots."

Moira shrank in a bit at his statement. Her eyes watered thinking of leaving friends, but mostly her home. Homeland. Inside, she screamed, *Why me? Why do I have to leave?* She'd heard the men and understood, but she didn't want to leave. Maybe if she thought of it as a vacation. *Yeah, that'd work.*

"Moira, where's your passport?" Justin asked after he ended his phone call.

Passport? All the talk had been about leaving Ireland, so a passport sounded like a normal thing she'd need. Yet her brain seemed to have short-circuited. She wished she could swish away the fog in her mind and focus on the larger problem that included her brother.

Justin had agreed to kill them. Or, so it seemed. The question was whether he was lying now, or had he lied to his boss? She wanted to trust him. Nay, she needed to do it. Turning toward her brother, he nodded as if to answer her unasked question. They'd trust him. Which meant, getting her butt in gear and moving.

"Moira?" Justin asked again.

"Um, I have it in my purse because I wasn't sure if I needed it as a second piece of identification to work today."

He stretched out his arm. "Give it to me."

Diana and her brother stood. "I'll grab mine," Declan said. "Did you already get the fake ones?"

Fake ones? She'd missed something crucial.

"Justin helped me get what I'd need before we left," Diana informed them before Moira could ask more about passports. For someone whose father wanted her dead, Diana appeared relatively calm. The crying aside. Then again, Moira was more prone to rant and rave, whereas Diana had been more on the quiet side.

"Okay, when you have the flight time, I'll call Danny and let him know we're on our way." Declan kissed

Diana softly. "I just need to grab a few things and we'll be ready." He strode out of the room.

Moira's mind ran through a list of what she'd need to travel. "I'll just need to drop by my flat to get a few things as well."

"No time," Justin informed her, as he shoved over the kitchen table. Glass shattered from the centerpiece that she'd bought for her parents one Christmas. She saw her heart shattering with it. If only they were here, none of this would be happening. Her father would've smoothed it over. He could fix anything.

Jumping up in fright, she screeched, "What are you doing?"

The look he gave her made her feel as if she'd asked a ridiculous question. "Trashing the place."

No. This was her brother's home. Her childhood home. He couldn't do this. Angry, she stepped forward.

"Stop, Moira. If I'm going to make it look like the three of you died, let me do this."

That stopped her in her tracks. He had said "look like." While it settled her somewhat, a sense of foreboding welled inside her gut.

A switch flicked in her boggled mind. What about her stuff? All her art and supplies. "Wait!" she nearly screamed. Not to stop him, but to get his full attention. This couldn't happen at her home. "What about my flat? I have a ton of money invested in my studio. I don't want you to destroy it."

"No time."

"Justin, I have commissions that are complete or in process, not to mention a small fortune in supplies." Plus, she'd been working on a few special pieces to show a friend of a friend's boyfriend who managed a gallery. If only she could have her own showing. It'd seemed so close. Plus, she could use the cash from the sales.

Looking away, a muscle in Justin's jaw ticked. "I'll have someone pack what they can before Boyle checks. Make me a list with locations of the items."

She skipped right after his assuredness of Boyle checking. "I can have Cassie and Quinn pack it for when I return. She can deliver the finished ones and can collect the outstanding payments for me."

"No." His quick, forceful response startled her. He softened before giving her a small smile. "No. No one can know you're leaving. Once I'm done, it'll appear the three of you fled, then died along the way. There's no coming back, Moira. I thought we agreed on that."

Moira swallowed hard. They hadn't said she'd never return. Had they? His words sounded so… final. "Okay," she managed to say, her mind processing everything, and it finally all clicked. Truthfully, she felt a bit of an idiot for not cycling through it faster. "So, you're not going to kill us like your boss wants," she said with still a bit of hope in her voice, although she'd resolved that in her mind.

"Of course not." Justin's incredulous response bolstered her confidence.

"And," her voice rose with the word, "you're saying

that I can never—ever—come back to Dublin. To my home. Because you're going to pretend to kill me"—she looked toward the office door where Diana had joined Declan. Pointing to the couple, she finished—"and them." Nodding, as if to answer her own unasked question, she pressed forward. "Why do I have to die? Can't I just move away and come back after a long time?"

Declan returned. "Moira. Quit fighting. You'll leave if I have to tie you up and carry you to the plane." Her brother's firm tone had her spine snapping with tiny explosions of anger. "We can talk more when we travel."

Knowing it'd be fruitless to argue, she acquiesced and did as Justin and Declan instructed. She allowed every bit of anger, frustration, and fear to build up inside her. Hopefully she wouldn't blow up on the flight and decompress the air pressure.

Within three hours of Moira overhearing the threat, they'd left Declan's home for possibly the last time, passed through private airport security—with the fake passports her brother had asked about—and boarded a Gulfstream.

Fingering the passport she'd been handed before boarding, Moira examined it closer. It was her passport picture. She guessed she could've shared it with Declan at some point. And, he had allowed her to keep Moira as her name. Now though, instead of Aiofe Moira Gallagher, she was Moira Lee Wright. With a roll of her eyes, she murmured, "Morally right."

"You've been planning this for a while," she said to

her brother, who sat on an ivory-colored sofa, as Diana slept with her head across his lap.

It'd taken a while for Declan to calm Diana enough to get her to rest for the sake of the baby. Understandably, the woman's emotions were shattered. With the length Diana's father would go to so she didn't marry Declan—murder—Moira wondered what Diana's childhood had been like. She'd always seemed so happy and put together.

Declan's hand didn't stop softly stroking Diana's blonde hair, but he looked up from the woman he loved. "We have. I'm sorry I didn't tell you."

The sharp pain in her heart from his betrayal pressed on her chest. She couldn't speak. He didn't owe her any explanations for keeping his and Diana's relationship secret, but the rest.... He owed her big time. He'd had a fake passport made for her!

"Originally, Diana and I were just going to slip away. We knew her father wouldn't allow a *garda*, a policeman, into the family. I'd never go on the take and would end up putting him away." He shrugged. "It'd just never work."

"You were going to leave me," she accused, "alone." Vulnerable. Nay, she wouldn't allow him to make her feel that way. "Yet, you had a passport for me. Why? Were you planning to tie me up and carry me away no matter what?" Tossing his words back at him hadn't made her feel better.

Declan heaved a sigh, then admitted, "Justin suggested it."

"Did he now?" She didn't know whether she wanted

to slap or hug Justin for taking care of her family. For ensuring her brother and Diana would have a chance at a life away from Boyle. There just seemed to be some high-handedness, but Justin was smooth.

Her brother shook his head, sadness seemed to overwhelm his features. "Based on all I know about Boyle, you wouldn't have been safe."

"Yet you didn't care that it'd put us all in danger when you decided to jump into Diana's bed," she snapped, then immediately felt contrite. That'd been uncalled for. As far as she knew, her brother didn't jump in and out of bed without thought. "Do you really love her or is it the baby? Is it all worth it?" Maybe she shouldn't ask him while Diana was there, as his answer could be fake—like their new identification—in case she was awake.

"I do love her. The baby just makes it all better."

Love sparkled in Declan's light green eyes with vivid blue-colored shards at the edges. Green eyes just like hers and their mother's. Yet when she really searched them, fear lurked there. Probably fear for her, Diana, and their unborn baby. He always did take on the role of protector for all.

What would happen to him and Diana now? Based on all she'd heard listening to him and Justin—and reading between the lines—the two would never be able to live openly without risk of being found by Boyle, who was, apparently, relentless in his vengeance. And for Diana, falling in love with a law officer was a betrayal her father would never allow to go unanswered. Spawn or not.

Exhaustion weighed on her. Her life had been turned upside down. She couldn't be mad at him for wanting to protect her by having documents ready in case they had to escape quickly. Especially since they had. If only he'd discussed it with her before today, it'd be an easier pill to swallow.

As if realizing how empty and alone she felt, Declan deftly maneuvered from under Diana, without waking her, and sat beside Moira on the small love seat she occupied.

"Can't we ever go home?" She'd asked this already and didn't expect a different answer, but the words fled her mouth. While she enjoyed independence, she didn't relish trying to start over somewhere new. Surely, she'd be able to go back to somewhere in Ireland at some point.

After he put his arm around her and she leaned her head on his shoulder. Safety, security, and love. Always how she felt with her big brother. "Nay, my *deirfiúr*. Not as long as Boyle lives." His resigned voice broke her heart.

Holding onto his shirt and tucking her head closer into his shoulder, she let him know, "I don't want to do this without you."

"You won't." He kissed the top of her head with such gentleness she wanted to cry. "Don't worry. We won't be alone. Danny, Justin's brother, will help us get settled and secure. Remember him?"

Yes, she remembered him. Although she remembered how handsome he looked the last time he'd visited. For her brother's benefit—so he didn't know she'd had a thing for Danny—she scrunched up her nose. "You mean the gangly kid?" That'd help Declan not realize she'd always had a crush on Danny. It'd started the first time he'd given her attention. It later grew from a child's crush to a teenager's lovesickness. She liked the idea of him, but she didn't know him and doubted that her crush had grown into anything more. They were adults now.

The rumble of laughter from Declan's chest made her want to laugh. She couldn't help the smile.

"He'll surprise you. I know you're mad about all this, but listen to me and listen well. Danny works in security and protection, so you listen to him. I don't want Boyle to find any of us."

Finally lifting her head, she settled back into the seat, although not having strong arms around her did feel lonely—even if they'd been her brother's and not a lover's. "Surely we'll be safe there using the fake identities?" While she wondered if Justin overreacted, she also knew to trust him. "Boyle doesn't know we've left Ireland."

He nodded. "I think we will be, but that doesn't mean you shouldn't keep that threat at the forefront in your mind. If Justin does it right, no one will even look for us. The IDs"—he looked at her sheepishly— "again, I'm sorry. Anyhow, it'll take work to find us."

"How do you think Justin will fake kill us?" A tingle of fear slid up her spine at those words.

"I think I might find a drop-off and push your car

over it," a sexy, male voice whispered near her ear. She hadn't noticed Justin come close. Then again, she'd always found his ability to sneak up on her scary. She'd been six the first time he'd frightened her doing that when she'd been sneaking a cookie in the kitchen after she'd been told no by the cook.

Dropping her hand from where she'd been rubbing her necklace without realizing it, almost as if guilty for touching it, she looked at him and smiled. "Sorry." Then shaking her head, she said firmly, "Won't they know I'm not in it?"

Justin continued around her seat to stand near them. "My hope is an unclaimed body is released around that time, so I can put her in the vehicle. If not, I'll find a way to make it appear like you've died." He shrugged as if talking about killing people was nothing more than a bother in the conversation. "Don't worry. I'll take care of it."

She ignored the whole corpse stealing thing because she didn't want to touch that and find out Justin was into some crazy things. "Why are you even going back? Won't he know you helped us? I mean, you're disappearing at the same time we do."

"Excuse me," Declan said, then stood. "I'll be right back."

After he headed to the loo—even a private plane had a tiny toilet—Justin slid in beside her and turned to face her. He reached up and, with two fingers under her chin, gazed into her eyes. "I'd go the ends of the earth for you,

Moira. I will do anything I can to keep you safe."

With a gulp of apprehension at his words, she witnessed desire flaming within them. Where had that come from? He'd never looked at her like he wanted her. Okay, maybe he had and, had once, entertained it, but lately, she hadn't paid his looks much attention. She couldn't deal with this now.

"If I'll be technically dead—" That brought another gulp. This time with nervousness. "—then why do I have to leave Ireland? Can't I just move to another town far away?" She'd never been outside her country and didn't wish to do it now. Traveling within Ireland appealed to her, but not *imeacht thar sáile*. She'd never been abroad.

Justin pulled back and chuckled. He shook his head. "No arguments, you'll go." Clasping her hand, he squeezed but didn't let it go. He held it like they were lovers and she didn't let go either. His strength comforted her.

"How will it work? I'll be a third wheel with my brother and Diana."

"Hmm." Grimacing, he said, "You could live with Danny."

Shocked at the suggestion he'd pawn her off on his baby brother, she pulled her hand from his and gasped. "I'm not living with a man I don't know."

"You know Danny."

She narrowed her gaze at the guarded tone in his voice. Why didn't he seem comfortable with that? With her staying with his brother? Was he jealous? Moira appraised him with the same eye she had after seeing him again after so long away. The man was sex personified. He'd always been the more traditionally handsome one of the brothers. Though, she'd always appreciated Danny's more subtle ruggedness. It probably had more to do with Justin's attention to her.

Fighting the urge to run her hands through Justin's short, dark blond hair, she reached up and ran a hand through her auburn locks instead. Grasping the hair tie on her wrist, she pulled the annoyingly straight hair back in a ponytail that extended to mid-shoulder. What she wouldn't give for some natural wave. At least it didn't have as much red in it as her brother's did. He personified the traditional Irish look of flaming red hair and green eyes.

"Declan made all the arrangements."

That surprised her. Somehow, she assumed Justin had been in control of this relocation. "Not you?"

"No." His jaw remained clenched, and she'd barely understood the words. "I don't think he trusted me in the beginning."

She'd noticed that rift between them. Thankfully, they'd reached a truce so Justin was helping them escape instead of actually killing them. Her mind spun again as to whether he actually would've done it. She'd seen him fight. He'd practically killed a man who'd grabbed Diana when under his watch. And, she'd overheard things that she probably shouldn't have that made her shudder. Aye, she believed he had a vicious streak in him.

Keeping her focus back on their plight, she shifted. "I'm worried about how I'll live, financially. I have some money saved, but I'm an *ealaíontóir*. I have a name that was building steam. I'm not comfortable using that fake passport to get a job. I don't want to get arrested."

"Just stay low-key. You can still be an artist. You'll just need to choose another name to sign your artwork. Declan has a checking account set up for you."

Her spine straightened. What? More preparation without her knowledge.

"Catch yourself on," her brother said as he approached.

What did he mean telling her not to be ridiculous? She had valid concerns.

"It's from the money our parents left us. You'll receive your share when you turn thirty, but I think given the circumstances, they wouldn't mind if I fronted some of it now."

Diana's cry of pain broke through the air as she woke. "Declan," she cried. "The baby." She doubled-up into the fetal position with her arms protecting her stomach. "Something's wrong."

In an instant, her brother was on his knees in front of Diana. "What is it?" His panicked voice evoked fear in Moira. Diana couldn't have problems with the baby. They were in the air. Over an ocean.

"Oohhh." The pain-filled moan brought over the male flight attendant, who'd been quietly reading a book as far from them as possible in the small cabin.

When Moira had questioned speaking with the man in the area, Justin had waved her off. "First, he's trained to ignore what is said or to keep quiet what he has heard. Second, he's a friend of mine, so he won't breathe a word."

With all the talk of Boyle finding them—and possibly torturing her to get to Diana—she didn't want to trust anyone.

The flight attendant, Stu, furrowed his brow while watching Diana. "Justin?"

Instead of responding to Stu, Justin directed his comment to her brother. "Declan, Stu has some medical training. Let him see her." Then he turned to Moira and extended his hand. "Let's give them some room."

Naw. She didn't want to leave. Her brother looked wretched, like he had when they'd lost their parents. Family stood with family.

Her hesitation must've resonated with her brother. He looked at her and nodded toward Justin. "Go on. I'm sure it's fine." Then his attention returned to Diana and her whimpering.

Moira allowed herself to be led away by Justin, although she kept her gaze on her brother. Nothing could happen to the baby. Not after what Declan and Diana had gone through to be together.

Turning on Justin, she whispered, "Why are you doing this?"

'This' was generic for many things, but Justin picked up on her overall meaning. He cleared his throat. "Your family is like a second family to me. If it's in my power, I'll never allow danger to darken your doorsteps."

Narrowing her eyes in scrutiny, she asked, "Are you sure you're not undercover for the DEA or something to bust Boyle?"

"You won't let that go, will you?" He shook his head at a question she'd asked more than once, since he'd admitted working for the drug kingpin. "You know that I no longer work for the DEA."

"But, he's bad." Like he didn't already know that. But Moira hoped he'd find now was the time to leave. He could stay with Danny and get a legit job back in the States.

"Don't confuse my good deed here with who I am." He looked down at her. "If this hadn't been the three of you, there'd have been no escape."

Not sure what else to say, she gulped then smiled. "Thank you for helping us, Justin."

He touched her cheek and she leaned into his touch. Justin was the only man she knew who she thought might be a killer one moment and the best man ever the next, yet her caring for him never changed. "Moira, don't do anything stupid that could get yourself killed like being plastered in the papers or becoming an internet sensation. One more time, I'm telling you to listen to Danny, even if you don't like what he says or does."

When Stu stood, Justin moved down the short aisle toward the three. Moira followed, hoping the news was good.

Declan remained on his knees, his hand running through Diana's hair.

"We need to get her to the hospital," Stu told Justin.

How the heck would they do that anytime soon? They were still hours from Baltimore.

"I'll check with the pilot, but we should be close to Boston." Stu didn't move but waited for Justin's approval.

Declan looked up at Justin with pleading eyes. "I know deviating from our plan isn't wise, but Diana has to have help."

"Do it," Justin demanded.

Stu rushed off. Presumably to divert the aircraft.

Watching her brother turn back to Diana and place his hand over her exposed barely there, four-month baby bump made her heart ache. Declan didn't need another crisis. He already had to protect her and Diana so the couple could stay alive.

"If you get us through his," Declan said absently, "we'll name our son after you."

Justin chuckled. "Poor kid."

Moira grabbed onto the fact she would have a niece or nephew soon. She'd not considered children of her own, but being an aunt sounded heavenly.

Stu returned to announce they'd land soon and walked away to secure the cabin.

The passengers settled in seats, buckling in for the unexpected visit to Boston. She wondered about the weather. Odd thing, but it'd popped into her mind. They'd removed their cold weather clothing to be prepared for the temperature increase in Maryland.

Miraculously, Justin had been true to his word and someone had dropped off her suitcases minutes before departure. She'd have clothes, toiletries, and, most importantly, her art supplies for the stopover.

Declan declared, "I'll call Danny when we land and let him know of our delay."

"Did you tell him that I was with you?" Justin asked.

"You asked me not to, so I didn't. Are you sure that's what you want? I know it's been a while."

"Yeah. He might not've agreed to help you if he'd known I was involved."

Moira started at that bit of information. Leaving their homeland and stopping over for a medical emergency wasn't enough? Danny and Justin weren't getting along; yet, he expected his baby brother to help. Her throat clogged at the fear that'd nestled itself there.

"Why wouldn't he help?" Inside, she wished she could take the question back. She'd learned long ago never to ask something you weren't sure you wanted the answer. And, while she was curious, she wasn't sure she wanted to actually know about a possible rift between brothers.

Justin closed his eyes and leaned back against the seat rest. At first, Moira thought he was ignoring her, then she heard his response.

"Because he blames me for our father's death."

Chapter Seven

Baltimore, Maryland

Cowboy whistled. "Son of a bitch. Weapons?"

Without taking their eyes from the activity on the HIS training ground before them, Danny nodded. Remembering what he'd landed Wayne into still fired his blood. It'd been a damn check ride, and it'd been one from hell. Then again, he wanted to kneel down and kiss the ground that they'd landed safely.

"Thank God I had my backup weapon. I didn't wear any other weapons since it was my evaluation with the FAA." With a shrug that Cowboy probably didn't notice, he added, "I didn't think I'd need it."

Nodding in agreement, Cowboy asked, "How long were you detained?"

Knowing Cowboy had probably already heard everything, Danny just grunted, "Too damn long."

While HIS had an "in" with the government, local law enforcement wasn't always happy when the men stepped on their turf and bullets flew. Hell, HIS agents weren't overjoyed about it either, but shit happened.

Thank goodness for Sebastian Davenport—the attorney HIS kept on retainer. He'd persuaded the deputies to wrap things up quickly and allow Danny, Boss, and Sugar to walk out of the building. While it'd been obvious self-defense, he couldn't wait for the grand jury to convene next month and decide. Danny hoped a "No Bill" was passed, so their actions would be considered justified, and the assholes who'd been shot couldn't turn around and sue him or any of the others.

"Those were some stupid fuckers," Cowboy added. "Most growers booby trap their crop and would've abandoned it instead of engage a downed aircrew since they knew help would arrive for the passengers."

"According to the arresting deputy, the growers hoped to relieve us of the bird. They thought it'd be great to transport their product with less hassle." Granted, none of those arrested had been qualified to fly a helicopter, but that hadn't stopped them from trying to steal the helo. Idiots.

Through his aviators, Danny watched Jason Hamilton—the sixteen-year-old adopted son of their big boss, Jesse Hamilton. Jason would have to consider the light breeze when sighting the target. Those attending today's training could enjoy it. June in Baltimore could be stifling, and they'd had an unusual heat wave park itself on their neighborhood.

"Well," Cowboy said with a drawl, "did you at least pass the exam?"

With it all behind him, Danny could finally laugh about the insane scenario that had been his check-ride. "Yeah. They didn't have criteria for not getting the examiner shot." The thought of getting back in the helo after the emergency landing unsettled him. His mind was already made up—he'd never fly again. He could've killed his passenger... and himself. They'd been damn lucky.

"Hell," Cowboy said, "I've jumped out of many birds as a PJ, and I must say that none had been because of an aircraft emergency. I'm damned thankful for that."

The HIS teams consisted of men and women with both military and law enforcement backgrounds. As the only former DEA agent, Danny brought network contacts to the table.

Granted, like every agent joining HIS—even the special operators—he completed the training put together by some of the special forces' warriors. Nothing compared to those weeks. They still ranked up there as the worst of his life. HIS called it GIN training. Their humor sucked, because it didn't involve alcohol. The agency's 'Got It or Not' program brought everyone up to snuff, especially law enforcement agents like him who'd never fast-roped from a helo, learned serious survival skills to include eating bugs—not the worst thing in the training—to keep the team elite.

Much to the special operators' desire, HIS had

evolved to accept more covert missions. Their previous relationships—especially with the FBI—had grown to an increased number of government jobs.

The report of a single rifle shot echoed through the air. Pulling his binoculars to his face, Danny grinned. He held out his hand to his fellow teammate and closest friend, Mike Vaughn, who went by the callsign Cowboy. "Looks like you owe me twenty bucks."

Instead of reaching into his BDU pants pocket for his wallet, Cowboy—always up for a challenge—countered, "Double or nothing he misses the kill shot on a moving target at a half-mile."

With a shake of his head and chuckle, Danny dropped his binoculars and knew he'd win once again. "Okay. Double or nothing that Jason hits the target." Jason had been sneaking into training when his dad was deployed on an op. The team gladly worked with him and kept it quiet as the teenager wanted to surprise Jesse. How he'd slipped the absences and training past Kate—Jason's adoptive mother, who was also a HIS agent—Danny had no idea. At some point, the Old Man—Jesse's callsign from the teams—found out about their secret, and the team survived his heated lecture reminding them their job was to protect the children, not put them through HIS training. After he'd cooled off and observed his son on the field, Jesse allowed Jason to join some of the basic training scenarios. Some. Jason had to go to college, not become an agent immediately.

They'd found a future sharpshooter in Jason. He had

a knack for the patience of the job. Pity he wasn't an agent because the teams needed more snipers.

Danny's grin stretched wide across his face as Cowboy immediately picked up on the change to the bet. "No, Ball Park. The bet is… misses the *kill* shot at *half a mile* on a *moving* target." He emphasized each word Danny had dropped.

The smile on Danny's face faded and he grumbled at the callsign Cowboy insisted on using for him. The remainder of HIS called him "Franks." He'd been a DEA agent after all. Not some special forces hero who earned a callsign. Such as Mike had been dubbed Cowboy by his fellow PJs while on active duty. At least Cowboy called him Franks on an op. Whether for brevity or continuity, Danny didn't care. The Ball Park Frank thing needed to be blasted from Cowboy's thoughts.

Instead of refuting Cowboy's callsign for him, Danny nodded in agreement for the bet. "I'll go with it because there are many times we want the tango alive."

Chuckling, Cowboy turned back to where the target was being changed to a dummy that'd move for the simulation. Pulling the binoculars up to his face, he scoffed. "I bet you'd prefer that. Then you can get your claws into the asshole."

With his background, Danny seamlessly eased into the role of interrogator for the team. While the skills he'd learned in the DEA were tough, the interrogation techniques taught to him by the former Army Rangers and Navy SEALs on the teams had thrown him for a loop. He hoped he'd never have to use them, but that wishful thinking was wasted. With the deeper roles HIS undertook, the tougher the adversaries. Also, the greater the risk to their lives. Someone had to do it, and if the government needed them to be the ones because their hands were tied, HIS would rise to the challenge without hesitation.

When the teams split into separate branches within the organization—investigation and security—he'd expected to be moved to the investigation team due to his background. Surprising everyone, the Hamilton brothers took over the investigative branch, leaving the security to the agents under the direction of two team leaders—Ken Patrick and Rob Grimes. In Danny's mind, it had something to do with the brothers marrying and having children. With the exception of Boss, Danny's team leader, and Joe Stone, the agents were unmarried. That made him wonder if it had been a secret qualification to join the organization.

Sliding a sideways glance to Cowboy, Danny figured the other agent would be the last to marry. Cowboy had grumbled about not wanting to settle down. He also remained vocal about not wanting kids. One day, Danny figured a woman would nail him down. And, to make Danny smile again, she'd have kids of her own.

Danny, on the other hand, desired a home that included a loving wife and children. Maybe four of them. Children, not wives.

"I wouldn't complain about it," Danny responded to

Cowboy's remark about interrogating a suspect. Hoping for airflow through his short hair, he lifted his camouflage cap from his head and reset it in the same position. A good broken-in hat kept it in place on an op. "Good old Uncle Sam generally prefers we just deliver them alive and leave the interrogation to the government."

Cowboy snorted. "Like that's stopped you before."

Danny's grin stretched across his face. This time with pride. "Damn straight."

"I reckon after the Marines, Jason will be a deadly shot."

Those years of practice—with his natural skill—would make him a sought-after sniper. "I hear Jesse's thinking of waving college for him." While agents weren't required to have a college degree—unless like some agencies where it was a job requirement—it'd been a Hamilton family standard. "Plus, I don't think he's told his parents he's considering the Marines instead of following in his dad's footsteps and joining the Army." Danny paused on that thought, then added, "Following either of his dads."

Jason's bio-dad had been a Navy SEAL and his stepfather had been an Army Ranger. Both tough careers to follow.

"Then," Cowboy said, "he can hurry his ass on back here because we need a sniper."

Danny grunted. Alpha team lost their sharpshooter when Sugar married Boss and left the teams. Bravo team had two snipers, but one was also the medic, which conflicted with his role on the field.

Hearing the "all clear" signal to Jason through his earpiece, Danny refocused on the target. Absently, he said, "I'm not sure it matters."

"Come on, come on," Cowboy chanted, as if Jason could hear.

Quirking an eyebrow, even though they both faced the action, Danny asked, "You're cheering him to fail at his task? I'm guessing this is more about not losing forty dollars."

In his peripheral vision, Danny caught Cowboy shrugging. "I'd never put money before bullets."

They stilled as the target jerked and the report of a rifle followed.

Cowboy lifted the binoculars he held and focused on the target. When he took a moment, Danny knew. Checking himself, Jason had hit center mass as directed by Jesse—a sniper himself. Like father, like son. Or stepfather and stepson. However one looked at it.

"Shit." Cowboy dropped the binoculars back to his side. "So, how's the dating going?"

A chuckle left Danny at the change of subject. "Smooth transition."

Reaching back for his wallet, Cowboy grinned. "Sugar still setting you up?"

Samantha had been tagged with Sugar as a callsign the moment she'd met the teams. Her voice was sweet as sugar. That southern accent did it every time. Damn, they missed her humor and skills.

"God, yes." He groaned at the thought of all the failures to find him the right woman. Especially Barbara.

"Still crazies?"

When Sugar left the teams, she knew he wanted to marry, so she made it her mission to find him the perfect woman. Although he doubted it would happen on a blind date, he'd agreed to please her. Secretly, he did have hope that one of those dates would work out. Heck, anyone on the team—including Cowboy—would've dated to please her. As Boss's wife, she held their respect, but as a former team member, she was held in high esteem.

Since then, he'd consented to six dates. It'd taken her time to find the women since she'd been new to Baltimore. When she'd said it'd be her mission, she'd meant it. She joined several gyms, met school teachers at her godson's school, chatted up women at the supermarket, and so the list went, so she could find someone for him. It did touch him that she put so much effort into it. Happily married women wanted all their friends to be the same. Some—like Sugar—went out of their way to make it happen.

After these dates—one of which he'd gone on a second date with, but that was it—he ended up blocking the women from his social media pages as they either clung, begged, or bitched about him. He'd also had to block the first few women's calls on his cell because Sugar had provided his phone number. After a serious discussion with her, she stopped that practice.

Danny should've been proud he'd been friendly enough they'd wanted to see him again, but he'd had no desire to deal with their shenanigans.

"Pretty much. She actually set me up with Barbara last night."

Cowboy stopped in the process of dropping the owed money into Danny's outstretched hand. "Barbie?" he asked in disbelief.

A smile tugged at the corners of Danny's mouth. He could laugh now, but had shuddered the night before. "Yep. One and the same."

After shaking his head, Cowboy slapped the money into Danny's palm. "How'd that happen? I'd think you'd have recognized that psycho bitch's name."

Cowboy had been privy to all the stupid shit Barbara had done after meeting Danny a few years back. She showed up wherever he was, called at all hours, harassed women he dated after her. At least she hadn't been violent. She did, however, need to learn how to deal with rejection.

Danny snorted. "I didn't even ask this time. Although it wouldn't have mattered. She gave Sugar a fake name. She knew Jen—the last blind date, and thought it might be me, so she pushed for the date."

"No shit."

No longer wishing to discuss the leech he hoped hadn't reattached herself to him, Danny checked his watch. 1400. Declan and Moira should be in the air. He'd made a plan with Declan to hide him, after leaving Ireland, until Diana's father was no longer an issue. It'd been easy since it truly involved finding them a place to stay, some security, and help settling in or finding a long-term location in Baltimore or elsewhere.

The 0900 call had been a surprise. The escape had been planned for a month from now. The Gallaghers arriving now created no problem except accommodations, but what caused the rush hadn't been discussed. He'd find out later today. They should arrive around 1800.

"Remember when I told you about my friends from Ireland arriving next month?"

Cowboy nodded. "Sure. We were going to discuss protection if they needed it."

"Well, they're arriving tonight."

"Is everything okay?"

With a shrug, Danny answered honestly, "I doubt it. They should be in the air is all I know."

"Need me?"

While he could probably use help with lifting bags and settling the group into his place, he didn't think security would be necessary. Yet…. "I don't think so. I'll let you know."

"You know I'm here for you." With a nod, Cowboy grunted at Doc's approach.

The team medic—a bear of a man—raised his brows questioningly. "You guys ready?"

No, he wasn't. In the stifling heat, they had to lug around forty pounds through the woods to practice a rescue and knew to expect an ambush from the Hamilton brothers.

Since their goal would be to slip in and out quietly,

everything would be hand-to-hand combat. While they had a strong team of agents, the brothers seemed almost superhuman at times. The brothers had years of practice at the moves they'd taught the teams, which meant they typically moved faster to put themselves on the offensive first.

"Hell yeah!" Cowboy shoved his binoculars in his backpack, lifted it, and slid it over his shoulders like it weighed nothing.

He'd called a cleaning service to have the house readied for Declan, so he had nothing else to do except wait for them to arrive.

Danny's distracted mind had nothing to do with the day at work and his boss requesting time off for family time. It had everything to do with the phone call he'd received while he'd neared the airport to pick up his guests. Declan's voice had been strained, and the fear in it blasted through the call. Danny had offered to meet them in Boston, but Declan declined.

Danny tossed the biography of Steve McQueen on the side table as he stood from his couch. Worry for his friends kept him from focusing on reading. There'd been no further communication from Declan. The status of Diana and their unborn child was unknown and that ate at him.

When the phone rang, he glanced down at his watch as he picked up the cell. Ten. Not too late to fly since it took less than an hour and a half from Boston.

Danny swiped a finger on the phone screen and asked,

"How is she?" before Declan could speak.

"She and the baby are okay. But Diana and I are going to stay in Boston for a bit so she can rest."

He didn't see a problem with that as the couple had just needed to leave Ireland and find a place to hide. However, his mind ran through former colleagues in the area that might provide protection should Declan decide they needed it. "Do you need me there?"

"No. We'll be fine for a while."

"What about Moira?" The kid had to be frightened with everything happening. *Kid*, he silently scoffed. She had to be—what? Twenty-seven or twenty-eight? Still….

"I'm sending her to you."

Considering the protectiveness Declan demonstrated for his baby sister, the idea they'd split up shocked Danny. "Alone? Are you mad?"

"She'll continue on the private jet, and she's not alone." Before Danny could ask who accompanied her, Declan hurried on. "Look, I need to go. Pick her up at midnight. Her escort won't be staying long. He works for Boyle, but trust him. He's on our side. At least in this endeavor." A brief hesitation told Danny there was more. "Oh, and Danny—"

The hackles rose on the back of Danny's neck. This didn't sound promising.

"I'm sorry." Declan disconnected the call before Danny could speak.

What the fuck?

One word kept playing in his mind. *Boyle.*

Throughout the evening, that name and Declan's "I'm sorry" ate at Danny. It'd worsened as the Gulfstream taxied at midnight. Normally, he'd admire the smooth operation on the ground with the crews working together in perfection, but his eyes remained glued to the cabin door.

It could mean nothing that Declan didn't mention the guard's name—he assumed a man, but knowing some badass women as he did with HIS, it could be a woman. It could easily be someone Danny didn't know. Yet, a niggling feeling that he'd missed something in the planning of the lovers' escape stuck with him. And, why was Declan sorry?

The cabin door popped up and slowly slid to the side. As stairs were lowered, Danny's eyes locked on the man guarding the door. His gut clenched and wanted to heave. His hope was that his eyes were deceiving him.

Justin—who he hadn't seen since their father's funeral—was Moira's guard. Declan's words came back to him— "He works for Boyle, but trust him."

It'd never come up, so Danny had never asked Declan who Diana's father was, nor had Declan shared it. He hadn't caught that slip before, but now that he had….

Son of a bitch. All this time, Danny had allowed guilt to eat at him for accusing his brother of being dirty and working for the criminal Danny suspected of targeting their father. Danny had been distraught because he'd been elsewhere with the DEA when his brother and father were involved in the deadly bust. Before then, he'd heard rumors that his brother was playing both sides but had ignored them. Until the day of their father's funeral when it all came to a boil in his mind.

After the mourners left, Danny had lit into Justin and all but accused him of murdering their father. His brother had disappeared after that, and Danny hadn't looked for him.

Watching the closeness of the Hamilton family had broken something in him, and he'd wanted to patch things up with his brother. Only, he'd never made the first move.

Yet, here Justin was—proving the agents right that he'd been playing both sides. With a fierce anger surging through him, Danny stepped forward and prepared to greet his guests.

One would be met with a hug while the other might be met with the end of his fist.

Just then a leggy brunette stepped into view and his anger took a step back. Gone was the scrawny teenager he remembered. This woman.... *Wow.* Little Moira had grown up. Then she smiled and her face brightened. She was an absolute stunner. Having her live with him didn't sound as easy as he'd originally thought. That buffer of her brother also residing with them was now gone. At least temporarily.

"Danny," she said, as she descended the few steps.

He pushed himself forward and when he reached her, he pulled her into a hug. Damn, she smelled good. Quickly, before his body reacted, he pushed her back.

"Moira, you've grown up." What a stupid thing to say. Of course she had. "I meant," he corrected, "you look beautiful."

Even in the shadowy moonlight, he caught the red creep up her neck and the blush that stole across her face endeared her to him. Damn, oh damn. Distance, he reminded himself.

Then his gaze landed on his brother, once again. He itched to reach out and sock the man, but he had escorted Moira safely into Danny's arms. "Justin," he said with a curtness he meant.

"Danny. I won't be staying but overnight, so the pilots can get some rest. I can stay at a hotel if you prefer."

Would he? He was royally pissed at his brother, but did he want him out of sight? No, he wanted answers and that meant keeping his brother close. He deserved answers. And he planned to get them. "No, I have room. Besides, we need to talk."

Justin appeared uncomfortable, but Danny didn't give a shit. If his brother was on the take and it caused their father's death, he'd kill him with his bare hands.

Chapter Eight

After an uncomfortable ride to his home and situating Moira and Justin in his spare rooms, Danny grabbed himself a much-deserved Natty Boh. Justin's appearance had been unexpected. So many nights he'd wanted to speak with his brother, to clear the air. Now that he was here, Danny wasn't sure what to say.

Even at the late hour, all three returned to the living room. With Moira and Justin on the couch—sitting too close for his liking—and Danny in his La-Z-Boy, he jumped right in. "What happened to move up the timeline?" He had no problem with his guests arriving early, well, except he had to work and couldn't entertain them. He just wanted to know what happened.

Moira responded, "Boyle found out about Declan and Diana. He found out she's pregnant."

Danny whistled at the implication, then a thought occurred to him, and he didn't like that his mind expected deviousness from his brother. "Did you tell your boss?" he asked Justin.

His brother winced. He must not have known Declan had revealed his employer. "No. I've worked hard to keep it secret. I'll have hell to pay for not telling Boyle about the relationship."

"You're going back?" Danny asked. Even though Declan had informed him Justin wasn't staying, he didn't expect him to go back to the asshole responsible for their father's death. "Why?"

"I have to."

"He has to kill us off," Moira offered, rather nonchalantly for the topic.

Justin shrugged. "I need to make it appear I killed them so they can all live freely without worrying about who might be after them. That'll also make up for me not telling the boss about the relationship."

"I can't believe you work for that asshole. You know he's responsible for our father's death. Sure, it was the US connection that actually did it, but he's their backer." Danny bolted from his seat, righteous anger building inside him, ready to blow. He walked to the end of the living room then back, before Justin spoke.

"And when I can prove it, I'll stop working for him."

That stopped Danny in his tracks. He turned on his brother. "You mean that you're only working for him to connect the dots to our dad's murder? What about the rumors you were playing both sides of the fence?"

"Rumors. That was until Dad died." His voice broke

speaking their father's name, and Danny wasn't sure how to react and respond.

Could he believe his brother after all this time? Was his brother really on the straight and narrow?

"Look, I was there when Dad was gunned down and couldn't do shit about it. The agency wouldn't let me do shit about it afterwards. So I chose my own route to find out the truth. It's just taking longer than I'd planned."

Moira reached out and clasped Justin's hand, and something inside Danny rebelled at the thought of the two of them together, an odd sensation for sure.

"There's something else going on. Someone is pulling strings to seize control of more than a drug pipeline. I just can't figure out who or what exactly is happening, but Boyle's been acting squirrely."

Danny dropped back down in his seat. He'd always been jealous that his older, perfect brother got to go on ops with their dad while Danny still did grunt work in the agency. The day their father had been murdered had been a day from hell. First, he'd lost his snitch, then he and his brother had argued about Danny's helicopter training, then the murder. And he hadn't been there to stop it.

Sure, they'd captured those who'd killed their dad, but deep down, Danny and his fellow agents knew the men weren't acting alone. Their father had been leading an op that had ties to Ireland. Yet, he hadn't been able to prove it.

Now, maybe his brother could prove it and bring

the mastermind behind the death to justice. Ironically, Justin had been named for justice. Their old man's play on what was important. When Danny came around, they just went with a name his mom liked.

"What can I do to help?" Really, there was no other appropriate answer. He couldn't hold on to all of the pain and anger at his brother after learning the truth. It surprised him how easy it was to let most of it go and how much lighter he felt.

Justin raised his and Moira's clasped hands and kissed the back of hers. "You can take care of the family. They mean everything to me."

Danny understood. Moira was off-limits. Damn if that didn't wrinkle his mood further. It shouldn't have, but he felt a connection with Moira since they were kids. He figured since a woman had been all but dropped into his waiting arms, then she had to be worth pursuing. So much for fate.

"Listen," Justin said and stood, bringing Moira up with him, "we need sleep, and Moira needs to adapt to your time zone."

"We'll finish talking in the morning." Danny watched Justin lead Moira up the stairs to the bedrooms. Why did they have separate rooms? Were they trying to fool him or something? He shook his head. It didn't matter. He needed sleep as well, so he trudged up the stairs to his own room. Tomorrow he'd show Moira the third floor and where she could put her studio. Anticipation flowed through him at how excited she'd be and thankful to him for the gift.

That eagerness dimmed somewhat since he couldn't wrap his mind around the idea that if his brother loved her so much, he wouldn't leave her. Then again, he was leaving her in the capable hands of his brother. No pressure.

* * * * *

Danny spent the last few hours of the night tossing and turning and was up before dawn. As he dressed, he smelled coffee and figured his brother had beat him to the punch. All night he'd thought on his brother and the situation. For so long, he'd been angry at Justin, thinking he'd been playing both sides and being a part of what got their father killed.

Finding out it wasn't true released most of the anger, but not all. The fact Justin hadn't confided in him set his blood to boiling. Then again, he'd given his brother a blistering at their father's funeral. Still. Justin had disappeared. Their mother would—

Their mother, she had to know Justin had reappeared, but she couldn't know what he was doing. She'd never been so happy as to see him and Justin leave the DEA. The fact Danny held a job with more risk didn't matter. It'd just been the heartbreak of losing her husband to the DEA; she didn't want to lose her children to them also.

When he joined his brother downstairs, Danny decided to tackle what was most important. "You have to see Mom. She's been worried about you."

"I can't," Justin said. "Not until I settle this."

"No. You have to see her. She's dying inside, losing you like she has. It's bad enough she blames me."

"She does?"

"Well, she hasn't said so, but I know she does. I mean, I go off on you at the funeral. Next thing we know, you've resigned and disappeared. What else is she to think?"

Justin rubbed his hand through his short hair. "All right. I'll go see her. But, Danny, first I have to go back. If for no other reason than to make Boyle think the three of them are dead. They don't deserve having to look over their shoulders."

"Fair enough. Admirable, actually. What else do you plan?"

"I'm going to keep digging until I can find proof the US pipeline originates with Boyle. I want a confession out of him admitting to having our father killed, but I'll go with finally connecting him. We know the leader had our dad killed. Those idiots who got arrested are loyal soldiers and nothing more. They'd never kill someone—especially a DEA agent—without orders."

Danny poured himself a cup of coffee, already knowing what his brother had said about the actual killer and his accomplishments and, like the DEA, suspected Boyle, yet no one had been able to definitively connect him. That'd be pretty awesome if his brother could do it. But also extremely dangerous.

"Aren't things going to be dangerous for you? I mean,

you didn't tell Boyle about Diana and Declan."

They sat at the table.

"Yeah, that's going to be a tough one, but I think I can win him over by providing proof they're dead."

Danny took a sip of coffee and almost burned his tongue. "And how are you going to do that?"

Justin looked aggrieved. "Jane and John Doe's from the morgue. Unfortunately, they have plenty, so if a few disappear, no alarm will sound."

Danny inwardly cringed at the idea but knew something had to be done. "Did he really want Moira too? She's just the sister. Is the man as bloodthirsty as that?"

After a sip, Justin set his cup down. "It's because she overheard something she shouldn't have. Here"—he reached in his pocket and removed his phone— "listen to this."

As the recording played, Danny's mind spun as to how this could be used. While it wasn't the connection they'd been seeking, this could bury the man. Based on those Moira identified in the room, partnering with a minister would be high-profile.

After the recording ended, Danny asked, "Last night you mentioned something bigger. Was this it?"

"No. This may sound odd considering my task, but I'm beginning to wonder if Boyle is actually in charge."

"You think someone else might be pulling the strings?"

"This"—Justin pointed to his phone— "struck me

as odd. Someone had to have set that up and it wasn't Boyle. I'd have known about it."

"Maybe he doesn't trust you as much as you'd like to think. Did he even ask you who Diana was seeing?"

Justin exhaled loudly. "No. That should've been a kicker since I was her assigned bodyguard."

"So maybe it's not safe for you to return. If he suspects you kept Diana's relationship secret, he might take it out on you."

"No. He called me to take them out. Granted, I'd already figured out there was a problem and had Diana at Declan's and ready to go when I received the call."

Danny took another sip of coffee contemplating. "I'll say it again. It might be too dangerous for you to return. You can lay false trails from here for their death."

"Yeah, but they'd never believe me if I disappear too. No, I have to chance it and return."

Danny had a sudden sinking feeling in his gut. His brother's life wasn't worth getting the man responsible for their father's death. But his brother was determined. "What can I do to help? At HIS, we've got a great group who can research your leads. We can also be there if you need us." He didn't have authorization to approve any of that, but he believed once he explained the situation to the brothers, they'd help.

Justin took a sip of coffee. "Like I said, take care of the family. Or at least Moira until Declan and Diana arrive." He palmed his mug and stared down in the murky liquid. "I spoke with Declan this morning. Diana's been admitted for observation." He looked up. "She might lose the baby."

Danny performed the sign of the cross and said a silent prayer for Diana, Declan, and the baby. He may not always make it to mass on Sundays, but he kept prayer close to his heart.

"Make sure to pray for me, not only when I go back, but for when I see Mom," Justin said.

Danny chuckled. "Yeah, you're going to need it when you see her. After she cries like a baby with happy tears, she'll probably light into you." Knowing the joy his mom would feel for seeing her other son made all the crazy plans melt away. Today would be about celebrating.

Chapter Nine

Moira's day began with another upheaval—although quietly—as Justin left to return to Ireland. With her brother in Boston, she was left alone with someone she felt she barely knew. Sure, they'd spent time together as children and teens, but this man seemed so different from the young man she'd sworn would be hers. She'd been stupid and lovesick then, but the thought of the vow sent butterflies to her stomach. This man didn't hold her heart, but with his looks and protectiveness, he held her interest.

"Moira," Danny said, snapping her from her memories and daydream. Before she could respond, he continued, "I have something to show you."

Her heartbeat ramped up at that. Curiosity drove her blood fast through her veins. She had no idea what he might show her, but she hoped she liked whatever it was.

"Are you finished with lunch?" he asked, before taking

his empty plate to the kitchen sink. "I think you'll like it. I knew it'd be perfect for your painting."

Painting. Something for her painting. Now that really got her excited. "I'm finished." She wasn't, but she wanted the surprise. Later, she'd grab a snack. Following Danny's lead, she brought her plate to the kitchen. She looked around for a bin to dump the rest of her sandwich but found none.

"Here." Danny reached out for her plate. "It's in the cabinet." He pulled out a handle and a garbage can slid out and slid in with the slightest push.

"Impressive," she told him.

"Hold that word for what I'm about to show you."

He grabbed her hand and nearly pulled her to the stairs. A bit nervous at the enthusiasm, but curious about the surprise, she closely followed, leaving her hand in his. It wasn't like she'd get lost in the place. Oh, it was large, but not that large.

Passing the second story, they climbed to the third. Danny opened the only door on the floor—as far as she could tell—and stepped back, smiling. He let go of her hand and waved her into the room in front of him.

When she stepped in the room, the amount of light hit her first. An abundance of natural light flooded the room from the windows lining the back wall. His home, while narrow, wasn't a terraced home, so he had windows on the sides, but it was built so close to his neighbors, the side light was not as rich.

Supreme happiness floated within her. She could

paint here. She could be happy in this one room while she waited for things to sort out. While she waited for her brother and Diana. While she waited for her life to become normal again. Painting soothed everything within her soul. And Danny had just given her the best gift she'd ever received—bar the stuffed rabbit her brother had given her as a child. She still had it, had, in fact, added it to the list of things packed from her home. But this, this was much grander.

"Well, what do you think?"

She spun around with her arms out to encompass the room, giggling like a little girl. "I love it. It's perfect."

"Just show me what needs to be lugged up here and you can get set up. Give me a list and I can have an easel, chair, and whatever else you need picked up easily enough. Then you can spend the afternoon making this yours."

"Afternoon…" She smiled. "Evening, night, straight through. I can't wait to get started."

Danny cleared his throat. The somber look told her she might not like what he had to say. She hoped he didn't assign rules to her painting.

"Tonight might not work. Remember, I didn't know you'd be here yet, so I agreed to some babysitting."

That certainly surprised her. He didn't seem the childminder type, then again, she didn't know this man. Only that he was generous. "Okay, I'll help."

"You won't need to, but I doubt the kids will leave you be. You'll be too much of a puzzle to Reagan and she's precocious. Not to mention little Amber who tries to copy her."

"It sounds fun."

"Are you sure? There's going to be seven children running around my house, ages baby to middle school."

She gulped but wanted to see Danny in this setting. Something about it tickled her curiosity about the man. Him and weans. Kids. "Oh wow, sure, I'm still game. I guess we'd best get the shopping done then. I'll need you to take me since I don't have a license or a car."

"I planned to anyway. Get your purse or whatever you plan to carry and let's get moving."

Later, Moira sat back in the comfy chair she'd selected for her temporary studio. The easel, while not the one she'd had in Ireland, worked well in the space. She and Danny had been limited to what was in the store, but she preferred to buy now instead of waiting for an online order because even two days without painting in that beautiful space would be horrible. She'd been able to purchase canvases and more paints. Thankfully, her brushes had been part of the inventory she'd demanded from her home in Ireland.

She sighed as she stood, then said goodnight to the room with the things that made her happy and content. She descended the stairs and met up with Danny, who was waiting in the living room.

"Again, I'm sorry. I agreed to this before I knew you'd be here."

Danny's apology was cute but unnecessary. She didn't

mind at all helping watch the weans. "I don't get how you are the choice as a childminder for wee ones."

With a shrug, he explained, "I like kids and offered one day to watch Ace, who is almost three now. After that, I became a babysitter for when the family goes out together. Now there are four one-year-olds, but with Reagan and Amber, I barely have anything to do. Those two act like mother hens. Truthfully, they're a little bossy. Cute bossy, but bossy."

Moira laughed at that visual. "Didn't you say Reagan had an older brother? Surely he could watch the weans."

Danny laughed. "He's a sixteen-year-old boy. He only cares about getting to first base. Besides, maybe the babies will have their first steps for us."

The doorbell rang and Moira braced herself for an evening as a childminder. Seven wee ones. She wasn't against it, but she hadn't been around babies enough, and she worried she might do the wrong thing.

As it turned out, all the weans were walking. Nay, not walking, sprinting. She, Amber, and Reagan each took a wee one to keep corralled in the living room with the others. Danny took two toddlers. The babies got into everything and they did it lightning fast. No wonder the family didn't get out together much. Who would watch this group? Well, besides Danny, who seemed as if he could've handled all the weans with ease. He brightened when playing with them. The man needed to have a family. It was obvious he craved one. Or at least did so when he was minding the babies.

With the wee ones finally asleep in Danny's room and Danny occupying three-year-old Ace, Moira and the older kids went back to the living room.

After getting them each a beverage, Moira sat, and Amber pulled herself up on the couch beside her. Then the little girl proceeded to impart her wisdom. "Mom says I can't live with a boy unless we're married or related. Are you related to Uncle Danny? Because if you are, then it's okay you live here, but if not, well, I guess you have to get married."

The logic of a six-year-old astounded her. She really didn't have words for a response that would pacify the girl. She desired Danny and living with him presented a challenge for her not to be forward since he was being so respectful, but married? Nay. She didn't care for the state of matrimony. Being free and single to live how she wanted suited her fine.

Reagan slid onto the love seat facing them. "Silly, that's only a rule made by your mom and dad. Real adults don't have to be married or related to live together. I heard Dad say people live in sin all the time. Uncle Ken and Aunt Sam did before they got married."

These parents were really messing with their kiddos' heads. She'd heard the men of this family were overprotective, but come on. Expecting it to be futile since the weans seemed confident in their parents' version, she tried to set the record straight. She did think it cute the kids all called Danny—and he said his teammates—Uncle. "Your uncle Danny is letting me stay here until my brother and his girlfriend arrive. We're not living in sin, getting married, or related. It is possible for two adults to be just roommates."

Reagan snorted. "Uncle Jake would never allow that for Amber. He said she couldn't even date until she was thirty. Imagine. Thirty is ancient. I mean, I don't want to date boys now, but Mom says I will one day, but it will be when I'm a teenager not thirty. I'll be half-dead by that age."

"Oh yeah, well, Uncle Jesse said you can't date until you're twenty-five. So there." Amber stuck out her tongue.

Reagan groaned and fell back in the cushions. "Twenty-five. Ancient."

Moira grinned and guessed that did seem ancient to a nine-year-old, but since Moira was twenty-eight, she was beginning to feel as prehistoric as the girls made her age sound.

"Are your brother and his girlfriend getting married? Because if not, they shouldn't be living here together either," Amber said.

As she'd expected, her explanation had gone in one ear and out the other. What the child's parents taught her stood firm in her mind. "They do plan to get married. They're having a wean." Too late she realized she might've opened up a whole other conversation.

Amber scrunched up her nose. "What's a wean?"

Moira tried to keep her Irish from her vocabulary, so she'd fit in better, but sometimes, it slipped out. "A baby."

"And they're not married?" Amber asked and truth be told, the child looked scandalized.

"Not yet. Her daddy didn't approve of my brother, so they couldn't get married before."

"But he approves now?" Reagan asked.

"Let's just say that he's not standing in the way any longer."

"Oh boy," Reagan said with a dramatic eye roll.

"What?" She couldn't imagine what she'd said to evoke that response.

"Anytime our parents start a sentence with 'let's just say,' it means they think we won't understand."

Well, she couldn't tell them Diana's father wanted them both dead instead of blessing their union. "Nay. Nothing like that for me."

Reagan nodded. "You've got a funny accent."

"Reagan," Amber chided, "you weren't supposed to mention that."

Why on earth? Oh, it must've been to keep from embarrassing her. Well, she couldn't get more embarrassed, so she exaggerated her accent, "Ye like how I sound, wee lasses?"

The girls fell into peals of laughter. Moira laughed along at the night she'd had so far.

Danny, with Ace clinging to him, stuck his head in the room. "Keep it down in there. You don't want to wake the kids." He ducked back out speaking to the little boy, "I swear those women…."

"I have a swear jar for the men who work for my dad.

So, if Uncle Danny cusses, you make sure he puts his money in the jar. I have to pay for college, after all."

The beauty of a wean's mind to switch from one topic to the next.

Chapter Ten

The past two weeks with Moira had been more fun than he could recall having in a long time. If he wasn't so damn scared of another crash, he'd have given her an aerial tour. It was a beautiful way to see the city. Maybe one day.

Declan had told him Diana was put on bedrest, and her situation was still cautious. So the two remained in Boston and asked that Moira stay with Danny, even though she wanted to be at her brother's side. To help keep her mind off the situation, he'd done what his mom did whenever she had something on her mind—he took Moira shopping.

Around town, she'd purchased the remainder of the supplies she needed for her studio, and he'd taken the time to show her around. They'd laughed, acted all touristy, and chatted about their younger days. As he'd expected, she fell in love with the first Irish pub they visited. They never made it to the other two. Something told him they'd spend a lot of time at this one, which worked out well because the teams also enjoyed hanging out there.

Watching Moira put delectable looking rolls in the oven, he moved to the bar in his kitchen and sat. With her back to the counter, she chopped vegetables with near precision. He reached over to snag a carrot, and she slapped his hand before he reached the vegetable. Chuckling, he held up his hands. "Okay. I won't," he lied. It made her look so fierce and protective that he'd have to attempt a steal again.

Pushing all her buttons made him smile. A lightness in his gut only emphasized the joy being around her created. He'd call it lighthearted… comfortable… close. Yes, it'd turned into a friendship that'd gone beyond what they'd experienced in their youth. It didn't mean he didn't still want the woman. He craved her with every bone in his body. Speaking of bone, ashamedly, his hard-on was ever present around her. Either she didn't notice the bulge in his jeans, or she didn't speak of it. Still, since she was his brother's girl, he wouldn't take advantage, but the desire to have her was slowly killing him.

It was coming to the end of the few days he'd had off. "Moira, when I go back to work"—her knife stopped a moment, then began again— "I need to make sure you've got everything you need."

Although she didn't look up, he saw a brightness to her face before she asked, "The car?"

"No, Moira. I've told you that you can't drive here. That driver's license won't make it through a police stop. Then you'd get arrested. Then your real passport would need to be used. Then you'd probably trigger something in the system that showed a trail." Again, he wished they could do more for her identification, but it'd been quick providing her a driver's license to match the passport Justin had forged. The license hadn't been for driving but for easy ID when needed. To ease his mind, he may need to speak with Jesse about helping her technically disappear and getting her documents that would hold up to scrutiny.

The brightness quickly faded, and he wanted to jump over the counter and hold her tight, promising to always take care of her.

He hated to ruin her happiness. To him, she was a breath of fresh air. Everything was new to her in the sense of how the US set their stores up. The sights, which he'd seen before, excited her, and she talked of painting a canvas of the town.

"Let's talk about money. I'll give you some cash and my card for whatever you need."

She shook her head. "I thought I told you that Declan put money into an account for me."

With his brows taking a deep dive, he wondered if she understood the change in currency. He also wondered why Declan had decided to remain in Boston, leaving his sister to a family friend rather than asking for her to join them. It was nosy, but he needed to know she wouldn't run out of money. "How much?"

She told him a figure, and his mouth dropped.

"See," she said confidently, "more than enough, and he plans to keep it full for me."

He swallowed a couple times, battling the lump lodged in his throat. He'd known the family was well off, but not that much to have coming in regularly. Then again… "Where did your brother get so much money?"

She shrugged. "He said it was from our parents, and soon, I come into my full inheritance." Her body tightened and that made him want to tickle her to find out the reason. That had been their way when they were kids. Now, he figured it would be inappropriate.

"What is it?" He reached over and snagged a cut potato.

"You shouldn't eat that raw."

Grinning—something he kept doing with her, he probed again, "What is it?"

When she slammed down the knife on the cutting board and looked at him with fire in her eyes, he almost wished he hadn't pushed. This emotion was something he hadn't seen and wasn't sure what it meant.

"I also have to be married to collect it."

After his initial shock, he laughed, then tossed her a grin. Even figuring his brother had been tagged for the job, he offered, "If you don't have anyone else by then, I'll marry you." Where the hell had that come from and why didn't it scare him? "Friends do it all the time."

Her nervous laugh left him wondering whether he'd

said the right thing or not. Surely, she had to know it was a joke. Although…. No, he wouldn't think of something so far out there. When he found the right woman, he'd marry. But Moira was a friend he wanted to make happy. Oh, and have twisting-in-the-sheets sex with.

Picking up the knife and slicing, she took a moment before she spoke. "Thanks, but I won't marry just for the money. I made a really good living in Ireland painting and can do the same when I return."

She'd leave. Panic took hold of him and walloped his heart into beating overtime. A thought occurred to him. "If this isn't over by then"—she looked at him sharply, but he wouldn't stop pushing— "and you're married, how can you collect the money without alerting anyone?"

She waved her hand with the knife—which he kept his eye on—as if his question was inconsequential, then seemed to think about it. "I hadn't thought about that. Since I'll be supposedly dead, Declan's my beneficiary, so I guess he has the money. Well, he'll be dead too." She bit her outer lip, and Danny wanted to climb over the counter and help her. After thinking it over, she shrugged and returned to her task. "Declan will work it out when the time comes."

He added to his list to ask Joe or Devon how secure the accounts were she was using. He couldn't let something so simple bite them in the ass. Maybe they should transfer the money to a new account in her fake name and do it while routing and bouncing it enough to hide every converted dollar. How does that work with the general inheritance if both of them are dead?

His DEA knowledge on moving money wasn't enough to answer those questions. According to Jesse—who was also a former FBI agent—and Devon Hamilton—former CIA and computer guru—and Boss, it'd been that DEA background that had made him so valuable to HIS. Yet, they hadn't needed him often enough to make him feel useful.

"Moira, I'm leaving you money to spend. Don't touch the account your brother established until I do some research."

She stilled. "Why?"

He exhaled loudly. "Nothing. I just want everything to be safe. I want to speak with someone who is well-versed in accounts. Until then, we should proceed with caution on anything tying you to Ireland."

Watching him and appearing to consider what he'd said, she finally nodded. "Okay. I wish this situation was done and over with."

He agreed with that. While her situation involved threats from overseas, his hands were tied. However, since it was Boyle who was involved, he'd find out if he knew the agent stationed in Ireland and use him or her for information. Shaking his head to wonder about that later, he leaned over the bar and sniffed.

Moira laughed. "I'm still cutting it up."

Since she'd arrived, they'd taken turns cooking, but her way was by far the best. "The smell of the bread is making my stomach growl."

She glanced at the oven. "Potato and cheddar rolls. I enjoy it so much more than soda bread, but I love that too," she rushed to add.

"And, what're you making?" He pointed to the pot she'd dumped cubes of meat into.

"A simple stew. I haven't cooked it for you yet."

He rubbed his belly but decided he wanted to have some fun with her since he hadn't heard a little Irish rant in a few days. "Hm. Is it as good as your mom's? Because she made the best Irish stew I've ever eaten." He shook his head, watching the pink creep up her face. "No, I can't believe anyone could cook it that well."

For a moment, he wondered if he'd gone too far and insulted her, without her realizing he was joking. Before he could make that point clear, she turned the spoon on him and began to rant. Mostly in English, but some Irish and Gaelic slipped in.

His grin spread across his face, and his heart lightened. She was magnificent in beauty and spirit. He drank in everything about her.

She spoke rapidly, and he couldn't keep up. He translated some of her Gaelic, although he wished he hadn't been able to. "Ungrateful." "Rat's ass." He hoped that meant she didn't give a rat's ass versus calling him that. "Poison." That one made him a little nervous. He had to put an end to her tirade, but when he raised his hand to stop her, she just spoke faster, and her accent thickened, ending his ability to understand her words.

Ignoring her verbal assault, that he'd thought would've

been joking back and forth, he stood, took the few steps to the refrigerator, and opened it. Like nothing was amiss, he asked, "Want something while I'm pouring?"

She stopped speaking as if just realizing he'd left the seat. When she didn't answer immediately, he looked at her beyond the open refrigerator door and quirked an eyebrow in question. She glared at him with her hand on one hip and the spoon still pointing at him. "You did that on purpose, didn't you? You, you—"

"Rat's ass?" he finished for her and laughed until he saw her fighting a smile.

Her embarrassment was even more attractive than her raging.

He chuckled and winked at her. "I'm having sweet tea. Want some?"

Controlled, she turned back to the stove and stirred the meat. "Is that all they drink where you grew up in Georgia?"

"Hell, yeah," he replied without a thought. "Want some?"

She wrinkled her nose. "I'd like a glass of wine."

"Red or white?"

Her incredulous look made him want to laugh also. As he thought about it, since she'd moved in, he'd laughed more than he had in as long as he could remember. All he did was work and hang out with other agents. He'd avoided women because he tended to find the ones he couldn't connect with and ones who became needy.

Bringing himself out of that morose thought, he

wondered if she'd answered more than once. "Red, we're having meat."

Stupid statement, he also knew she'd stocked up with Irish wines. Every time they'd entered the Irish pub, *Sláinte*, he caught some silent communication with her and the owner. Not only had the man put her in contact with a store that carried fine Irish wines, but, because the owner referred her, her wine was delivered.

Danny knew she visited the bar when he'd had meetings and training. Having her country's music, food, and togetherness seemed to help her acclimate. She'd kept to the area and didn't balk at his security restrictions. They had no direct threat, but he'd purposefully omitted telling her about the men he'd hired to watch her, so she could feel independent but remain safe.

While the meal finished cooking, he pulled out his laptop and sat on the couch. It'd been a few days since he'd chatted with Justin. According to Justin, Boyle bought the fake deaths. The man hadn't even choked up over his own daughter's death. A daughter he'd loved until he found out she was in love with a police officer.

In an effort to keep in touch, he and Justin had set up secure email. It wouldn't be instant communication, but it'd be something to keep each other updated. When he logged in, nothing new appeared. Danny silently swore. They had a schedule, and Justin had missed his update. Either Justin worried someone would trace their communication, or he— Danny swallowed that thought. If Justin had been questioned, tortured, or worse, he wouldn't be able to warn Moira or Declan.

Danny kept his hope that nothing had changed with Boyle's thoughts, but he still felt better keeping a small security detail on her.

Before he logged out, a new message appeared from Justin. Shouldn't he be sleeping? Danny glanced at his watch, figured the time difference and worried.

Don't forget to water the roses for me.

In a reply to the email, he typed, *Should I add fertilizer?*

The quick reply put him at ease—a little. *No. I think they're fine without it.*

With the conversation over, Danny deleted the message and double deleted it how Devon had shown him to make sure it couldn't easily be retrieved.

The aroma coming from the kitchen made his stomach growl as he finished shutting everything down. From his position, he watched her as she pulled out the bread, which made his mouth water. Maybe it was her bending over the stove, that—

He shouldn't go there. The good news was, according to his brother, there was no word of Boyle suspecting Moira or her brother were still alive. Technically, they were safe. He'd still contact the DEA agent in Ireland. Maybe he could pull some information that Justin couldn't share, due to communication limitations.

After putting away his laptop, he joined her in the open kitchen-dining area for supper. She'd allowed him to set the table, which made him feel like less of a dud making her cook in his house. It'd been an agreed-upon pattern, but sitting while someone cooked for him was hard. As he imagined it was for her also, especially in a strange house.

Through an excellent supper, he told stories of his teammates and they laughed at the antics of the crew. She looked remarkably enticing, even though he doubted she'd tried. She had that natural beauty appeal down pat.

It'd been tough keeping his growing feelings at bay. The draw to her had begun when he'd spotted her stepping out of the plane. After spending time with her, the more he'd learned about her, the deeper his cravings. It'd also told him that he needed time away from her for all the reasons he'd stated, plus the fact she was taken and didn't give him the impression she reciprocated his feelings. Abruptly, he stood and tossed his napkin to the table. "I'll help clean up."

She looked at him funny. "Fine," she agreed softly.

Together, they cleared the table and handwashed the dishes after a fight over who washed and dried. He rarely used his dishwasher as it took too many days to fill.

"You can dry," she said. "Because your dishes aren't clean enough when you wash."

With a hand to his heart and a step back in feigned horror, he didn't agree, but it didn't matter. They'd get clean either way.

"I made some friends at the gallery down the street." She handed him a white plate. He wasn't very creative with his decor. Maybe she could help him spruce the place up some. He'd love her hand in making his house a home.

Wiping the plate, he nodded. "Wait. You what? When was this?" He hadn't received that in a report from his men.

"Laura and Luke."

His hand tightened on the next plate she'd handed him. Luke? "Are they a couple or something?" *Please say yes,* he thought, because he didn't wear jealousy well.

With a swift shake of her head, she said, "Nay."

Before he could probe more, they turned toward each other and Moira's momentum brought her into his chest with her hands between them. Instantly, he grabbed the sides of her waist to steady her.

Fuck me. His breath caught and his heart squeezed as he held her against him. Gazing down into her bright eyes and watching them slowly darken sent heat south, tightening his jeans. All he wanted to do was take her into his arms and carry her to bed. He almost felt done in when she licked her lips. As if not in control, he dipped his head to kiss the ever-loving hell of her, but he came to a screeching halt. He couldn't kiss his brother's girl. But— "I want to kiss you so bad it hurts."

Her delayed answer began to shatter the moment. He released his tight hold on her, so she could step back if she wished. But he didn't remove his hands. "I… um… I'm not sure—" Disappointment shined in her eyes when he pulled back and dropped his hands. The heat from her body and touch evaporated, making him want to grab her back.

It was possible they should've had this conversation earlier, but it was always an awkward conversation to have. Surprising her by taking her hand, he led her to the table and guided her to a chair beside him.

The jumbled thoughts in his head chose their own path to his mouth, ignoring his honor and integrity. "Moira, there's heat between us. I can't hide anymore that I want you in my bed. But I know you're not here by choice."

"I um—"

Reaching out with his free hand, he placed two fingers over her lips. "It's okay. You don't need to say anything. I won't push. Now—" He sighed and dropped his hand from her mouth. "—if Justin takes out Boyle, are you going back to Ireland?"

While she looked at him a bit strangely, she nodded. "Of course. It's my home."

"Have you ever considered remaining in the States? I mean, you can stay here as long as you'd like."

"I'd like to visit from time to time. I do love it here." While the joy in her eyes evaporated, she continued, "You should come visit me once I'm set back up." A cute blush filled her cheeks, and she lowered a head a tad. "I only have a one-bedroom flat, so you'd have to stay with Declan—if he returns—or in a hotel."

Undaunted by her not inviting him to stay with her, he wouldn't give up getting her to stay. With his hand still in hers, he asked, "What if you found a boyfriend or fell in love? Would you stay then?" Before he said the last word, he wondered if he'd overplayed his hand. Although, he really didn't have a good hand to play.

She jerked her hand from his. "Danny, what's this all about?"

He dropped his brows as his spirit sank at the concern in her voice. No, her tone held more anger and frustration than anything else. Not ready to admit his feelings without speaking with his brother, he decided it best to drop the subject for now. "Nothing."

"Is that all? I'd like to make some plans with my friends for tomorrow. Low key. I promise." Her statement told him the conversation about them had abruptly ended even though it'd never really started. He'd screwed up and lost all chance of turning their conversation into a fun, personal chat to continue getting to know each other better. Oh, and winning her over.

Surprised, he responded, "Sure."

Once she left the dining room, he dropped his head in his hands, elbows resting on the table. He wanted to continue to be her friend, more than anything else, so he wracked his brain on how he could keep his lower brain from making the decisions.

Only one thing would do that.

Chapter Eleven

"I don't like this, Franks," Cowboy said quietly through the comms.

Neither did Danny. It was too quiet. The intel they'd received on this government-sanctioned op sucked monkey balls. Arthur Hall, FBI Deputy Director, and HIS worked together on many ops. Danny Franks never asked why. He did what needed to be done.

This was supposed to be an easy snatch and grab job. Not even snatch. Someone brought the boy to them. Easy for the four of them. Not breaking their arms to pat themselves on their backs, but he, Cowboy, Doc, and Stone knew how to win. This time, something wasn't right. The air reeked of it. The heavy pressure of getting the boy and team to safety rested on his chest, making each breath painful.

Why the agency—any of them—had farmed this out should've set alarm bells ringing in his head when they had off-the-books black ops that could be done with their hands tied behind their backs. Uncle Sam was, at least, providing air transport out of here.

Reaching down beside him, he checked the little boy's pulse for about the hundredth time. Doc said he'd sleep until they got him nearly home, and that worked for Danny since he'd yet to hear their ride approach.

When the men returned from patrol, he'd find out what disturbed him about this op. "We'll be fine." Together, they'd always find a way.

Stone reported in first from his recon of the area behind the structure. "I'd say we're going to be rockin' more than we thought."

"If I didn't say it before, thanks for joining the party, Stone." Without him, they'd been benched for this op, and as much as he liked being around Moira, this kid needed them.

Cowboy didn't wait a beat before he got in some good-natured jesting. "After riding that desk, did you put on your big boy pants to enter our playground?"

Doc reported in, breaking off anything Stone said in retort. "They've got a fucking army arriving."

Shit. How did their contact not tell them that? Dammit, they were a quarter mile away from their extraction point and were nearly boxed in. Why not protect the boy in the first place, instead of bringing in the troops to take him back?

Danny grabbed the bill of his camo cap, yanked it off, then shoved it back on his head. His mind spun fast through idea after idea. No one said it, but they should've heard the helo by now, which meant they had to fight their way to a secure location and wait for backup transport. He'd be kicking Arthur in the ass for leaving them like this with an innocent child under their protection.

If HIS had their own helo, he could've flown them in and out. No waiting. Wait, did he say he'd fly it? Impossible.

"I found one gap in their coverage," Doc stated, "but I can't guarantee it still holds."

"Ditto," Stone added.

Danny's gut churned. The leader in him screamed setup. Their target knew this team would be there. Arthur had a leak because Danny knew HIS didn't. Shit, it could've been a leak elsewhere since the troops were trucked in. Until Arthur found the traitor, Danny would remain wary.

His blood pulsed with a surge of adrenaline in a prepared-to-fight mode, but he wanted the team to be on the same sheet of music. "How many tangos behind us and how large were the gaps?" he asked in a take-charge voice. "Enough for us to slip through?"

Doc answered first. "Roger."

"Negative," Stone said in a clipped voice.

"Doc?" he prompted.

"Twenty. Ten each side. Either leaving the exit open for us to walk into their trap or closing in on us."

Definite setup. He hated making the hard decision, but he had to so they could run a successful op. "Well, boys and girls—" Danny started.

"There ain't no fucking girls on our team anymore," Cowboy corrected him.

"I don't know, Cowboy," Stone taunted, "you seem to get your panties in a wad quite often."

Too worried about them getting out of here to their extraction point, their friendly banter slid over him, but having it was normal until go-time. "Okay, boys—and I use that word lightly—I'm not saying anything you're not thinking. This reeks setup. First, our ride isn't on time, and the enemy provides a perfect path back to them? Only an idiot wouldn't catch that. Standby."

Slipping his backpack to the ground, he slid the zipper, greased, so it wouldn't make a sound, opened, pulled out the sat phone, and dialed the op line. As expected, the answer came before the first ring ended.

"Go," AJ Hamilton—youngest Hamilton brother—clipped.

"We don't have a bird or much time," Danny stated briskly.

"What do you mean?"

AJ's muffled voice called for Devon to the phone while using another to call about the transport. When would AJ learn to completely cover the mouthpiece when expecting it to mute? Danny shook his head at that.

A second click on the phone line told him Devon—who a few sometimes referred to as Big Voice—had joined the call. Good. He wouldn't have to repeat anything and Devon would be working that computer of his.

"We're boxed in." The rapidly coiling tension in his gut nearly paralyzed him. He'd led his men into a death, capture, or torture situation unless they got the bird where they had a smaller gunfight to make their exit.

When they'd seen two guards roaming the area, they were too far away to waste ammo. On their planned route, they found a location to dig in and wait. He didn't like being so close to a drop-off on the one side because they could get pinned down if things didn't go as planned.

"We've got the package but no ride."

"Shit."

"Get us a ride. I can get us somewhere for a while, then I'll have to walk our asses back home." The low growl in his voice came from deep within and controlled the depth of his surging anger.

"They're not there?" AJ snapped.

To the team, he ordered, "Close recon. No heroes. Watch your six."

Doc moved beside him and attached a harness to the little five-year-old sleeping boy and attached that to his chest. With Doc being the largest and the kid's legs the shortest, it made sense to connect him for a safer carry.

"No, we'd hear the bird if it was close, AJ," Danny belatedly answered his question. "And it's pretty quiet. Except for the stink of a setup."

"Why do you think setup?" AJ said.

Danny snorted. Thank goodness Devon was on the ball with getting their ride. "They showed up after we collected the boy and went straight for us, not the house."

"Fuck."

"I second that." Danny wondered why Devon hadn't already had something for them. He always did.

Speak of the devil. Devon always came through for them. "Your backup is there."

"The fuck you say. It's quiet. No extra bodies around unless they're ghosts." Then it hit him. Spooks. They were pretty much ghosts. "Got it."

"They're in a bird hovering near your location," Devon informed him.

He wished the two brothers were here to realize what they said wasn't true. "Impossible. It's too quiet not to hear a bird." They rode in on one near their current spot. There wasn't one near.

He could hear the smile in Devon's voice. "Trust me."

A shiver of fear slid up his spine resting on his shoulders where he kept the lives of his men, but he did extend that trust.

To the team, he ordered, "On me."

Always the 'you can't bring me too much intel' guy, Devon instructed, "Get me all the intel you can. Nothing is too small."

Like they hadn't heard that before. Gunfire ripped his attention away. "Sitrep." His heart pounded. He needed the situation reports from his returning team members. Maybe they could fight their way out, but probably not.

"These fuckers are closing in," Cowboy whispered in his mic.

"Our bird's nearby."

Danny's mind whirled for a long moment. If they could— "Are any holes still open?"

"Negative," Doc said.

"Negative," Stone added.

"Who took the gunfire?"

Each man denied it, which made things more Charlie Foxtrot—clusterfuck.

Fuck! His trust was wavering. He had to get his team and their package out of here, and it was too late to turn back.

Devon came back on the phone when Danny was about to hang up. "They're on the cliff. Just north of where you arrived."

"Hell no!" he almost screamed into the phone. "We'll get pinned down."

"Your bird will be there before you make it. Trust me, Danny," Devon requested once again.

With a sigh that couldn't wash away the cold sweat covering his body, he remembered Devon had never steered them wrong. "Okay, we're moving." He disconnected, tossed the sat phone in his backpack, and hurriedly slipped it over his shoulders. Gut deep worry that he would bring them to their death, stuck at the cliff.

"We gotta blow this joint and fast," Cowboy stated, breathing a little heavy.

"Together, we head to the cliff."

A frustrated quiet filled the air, so Danny explained, "Devon says they're there."

They headed at a fast yet smart clip in the forested part toward the cliff. His heart beat fast and not because of the exertion. Not only were they skirting guards in the woods, they'd be vulnerable in the open where they'd board the helo.

He couldn't wait for his team leader to get his ass back to work. Filling in for Boss sucked. Just plain sucked.

At the edge of the cover, they knelt to keep from being seen. While Doc—because he had the package—turned from the danger and watched for their ride, the other three had their backs to him prepared for anything.

By now they should hear the whomp-whomp of the rotors bouncing off the walls of the ravine. Nothing. Christ. Devon couldn't be wrong.

They didn't need this problem. The four could probably do some damage, even with limited ammo and supplies, but having an unconscious five-year-old on for the ride decreased his confidence in their success. Then they'd still be without a ride.

A small displacement of air warned him before he heard the faint whirl of a helicopter. He whipped his head around and his mind almost couldn't process the abnormality. What the fuck had Arthur sent?

Then he saw it float above the ravine and land one skid on the ground for them to board. Holy Christ. He'd heard these birds existed, but no one would ever admit it. Stealth-like.

When shots came from the bird, he stiffened a moment with a quick thought of friend or foe, but none of his men dropped, so he took that as a good sign.

He called to his team, "Hot loading!"

Cowboy, a former Air Force Pararescueman, quickly jumped in. "I'll break 'em in."

"Good, you go first. Help Doc."

When Cowboy opened his mouth to say whatever it was, he commanded him, "Go, go, go."

Danny had to hope everything went right because the gunfight was closing in on them and their only free space was the drop-off.

After Stone made it, Cowboy's voice halted him. "It's too hot. We're swinging around for you. Hang tight."

"Hang tight" he wanted to mimic. Alone, adrenaline took over. He hot-loaded his weapon—ejecting his clip and quickly replacing it with another—and fired at the nearest tango. Without the sniper on the bird taking out threats, he was busy, which meant his hiding spot had been compromised.

Knowing what to listen for, he heard as the bird neared his position.

"They've got you covered, Ball Park. You're going to like it. It's a sweet ride. Now we gotta blow this popsicle stand. And I've rolled out the red carpet for you."

He grinned. Cowboy always brought levity when needed and knew he loved all things helicopter, but his smile quickly froze. Did he say "roll out the red carpet?" Oh, holy fuck. Only Cowboy would call one maneuver that.

Swallowing back his fear, he made the dash, found

the ropes, and anchored the carabiners on his harness to the SPIE rope and the safety line, wished he had goggles, reminded himself he never wanted to do crap like this on a regular basis, then walked forward, kicking off the cliff into nothing.

Chapter Twelve

The moment the helicopter touched ground in Maryland, Danny exited first and stalked to HQ. He'd only barely noticed that their ride had powered down. He'd eagerly checked it out during the flight and a refueling stopover. HIS needed one of these birds because they were about the next best thing to sliced bread. It sucked because the helo technically didn't exist, but a man could crave adventure.

He started for a moment. Had they landed on a helicopter pad in the making? Hope jumped up his chest at the thought. He hoped one day he could bring the men and women back and forth from ops. Get them out of all kinds of situations whether light or deadly. There he went again thinking he'd fly, knowing that was unlikely.

At the heavy entry door, with his mind back in the game, he punched in his personal code. When the door opened, he turned to make sure it closed behind him, but his team brought up the rear.

"Doc, check him out and get him to whoever's here to collect him. Everyone else hit the showers. I'll handle this." As Alpha team assistant team leader, Danny was responsible for everything—good or bad—that happened on an op under his command. This time, he hadn't planned backup transport and somehow brought a small army into their rescue mission.

As he reached the war room, he took long strides, not even greeting Devon who looked as tired as Danny felt. His insides burned with a rage that could make the largest bonfire ever. When he found the office he sought, he entered, not wasting his time playing games.

Slapping his hands on the desk, Danny leaned his head down to look at AJ.

"We go on no more ops with just the four of us without a sniper," he said firmly. "If we hadn't had some black ops help, all four us wouldn't be walking back in. And the FBI had its own group of spooks. Why weren't they doing this shit instead of swooping in like an avenging angel and providing transport that doesn't even belong to them?" His anger, frustration, and finally sarcasm bled into his voice and he wouldn't change it a bit.

Alpha team had been prepared for the op. Although Cowboy had wanted to barge in, toss a few flash grenades, they'd agreed to accept the boy from his nanny. With no expected army, two of them could've handled it.

AJ ran his hand through his dark hair, and Danny couldn't tell if it was frustration or something else on his face. "I know." His soft tone warred with what Danny thought he'd seen. His stance in the meeting strengthened when AJ leaned back in his chair and crossed his arms over his chest, like they weren't discussing something that hadn't been life or death.

"Did your help arrive? Okay." AJ looked sheepishly. "I guess they did if you're here."

Danny also remained standing with crossed his arms, his eyes narrowed. He nodded although it'd been unnecessary. "Yep. I would've liked them earlier."

"Arthur called and told me he'd sent them but didn't know if they'd make it for cleanup."

"Speaking of cleanup, that's exactly what they'd have been doing for us if we hadn't had them. Why was this a setup?" It still didn't add up to him and that bothered him down to his toes.

Ignoring his important question, AJ aggravated him more by asking, "What did you think of the snipers?"

About ready to jump over the desk to keep AJ on track, Danny forced himself to shrug. "They were fine. They kept our asses alive. But I'm more worried about what we left."

AJ waved off his words. "Before we forced Ken on medical leave, he approved Alpha team two snipers—which is what we want per team." AJ shook his head. "I think the man is superhuman or something, working so long injured."

It had taken a lot to finally get Ken to take medical leave after being shot more than once. If it hadn't been for Sugar, he probably wouldn't have taken the time. The problem was that she'd been their sniper and decided to keep one parent out of the action with the boy they were raising.

AJ picked up a bag of chips and offered him some. Danny declined and almost snatched them from him because last he'd heard, AJ's wife said he was getting flabby in the gut, so junk food went out the window.

Somehow discerning Danny's thoughts, AJ explained how his wife didn't rule the roost and if he wanted—

Danny tuned out. He needed to give a full debrief, shower, and get home to Moira. He needed to see her and know she was okay. There'd been no message from the former DEA buddy he'd hired to covertly watch her. He took the silence as a positive sign.

AJ now discussed his son. Danny admitted Ace was a good and smart kid. But he'd had enough. He slammed his hands on the desk again, this time making AJ jump. "AJ, focus. You said you had two new sharpshooters for the team? Where the hell were they tonight?"

Looking at AJ, finding the corner of his lips curling into a smirk, caused Danny to feel even more nauseous. You never knew what to expect from the runt of the Hamilton men. It appeared AJ had a secret he was eager to share.

"Where were they tonight? They were covering your six."

Thrown by that statement, Danny staggered back to the chair facing the desk. It took a moment to process exactly what he meant. "Are you telling me two of those 'I-don't-exist' agents are joining us?" Not that HIS was a step-down, but…?

Somehow in the time he'd pondered things, AJ had put away the chips and turned serious. "Okay. Yes, two snipers are coming our way and will be on Alpha team. It gets better. One sharpshooter is an explosives expert while the other, his twin, is a top-notch handler."

"Since they're spooks, maybe we should split them up."

"I don't split from my sister," a deep voice with a hard edge said from behind him.

Danny spun around to face the snipers from the helo and Alpha team's newest sharpshooters. While you'd never mix the twins up, it was obvious they were brother and sister. Now. On the flight, she'd done a great job hiding the fact she was a woman. Like him, the siblings hadn't showered and looked to be carrying gear.

Peering to the side, Danny caught sight of three sweaty, mushed camo-painted men. Either his team had come back to support him or they'd followed the spooks. Either way, he appreciated it. And now he knew AJ had been stalling instead of being an idiot.

AJ scooted around the desk in the small office and unnecessarily introduced them at the doorway, obviously noting the rest of the team waiting. He turned back to Danny with a quirk of his brow, and Danny chose to ignore any implied question with that expression.

They'd spoken briefly on the bird, but mostly just the

thank you for arriving when they had and not dropping Danny as he flew behind him on a rope. Both gave a strong handshake, but there was no denying the brother's grip had a 'touch my sister and I'll kill you' feel.

"What the fuck?" Cowboy opened his mouth to say more and Danny cringed. The team didn't know them yet. The siblings had said few words on their return flight. "Did we just start taking the first people who show up?"

The twins looked at Cowboy, and he looked down at Jane, then cocked the smile he used to pick up women. Danny knew his next words would be wrong. So very wrong. He reached to get Cowboy's attention and stop him, but he was too late.

"Hello, sweet cheeks."

A stunned and nearly unconscious Cowboy slid down the wall to rest on the floor. Danny didn't see the motion but heard the crack of a fist hitting a jaw. By the bewildered looks of his team, they'd also missed it. Cowboy would learn not to mess with Jane with her brother around. The quick movements went unnoticed. Internally, he shook his head in satisfaction. He looked forward to having these two on the team.

"Great shot," John said.

Jane looked up at him, nodded then smiled.

Danny glanced at the wide eyes of his team and her approval. They'd worked with tough women before, so he shouldn't have assumed her brother was the one to knock out Cowboy.

Putting his arm over his sister's shoulders, they turned

and moved toward the locker rooms. Danny looked down at Cowboy again and spun back to AJ. He stated, not asked, "We're calling it a day." With that, he turned back to Cowboy, who peeked through half-lidded eyes and then jumped agilely to his feet.

"When are you going to learn?" Danny grumbled in frustration. He needed to get home, not caught up in Cowboy's way to welcome new team members.

"Never." A broad grin accompanied that statement. "I could tell when she was shooting that girl has got a lot of rage in her."

As he'd guessed, Cowboy had faked going down and knew she'd thrown the punch. Danny pinched the bridge of his nose with his thumb and forefinger. "No," he said and reinforced it with stronger ones, "No. No. Absolutely not. We will not have another agent-to-agent relationship on this team."

Checking the movement of his jaw, Cowboy managed to laugh. "Oh, hell no. I like my dick too much to have her brother slice it off while I'm sleeping."

"I doubt he'd wait until you slept."

Whistling, and as if nothing had happened, Cowboy walked to the locker room. "Don't leave without me. You promised to let me meet your charge."

A small frenzy rode its way through him. He'd put off Cowboy meeting Moira for these past two months. At some point, Cowboy would just show up if he kept saying no, so best he do it on his terms.

After Danny provided an abbreviated debrief to AJ

and showered, Cowboy had cleaned both of their gear, prepping them for no-notice ops. Leaving HQ, Cowboy sat beside Danny in Danny's truck, prattling on about the bar and women. Danny's brain was too tired to process what he said, until he hit on something that floated in his mind also.

"Why do you think two of Arthur's black ops are joining us?"

"We could ask them," Danny offered as a solution Cowboy ignored.

"Do you think they're spying on us?" He whispered the question like they were being bugged.

It couldn't be the money because although HIS agents were highly paid, black ops had to make a crapload more. Even though they had Russian accents and generic names, he wouldn't peg them for spies. Besides, why would Arthur offer up two of his assets when a bug or two would get him everything the twins could uncover? No, he guessed something happened that made them want to leave the darkness, and Arthur valued their abilities and wanted them working for the good guys. At least he hoped.

Moira hadn't answered Danny's earlier call, so he could warn her he'd be bringing home company. Women liked it when men warned them, didn't they? He figured she was lost in painting because she didn't take her phone upstairs with her. She'd explained it disrupted her creative muse. Whatever that was.

When they arrived at his home, neither men had

spoken since the two black ops entered their mind. Admittedly, Danny's had switched to Moira and his brother. He didn't like the images in his mind. Mostly that a threat still existed and he couldn't find it.

Due to the late hour, the house was dark. He wished she'd kept a light on for him.

He and Cowboy tried to remain quiet as they entered, but they were far from it. In the kitchen, packs were dropped, and Cowboy perused the contents of the refrigerator for their late dinner. Since Moira usually cooked enough for an army, they'd bypassed the fast food places on the way.

"Son of a bitch," Danny yelled while he crumbled a sheet of paper, wanting to rip it apart, piece by piece, erasing it along with the situation that went with it. Instead, he tossed it across the room with all his strength from his old pitcher hand. "She's gone."

Cowboy pulled his head from the freezer and looked at him quizzically. "What'd you mean gone? Like to a party? To the store?"

"Don't act like you don't know what the fuck 'gone' means." He'd used the F word way too often today. He tried to avoid using the word—Reagan's swear jar or not.

Before Cowboy could respond, Danny hit a speed-dial button and held the phone to his ear. When her voice mail came on, pressure on his chest hit him hard. "Hey, Moira, just checking in. Call me." He paused and dialed another number. While waiting for the answer, he asked—to no one in particular, "Why hadn't she called me before she left?"

Cowboy, of course, had to respond. "Dude, she knew you were busy. Maybe she thought she shouldn't."

"But I've explain—"

"Franks, I'm glad you called." Mark Kelly's voice sounded weak to Danny's ears. His pulse pounded so loud his ears ached.

"Kelly, what's going on? Where's Moira?"

A groan preceded the answer. "I left you a message."

Danny pulled back his phone to check the message icon. Nothing. "I didn't get it. What's going on?"

"I'm sorry. I was in a major car accident a couple days ago and am still in the hospital."

Pacing, Danny slid his fingers through his hair, over and over again. "How are you?"

"I'll live."

"Do you think it could be related?" Not that he'd had any intel that Moira was in danger. Last he knew, Boyle thought she was dead.

"I don't think so since it was a drunk that hit me."

"You'll let me know if you need anything?"

"Of course I will. Listen, I tried to call Jax to cover for me."

A smidge of relief hit him amidst the horrible situation. Silence for too long took away that relief.

"Dead. Self-inflicted gunshot wound."

His gut sank at the blow. He'd thought Jax had improved. He never considered he'd commit suicide. Then again, how often did someone believe that of their friend? Spots danced before his eyes at the thought.

"I called everyone I knew. They all had a job for this weekend. I phoned to let you know no one was watching her."

Pinching the bridge of his nose, Danny heaved out a breath. "It's not your fault. I want you to rest and recuperate. Oh, Kelly, I'll see what's needed for Jax."

"Thanks, man. I'll call you when I'm released."

Nodding even though Kelly couldn't see, Danny, in a reassuring voice, thanked his friend and ended the call.

He wanted to throw his phone against the wall, but he barely restrained himself. In an effort to see if he did have a voice mail that didn't show, he called, entered his pin, and was informed he had no new messages. He'd have to have a chat with the carrier.

Tapping his phone against his forehead, as if he could pound in the answer, a thought popped into his head. With more confidence, he made the next call. "Are you still at HQ?"

With a slight hesitation, Stone responded, "Just walked out the door. What do you need?"

Even though, as far as he knew, there was no threat to her, he couldn't stop himself. "She's gone. Would you go back inside, pull up the tracker in her purse, and let me know where she is?"

Cowboy's loud declaration drowned out Stone's reply. "Dude, even I know better than that." He shook his head and chuckled as if enjoying himself. "You are so fucked."

Chapter Thirteen

"Why can't she stay where I put her? She has free rein in Fells Point, but is that good enough? Apparently not."

Fear like he'd never known coiled in his gut, ready to strike, as the drive to the Timonium Fair Grounds tightened the knot in his stomach. The fact she hadn't gone far set a drip of relief flowing through him. However, the fact she went at all pissed him off. Did she not care about her safety? Although they hadn't heard of a threat, it didn't mean it didn't exist. He knew she felt safe since Boyle thought her dead. Which, technically, meant she was safe. But he had his own way to play the odds.

He didn't have a choice about leaving her though. He had to work. Ken was due back soon, so he'd try to work something out. He wasn't sure he really needed someone watching her. As things stood, Boyle believed her dead. Besides, he couldn't afford to give her guards forever. Ultimately, he had to allow her to enjoy her life. However, tonight wasn't the night.

And that's why he put his foot farther down on the gas pedal.

Looking over at Cowboy, it became obvious they couldn't afford to be pulled over since, in addition to their concealed carry weapons, they had more of their gear.

Cowboy must've had the same thoughts. "Dude, you got a case in here?"

He felt insulted at the question. "Of course I do. There are two open handgun spaces for the ones I'm carrying." Danny glanced over at Cowboy. "Do you?" He knew the answer but felt he should ask.

His answer came quick. "Of course. But they're in my truck."

Laughing, he shook his head again. Whatever woman nailed him down had her work cut out for her. "Not every male does. Just the awesome ones like us."

"Hell yeah!"

Cowboy fidgeted with the temperature controls, and Danny wanted to slap his big hand.

"What's your plan for her? I could toss her over my knees and spank her for you."

With jealousy surging through him, if he could, he'd push Cowboy out the door, even while the car was in motion. Even if he succeeded, Cowboy would be waiting at the next stop, grinning his ass off like a lucky bastard.

That was partly why he'd not allowed Cowboy to visit

or hang out while Moira was around. While growing close as friends, he and Moira had a few moments of more than that. That's why the thought of turning her over his knees and spanking her naked butt until it was pink and he could soothe it with a rub from his hands was what he wanted to do, and curse anyone else who wanted to see even her panties.

Knowing she had his brother, Danny hadn't pushed, even though they'd almost kissed. It sucked balls that she hadn't answered his question about staying for love. What concerned him was that he worried she'd change her mind after meeting Cowboy. Women flocked to the agent for some strange reason. No, she might fall for his charm like every woman, but Ireland was her love.

Straining to keep the anger out of his voice for Cowboy's offer of assistance, he ground his teeth and all but growled, "No. We don't need that."

In his peripheral vision, he caught Cowboy's shrug. "All right. Just sayin' that I'll be there for you, bro. Always willing to take one for the team."

Danny snorted and just like that, his jealousy of Cowboy slid to nearly nothing. That fifteen minutes could seem like another lifetime.

"How do you think she got here? She didn't drive, did she?"

He hoped not because he'd told her more than once her new license wasn't actually valid. "She rode with Luke and Laura. At least, in her note, she'd said she was with them."

"Are you going to get more guys to watch her when you're gone?"

"Yes. No. I haven't decided." He had to reevaluate the situation. There had been no sign of a problem locally or in Ireland. Yet he liked erring on the side of caution.

"What about the drug dealer? Any word?"

Tired of waiting, Danny had contacted his friend DEA Agent Lance Ting, who was working with authorities in Ireland. Danny had told Lance some of what Moira had seen and heard. Justin had insisted not all was released. "Nothing yet."

Sitting in typical Baltimore traffic, Danny tapped his fingers on the steering wheel. Cowboy turned in his seat. "Thanks for letting me tag along."

He smiled at his friend who was only going because he was a dawg. "Truthfully, I'm glad to have the company."

The traffic in their lane hadn't moved in far too long. The other lanes were at least inching along, but not theirs. "An accident."

"I'd agree," Cowboy said, straining to see what he could out the window.

Danny put on his left blinker and tried to find a hole in the creeping traffic in the next lane. After several minutes of no openings, he slapped his steering wheel in frustration. "Doesn't anyone have any driving courtesy anymore?"

"Then it's time you forgot yours. Be a shit and cut someone off."

"I'm just not like that."

"Then you've got three options. Get over quickly. Let me drive and get over it. Or I can go block traffic for you to get your granny-ass over."

Administering a punch to Cowboy's bicep would've released the tension if he hadn't almost broken his hand. Those damn special ops guys.

"I thought you were worried about Moira's safety?"

That got through to him. He'd make a hole and they'd get through the rest of this traffic to make sure his woman was safe. Then he'd figure out how to make Justin and Moira see it that way.

Chapter Fourteen

Closing up her booth for the night, Moira looked forward to the bands scheduled to play. That afternoon she'd spoken with her brother. Diana had improved, but they decided to remain in Boston. It was where the two planned to build new lives. They'd yet to figure out how to accomplish many things without a real identity, but, like her, thought once Justin brought down Boyle, they'd be free.

Laura and Luke arrived and helped her pull down the last of her Irish landscape paintings. She'd had an excellent day—better than she'd expected, which meant she might sell out of her artwork before the Irish Festival ended.

Although many of the people attending weren't Irish, a sense of home bled into her every pore, making her mourn for what she'd lost. Instead of allowing the drowning emotions to grab hold of her soul, she reminded herself that she'd eventually return home. She trusted Justin to make that possible for both her and her brother.

That thought tried to drag her down. She'd made friends in Baltimore who she'd come to love. But it wasn't her home. It was a temporary Band-Aid to keep her alive while Justin cleared things up.

"All done," Luke said, tossing his hands on his hips like Superman.

Pinning a smile on her face, she looked between him and Laura. "Thank you so much. You're great friends." From her experience that was true. While Cassie had been a great friend, she would've stood there chatting instead of helping Moira.

Laura narrowed her eyes at Moira. "What's wrong? I know that fake smile when I see it."

Luke nodded.

Having Danny with her would've made her smile, but he had to work. She'd left him a note stating she'd left with her friends in case he returned from his mission early. She knew they'd enjoy themselves laughing and dancing together. Assuming he could dance. Maybe next time. It occurred to her that she hadn't told him where the three of them had gone. After a moment, she shrugged. She'd probably be back in Baltimore before he returned.

"I just wished I'd had time to visit some of the vendors, but I was a *wee* bit busy." Her heavy purse attested to that.

Her friends looked at each other, and she knew they

didn't believe her reason for the fake smile. She also knew they wouldn't push. They'd wait for her to come to them when she was ready.

"Let's go," Laura urged. "They're a few booths still open."

Moira tucked away the last of her supplies and felt comfortable leaving them for a few minutes. "Let's do it."

If only they knew that by walking single file, Laura and Luke had positioned her in the middle, as if they were security guards protecting her. Moving slowly along a table covered with beautiful glass figurines, an older woman proudly informed them that her husband crafted them all.

After narrowing her eyes at Moira, the woman asked, "You're that *ealaíontóir* on the end. Aren't you?" Her Irish accent hit Moira as authentic as well as her use of the language.

Pride in her art could never overcome her shyness when someone asked her if she was an artist. She had no idea why it felt boastful if she responded. Boastful was the last thing she wanted to be as an artist. Pasting on that fake smile, she nodded.

Reaching her hand over the table, the vendor introduced herself. "I'm Moira Kilkenny Johnson." She chuckled. "I married an American. My love for my country was strong but not as strong as my love for my husband." Her smile broadened. "Thirty-nine years." The wistful look on the woman's face lit some envy in Moira.

Would she actually ever find that kind of love? If so, in Ireland or the US? When she thought of that, Danny's face came into view. While in the past, her mind whirled through men who'd asked her out or she'd dated. The warm feeling for her Irish potentials didn't exist.

"My name's Moira as well," she answered, without thinking, catching herself before she disclosed her real surname. Danny had instilled in her that she had to stick with her new identity, no matter the case. "It was nice to meet you. You have a lovely booth. With it being so late, I'd also like to see what other booths are open."

The older woman's excitement about all the booths had her rattling them off like children with all their offerings. Thanking her, the three of them moved along, passing clothing booths, knick-knacks, and more. When they spotted a novelty booth, they rushed over, she and Laura laughing before they arrived.

Luke groaned. "I can't decide if I'll enjoy this or not."

With a wry smile, Moira laughed. "Oh, you'll enjoy it, or I'll make you sit at my booth all day tomorrow as my assistant."

In a look of mock playfulness, Luke placed his hand on his chest and widened his eyes with laughter in them. "Oh, the horror. I can't sit at your table all day. There's entertainment to enjoy. And possible men to attract." He winked at her.

Moira's smile changed into one of satisfaction. With Luke wanting to mingle, he'd sit for a bit with her, but he'd never make it all day. Although since two-thirds of her paintings sold today, she might not be sitting all day. *That would be wonderful. Although Justin had said they were safe, Danny wanted her to live as if she wasn't. There were days when she didn't know what to think.*

Two women she'd place not much older than herself greeted her. "You're one of the artists," one of the women identified her in a friendly voice.

"*Aye*. We'd like to enjoy the items you have displayed."

"Well, of course. We have people do that all day. Truly if someone is playing with something, it draws other people's interest."

As relief soaked through her body, Moira thought on the kindness of the people working this event. She'd known nothing in Ireland that matched this. Aye, they had great festivals, but they leaned to mostly celebration in general. These Irish-Americans were celebrating their heritage as if they were on Irish soil.

As Moira and Laura handed each other the most ludicrous of Irish novelty items, they donned them and turned to Luke, who hadn't touched a thing. She gave him an evil eye, as best she could, and he held his phone. "I'll be the one to remind you how foolish you look." He winked. "Without being wasted."

She did imagine they were probably worse than silly, but it was fun. Her first outfit to remember started with her head gear. Wearing a hideous fake paper crown shaped in a four-leaf clover that stated "Kiss me, I'm Irish" across it, she couldn't decide what accessory was worse. Below the crown, she'd been handed bright green glasses with horizontal green stripes every inch or so. The design, like most things, were four leaf clovers, and the stripes made the glasses unusable. Around her neck, Laura wrapped a thick boa made with something close to tinsel.

To top it off, Laura handed her a tube of lipstick. Looking at her friend, Moira wondered how much she'd drank because Laura had once commented on the fact she didn't wear lipstick. Her favorite was a light to clear lip gloss.

Moira must've shown her confusion because both of her friends laughed. They didn't laugh hard at her fun outfit, but they laughed hard at a tube of lipstick. What type of surprise should she expect?

Laura waved her hand at Moira in a "hurry up" gesture. "Go ahead. It's a necessity for our outfits." Laura's assertion it would be paid for had her examining the tube.

Unease gripped her at what the tube contained. Then she silently laughed at herself for being so foolish. Her friends were only having fun with her.

Opening the tube and carefully peeking in caused her friends to laugh even more. Moira twirled the base and a tube of green lipstick appeared. Green. After this festival, she'd probably remove green from her palette because she wouldn't be able to look at it for a long while.

"Are you kidding me?" Moira twirled the lipstick down into its tube and handed it back to Laura. Saying the first thing that came to mind as to why she couldn't wear it, she blurted, "I don't want to take yours. It's okay. Next year, I'll remember to buy some."

Laura held her hands up and shook her head. "Oh, this is yours. I have mine in my pocket." She reached down, pulled it out and, in the small mirror, probably designed for patrons to view their silliness, Laura applied the lipstick, rubbed her lips together, then opening them with a pop. "Before you ask, yes, I paid for them."

Seeing no way out of copying Laura, she moved to the mirror and raised the lipstick again. *Come on.* Who thought of that color for their lips?

She closed her eyes for moment to kickstart her into doing this little thing. She knew she'd look ridiculous and maybe that was her hang-up. Their goal was to have fun. With that, she applied the lipstick, popped her lips together to blend it, and stared at her green lips in the mirror. It was worse than she'd thought. She had to get the hideous color off her mouth.

Reaching into her purse to grab a tissue and wipe her lips clean, someone bumped her from behind, knocking her a bit off balance. Reflexively, she jerked her head up and saw an older man weaving down the aisle. She shook her head and thought of how she'd not been staying aware of her surroundings like Danny had taught her. It'd been easier in her booth, but moving around, well, she couldn't let her guard down. Granted, Danny didn't expect that trouble had followed her, but she had promised to listen to him on all-things security.

Such as, he'd said that he wanted someone with her

all the times. He hadn't specified who, so she'd thought Laura and Luke would do. Realizing it could be easier for someone to sneak up on her than she expected, she wished it was Danny though. Not only did she trust him, but they had a friendship that made her want them to be more.

With a sense of unease in her stomach, she scanned the room while asking, "Are we ready for pictures?" With Laura's and Luke's grins, Moira moaned. Something told her she wouldn't be wiping off the lipstick anytime soon.

After Luke took what felt like a hundred pictures of her and Laura, while they posed in all kinds of silly positions, the two of them began switching items and grabbing more from the table. Moira's laugh had been so belly deep that she'd felt freer than she'd expected to again before she'd left Ireland. No, she'd felt that free with Danny. She wanted to show him she could survive without constant watching. She understood if danger touched American soil, her security would change. Until then, she'd remain vigilant while enjoying herself.

The big plastic clover clamp earrings caught her eye. She had to wear them, just had to.

The woman running the booth laughed and walked to her.

"Let me." One of the women came over to her with a sticker and she stiffened.

When she reached toward her face, Moira quickly stepped back, unsure of what to expect.

"Moira, it's okay. Look, I'm getting one right now."

Laura laughed.

In the groove of it, she nodded. "Go ahead—wait, is it permanent?" A slap to her forehead was warranted, but she held it back. Of course it wasn't permanent.

With a chuckle, the woman put it to her cheek before she answered, even though Moira had already figured it out. "No, it's not permanent."

After a few minutes of a wet rag on her cheek, Moira hurried to the mirror. This time, excitement lit her curiosity. Deciding she needed more green lipstick, she pulled it from her jeans pocket and reapplied, then laughed.

Luke and Laura went quiet and she wondered what they planned next. Even with her fear of this and that, she'd truly had fun. If only she could take them back to Ireland. Back to where though? She'd surely lost her small flat.

Blinking her eyes back into focus, she saw a head appear in the mirror behind her. She squeaked and jumped back, but not before she witnessed her face in the mirror pale. How did he find her?

"Am I interrupting?"

At the familiar voice, she whirled around and lost her balance. She'd never heard this level of anger coming from the man with the heavy scowl. Her chest tightened with fear and relief at seeing him. "Hi," she said breathlessly and wished her voice had sounded stronger and less 'damsel in distress.'

Danny's brooding look and raised eyebrow didn't

stop Moira from wanting to throw her arms around him, but she refrained. Considering he'd tracked her down, he might not be in a welcoming mood. Concern for that mood set her system on alert.

Glancing to the side of Danny, she noticed another man and smiled. "Hi, I'm Moira." That smile and twinkle in his eyes told her he was trouble. "Wait, don't tell me. You're Cowboy." She didn't expect too many of Danny's friends to wear cowboy hats in Maryland.

"Yes, ma'am. I certainly am. And it's a pleasure to finally meet you, little darlin'."

"Oh, Christ," Danny said in a low sigh.

When Danny's gaze swung back to her, rapidly coiling tension in her stomach loosened, wreaking havoc on her nervous system. She'd done nothing wrong. She'd followed his instructions, even though she'd questioned her decision, but he hadn't complained before when she spent time with her friends. Come to think of it, why was he here? Had something happened to her brother since she'd spoken with him? Why hadn't someone called her? Then again, they could've, and she hadn't heard the ringer. The bands had drowned out smaller sounds.

"Why are you here? Have you heard something from my brother? Is he okay?" She reached in her pocket to check the phone she should've looked at sooner.

In answer to her questions, he grunted, "Come on, we're leaving."

Realizing Cowboy spoke to Luke and he looked sick to his stomach, she turned back to Danny. "What's going on here? Why is Cowboy harassing Luke? Now that you're here, why do I have to go home?"

Laura approached. "I can see you've got a ride, but are you still watching Dublin 5 with Luke and me?"

She did still want to listen to the band, but she also wanted to be with Danny. Maybe she could have both. "Can we stay and listen?"

His jaw working but not grinding told her he was considering it.

Looking at his watch and the growing crowd around the stage nearest them, he asked, "What time do they play?"

"Half twelve." She remembered she'd used an Irish phrase and corrected herself. "Twelve-thirty."

"No," he said without hesitation. Actually, he'd barely said no when he clipped, "Grab your purse and let's go. Oh, you might want to give back some of that green."

She witnessed a quick quirk of his lips.

Cowboy returned from speaking with Luke, and he and Danny looked at each other and must've had some mental telepathy going because when Danny turned back and after Cowboy walked off, he demanded, "Take me to your booth. We're leaving."

Chapter Fifteen

At the sight of her booth and the few paintings, the thought of taking her over his knee became more of a probability. He couldn't decide if she'd been defiant or didn't understand what would happen if she was found by the wrong people.

He wanted to kick something. "Dammit, Moira. They have your signature on them. I thought we discussed you'd have to use something else."

"Those are paintings I brought with me. I couldn't change my signature."

His head dropped while his thumb and forefinger held the bridge of his nose, reminding himself she might not understand. Dropping his hand and looking up, he willed himself to be patient. "Not everyone that attends are locals. Those who bought your paintings might show friends, display them prominently in their home or office, or even send them to a friend in Ireland." To prevent the rebuttal he saw building in her, he raised his hands to cut her off. "Don't try to interrupt me and say those things don't matter, because any of them might post their new acquisition on social media, along with the painter's name."

Hell. He'd made her eyes water, which was one step away from crying. "My intent wasn't to upset you, Moira. I just need you to be more careful." Wanting to give her comfort, he stepped close, then at the last moment, he slid his hands up and down her arms. They stood so close that her green-colored lips called to him. Transfixed, it took a moment for Cowboy to break their searching gazes. Searching for what, he wasn't sure.

"Let's get this together and go," Cowboy insisted, trying to collect all of her paintings under one arm. "We didn't get to eat."

That snapped her attention back to her work. "Nay. Nay. Don't carry those like that."

As he watched Moira and Cowboy argue about everything, he pulled Luke aside.

"Look," Luke said, "I'm really sorry. I didn't know she shouldn't leave the area where we live."

It appeared Cowboy had had a nice chat with Luke. "She's not on a lockdown, but I'd rather be safe than sorry. I'm asking if you saw anyone paying her special attention or always coming to her with crowds, or anything like that? Think good before you answer."

After what appeared to be deep thought, he shook his head. "I didn't see anyone like that."

That relieved him greatly. "How many days have you been here?" Based on the date of his car accident, Mark had given him that answer, but he wondered if he'd get the truth.

"This is our second day."

"Why didn't you come home to sleep instead of camping out here?"

His face brightened. "It's so much fun to camp out with everyone. The fun almost never ends."

Danny wanted to tell him this was the Ritz compared to some of the camping he'd done with HIS. He didn't want to get into a long conversation, so he opted instead to say, "Thank you for watching out for Moira."

Luke blushed a little. Actually blushed. Danny chose to ignore it so as not to embarrass the man any further.

"I was just doing what any friend would do."

Danny slapped him on the shoulder blade to express his gratitude. "I appreciate it, all the same." He turned and walked to Moira. Now they just had to make it home where he could breathe easy.

His two travel companions had somehow agreed on packing. They even smiled at each other after the fighting they'd done. Damn Cowboy and his ability to charm any woman. He didn't see it, but women did.

"Let's go." Danny hurried them along.

Cowboy led them to the parking lot, straight to Danny's vehicle.

After loading the truck and tying down the easels in the bed, he had to suffer through another argument between his travel companions about who would sit in the back seat. Most arguments like that were for front seat, but he'd yet to see either of them do things normally.

Growling, Danny interrupted, "Moira, front seat. Cowboy, back seat. No arguments. Now let's move." More than likely he came across curt, but he wanted to get on the road.

Settled in, Cowboy leaned forward until he was between the two of them in the front.

"You sure are pretty. Now I see why Ball Park won't let anyone near you."

Danny reminded himself that the next physical training session in the ring, he'd call upon Cowboy, so he could take his frustration out on him.

"Ball Park?" she asked, giving her full attention to Cowboy.

In the rearview mirror, he saw Cowboy sit back and grin at him before he leaned toward Moira again. "Yeah. 'Ball Park' like Ball Park Franks."

Cowboy's happy bubble was about to take a hit and that pleased Danny.

"I don't know who this is? Is he related to Danny?"

Danny couldn't help but laugh and realized his mistake too late. "No, Moira. I wasn't laughing at you. It was at Cowboy because his joke took a nosedive."

"Nah," he drawled. "As long as I'm talking to the pretty lady, laughing at me won't matter."

Danny rolled his eyes. How could women buy into this drivel? Come to think of it, Cowboy didn't have a woman right now or he wouldn't have come with him. As long as the man only joked with Moira, they'd be okay.

"Why Cowboy?" she asked, studying him and then pointing to his head. "Is it the cowboy hat?"

"It's just what people call me."

"What's your name?" she asked.

Danny checked in the rearview mirror again because Cowboy had leaned back as if to battle some demons. His name wasn't unusual, so Danny couldn't understand why he didn't share. He'd yet to understand why his friend was too chicken to say one four letter word.

"Mike. It's Mike."

"I like it for you. I will call you Mike."

Danny saw Cowboy about to argue, so to keep him from saying something that might upset her, he asked, "Did you enjoy yourself?"

He liked her excited, like she was about her time at the festival. Her cheeks lightly blushing, her eyes brimming with happiness, and even her hands moving at a fast rate to get her point across.

"Yes. Luke and Laura are fun and included me in everything."

Cowboy leaned forward again. "Tell me about this artist that was unhappy with you."

Jerking his head to look at her, Danny heard the thunk, thunk, thunk telling him he'd driven off the edge of the roadway. Luke hadn't mentioned there being a problem to Danny. Maybe Luke figured since he'd told Cowboy, he didn't need to repeat the information. But then again, maybe this artist didn't match what Danny had asked. Cowboy's question to Moira explained where Cowboy had ended up after he'd done a search of the area.

Before she spoke, she sighed. "I think he's been the only artist at the local festival for years. Since I sold more paintings than him, he got upset."

"Upset how?" Cowboy and Danny asked simultaneously.

The look from her should've been expected. "No, we're not crazy," Danny said. "So answer us."

He felt more than saw her shrug. "Mostly when I had a crowd, he'd walk over and tell them there were more at his table. Some people went over and back to my table, unhappy because they thought it was more of my work."

"That asshole," Cowboy said first. "Was he hostile?"

"*Naw.* But he was *sleeveen."* When neither said a word, she added, "A sly person."

Filing that information away until he and Cowboy could talk, he asked, "Did you meet others from Ireland?"

"Oh, aye. I found out they get together every now and then. Can I go?" she pleaded with him. Sure, now she asked.

"Would it be a problem if I went as a friend or as a date?" Why did he ask that last part? They'd been doing things together as friends since she arrived.

She hesitated and her answer was so low, he almost had to ask Cowboy to translate. "A date is fine."

Shock zinged its way through his insides, and a smile widened until his cheeks hurt.

Cowboy slapped him on the front of his shoulder before sitting back. "I'm the master," he said.

Leaning closer to Moira, Danny asked, "Are you sure?" Heart pounding, he hoped for an affirmative answer. He didn't want to screw it up. It was a shitty thing to do to his brother, but his heart was telling him he and Moira were right for each other.

When she quickly turned to him, she nodded with a sweet smile.

Cowboy's movement caught his eye. His friend leaned back in his seat, taking a finger to lift his cowboy hat. "Yep, the master."

Chapter Sixteen

Although he'd rather be with Moira, Danny met with Cowboy and Doc for after-hours drinks. After Cowboy asked the server for another round for the three of them, he turned to Danny. "Why the hell aren't you with that pretty little thing? Last night she said she'd date you."

Danny remembered that also. However, it'd kept him awake most of the night worrying about his brother. He wanted Moira, but he didn't want to go behind his brother's back, who couldn't be here, especially because he'd left to make her safer. "I need to talk to my brother first," he admitted.

"Screw your brother," Cowboy asserted. "He's not here. He left her with you."

"Exactly. He left her in my care. Not to steal her away." And that'd be what he was doing since they had no idea when Justin might return. Or, if he'd make it home. Justin was playing a dangerous game that Danny wished he wasn't. Bringing their father's killer to justice wasn't worth his brother's life. But to steal his girl during the process, that would make him a massive asshole.

"Ask him," Doc suggested, "next time you chat with him. Heck, ask her. Things may not be as serious as you think."

What would Moira say? He'd hate for her to say she'd date both him and his brother. He'd also hate to hear she broke up with Justin to date him. The man who was present. That would be like a kick to the gut. "No, it needs to be my brother." That was the only right way to settle the matter. Exactly how he'd code that in a secure message, he didn't know.

"What do you think of the newbies?" Under his breath, Cowboy said, "Damn Russian spies."

Danny chuckled but worried at the animosity Cowboy had for John and Jane. What ridiculous names, John and Jane Smith. So phony. Yet, he guessed using their real names with the government wouldn't have worked. Too many doors would've been shut on them before they had the chance to step inside.

"And a munitions expert," Cowboy grumbled, after taking a hefty swig of his beer. "I'm the munitions expert on our team." He took another swig.

"He's not here to take your spot. He's primarily a sharpshooter. Heck, they're only temporary anyhow."

Cowboy brightened at that. "They are, aren't they? Pity. That Jane is one fine woman."

Danny decided to ignore that comment. "You need

to be prepared. The brothers plan to put two munitions experts on each team. Two of everything if they can do it." Here he sat with Doc whose specialty was evident by his name and Cowboy who was their explosive ordinance expert. Again, he brought nothing to the group. Maybe he should learn explosives and be another expert on the team. No, he had no desire to blow himself up with his own stupidity. He was an interrogator. Yet, everyone had some interrogation skills, so he wasn't all that special. Maybe if he could convince himself to fly again….

"We'll have larger teams then," Doc said. "But I heard they won't have two medics on each team."

Setting his beer down on the table, Danny said, "Maybe we'll get someone with more experience than Stone."

"Stone has no experience. He's a computer geek." Cowboy laughed.

"He did slide right into the job at HQ." Danny finished his beer. "Ready?"

Beer mugs hit the table, and the three men stood. As they made to exit the Irish Pub with Danny in the lead, someone bolted in the door, right into his chest, almost knocking him down.

"Moira."

"Hide me," she insisted. "Two men," she said between raspy breaths, "chasing me."

Without pause, Danny moved them away from the entrance toward the rear door of the pub. Before they made it, Cowboy said, "Tallyho," noting he'd caught sight of the potential threat. The men had entered. "Showbiz," Cowboy suggested.

Danny agreed to the protective tactic Cowboy had designed and recommended. They were inside, had no weapons and, whenever possible, they would peacefully neutralize a threat when they had an innocent with them. And they had no idea if the men who'd entered had weapons. So, he played along with Cowboy's suggestion. One, because it was a smart idea, and two, because he wanted the excuse to kiss her. And that's what he'd be doing. He turned her with her back facing the wall and whispered, "Play along."

Wide-eyed, she nodded.

He pulled her close and kissed her. Not with all the pent-up desire for her since he had to retain some focus and perspective about what was happening around him. They only had to pull off lovers who'd had a bit too much to drink and were making out. Yet he wanted so much more.

Her mouth opened under his and either she was a great actress, or she wanted the kiss as much as he did. Their tongues mated in the age-old song of passion. Her arms entwined around his neck, pulling them so close even a breath wouldn't have been able to slip through between them.

As expected, his cock thickened, wanting to take this make-out session to the next level.

Vaguely, he heard the men tell someone to step away, acting like bodyguards protecting one or both of their privacies. They assured the men they hadn't seen a woman run though, especially since their job was to see that their boss was not disturbed, not to watch for stray women. Cowboy laughed and told them unless she was hot, then their boss might want to meet her tomorrow night. He was set for tonight.

After a few more minutes, someone tapped his shoulder. "Okay, Ball Park, we're set."

Reluctantly, he pulled back from Moira's soft lips and stared down at her with his ragged breathing. Her eyes were pools of desire. He had to speak with his brother ASAP.

"Bathroom," Moira said breathlessly, then slipped from between him and the wall and went into the ladies' restroom. He watched the door for a moment, then turned to his teammates. "So?"

"I recognized one of them. Underground. Either she was a chance grab, or someone contracted for her," Doc said.

"Fuck," Danny said. "Why can't this be easy? I have to work. I can't be there to watch out for her, and I haven't sought out anyone else to keep an eye on her."

When they spoke of the Underground, it was not Baltimore's Underground Science Space. No, it was where the worst of the worst operated and the law was useless. If someone contracted for her, then Boyle knew she was alive.

"I have to speak with Justin, no matter if it's out of our planned cycle. This is too important."

"Yeah," Cowboy said. "Maybe you'll ask him about the girl since you just made out with her." He snickered.

Maybe. Probably. They'd had no way to hide her otherwise. He looked around to see if she'd heard Cowboy's words but didn't see her near them. Realizing she'd taken so long in the ladies' room tightened his gut that she might be avoiding him now.

"Excuse me," Danny said to a woman walking their way. "Would you check on our friend for us, please? She's been in there a long time. She's about five foot six, auburn hair with lots of red in it, and is wearing jeans and a green shirt."

The woman walked back their way, shaking her head. "There's no one in there. Sorry."

Moira must've slipped by them when they were talking and left through the back door. Dammit. "Doesn't she realize it's not safe? Hell, she came in here running for her life."

"Maybe the kiss wasn't the best idea," Doc said, as the voice of reason. "How are you gonna find her now?"

It took a moment, then Danny remembered. "Oh, I have a way."

Chapter Seventeen

Jesus, Mary, Joseph, and all the Holy Martyrs! Not thinking clearly, Moira raced from the bar, wondering if she'd have a heart attack with hers beating so fast and—could it burst out her chest? She couldn't focus on that. She had to keep an eye out for anyone or anything she'd deem a threat. In the midst of her running for her life—that's how she felt—she brought a hand to her lips. They still tingled from the man who wasn't the gangly lad of her youth. Nay, he stood taller than her by about six inches, maybe more, maybe less. She wasn't a short woman. He hadn't needed to lean down too far, and she hadn't needed to step on her tiptoes. She'd call that perfect in her mind.

When she'd arrived—just like her brother had said—Danny had waited for her at the airport. Shock had been the word of the day. He'd turned into a man. A fine-looking man. A man who set her body into a jumble of erotic feelings until she wanted to walk up to him and say, "I'm yours for the taking."

Only, she didn't want her brother to learn she wanted to share one of his friends' bed. She didn't know if it'd be worse for her or for Danny. Better to suffer the desire silently, which sucked.

What she hadn't planned for had been that over the past few months, her attraction would have grown. After tonight, she had no idea how things would stand between them. But it was something she'd think about tomorrow.

After four blocks of foolishly running, constantly glancing back to ensure she hadn't been followed, Moira stopped. "Nay. Nay. Not now," she muttered, barely about to say the words. Frozen to the spot with legs slowly turning rubbery, she opened her purse. She fumbled around in her bag for her inhaler, only to panic when she couldn't find it. A full-blown "I'm going to die," paralyzing panic.

The last time she remembered using it was in the bathroom at the bar. She'd needed it then, because Danny had literally taken her breath away. The run had done it this time. While she'd ran, she admitted that she'd been frightened. It'd been stupid to leave Danny and his friends since they protected people, but they had chased off the men. At the time, getting away from Danny seemed more important. As her mind swirled, she knew how foolish she'd been to leave by herself.

Fear brushed through her and made a second stroke. She couldn't breathe. She was suffocating. This couldn't be happening. A door opened on the townhouse she'd fallen to her knees in front of. She'd made it to her friends' home.

A women's shrill voice had someone else running back inside. Were they calling the cops on her? Nay, they needed to call 911. "Get the inhaler Moira left here!"

"I—" She fought for her next breath, pain filling her chest at the effort. "I. Can't." She tried to gulp air but to no avail.

She recognized her good friend, Laura, who touched her arm and assured her she'd be okay. How could she say that? If they didn't get an ambulance here now, it might be too late.

Bare footsteps slapped across the walkway. "Here," Luke said.

"All right, Moira," Laura's soothing voice helped take off some of the edge, but it hurt not being able to catch a full breath. At any moment, she'd pass out.

Laura took her hand and placed the inhaler into it. Her hands shook so much, she couldn't make it work. *Jeanie Mac! It was too late.*

"Moira Wright, you stay with me," a voice demanded. Darkness surrounded her vision, and her ears rang. "Now, I'm taking your inhaler, and I'll administer your medicine."

Even with the authoritative tone Laura used, Moira wasn't giving up her inhaler. She'd already lost one tonight; she needed this one. Needed to get it to her mouth.

The inhaler was jerked from her grasp. "Dammit, Moira, you will not pass out on me. Open your mouth."

As if all her functions had ceased, she tried to open her mouth but failed.

"Open it, Luke."

"All right, Moira, here it comes. Take a breath."

The first squirt hit her throat since Luke had her mouth open so wide. Her jaw hurt. But not more than the elephant on her chest trying to kill her. She couldn't remember ever being this bad, except her first time. Her parents had looked scared before the doctor diagnosed her. Then he'd explained it was a lifelong illness, but there were things she could do to lessen the chances of an attack.

If she hadn't already been frightened, confused, and excited over Danny's kiss as well as running for blocks, she wouldn't have had this attack.

The breaths weren't coming. Harder and harder it became to get any air in her lungs. When the darkness rimming her gaze crept in closer, her panic grew.

Of course, she'd been instructed not to panic when an attack happened, but those doctors weren't the ones who couldn't breathe. Who wouldn't fight for what little air they could? With the lack of oxygen getting to her brain, she felt ready to allow the darkness to consume her gaze, so the pain, pressure, fear, and inability to control what happened to her would go away.

"Dammit, Moira, work with me. Once more," Laura directed. Her friend was a take charge kind of woman who treated her like she had been given paddles to shock her back to life.

"Inhale."

After the last squirt into her mouth, Luke let go of her jaw. She still couldn't breathe. It'd been too late. She couldn't afford to go to a hospital because her name could end up somewhere that would make her found. Which would contradict her death in Dublin.

Laura's face swam in front of hers. "Moira, calm down. You can breathe now, but you can't keep panicking. You've got to settle some and we'll get you through this."

Easy for her to say. Laura wasn't the one dying.

"Look at me, Moira. There you go. Take slow, easy breaths."

As she listened to the hypnotic voice, Moira obeyed and began to get her wits about her. The elephant squatting on her chest had moved on, but the burn remained. She knew it'd go away soon.

It took a few minutes, but Luke and Laura stayed with her as her attack passed. With much relief, Moira bent her head down and regained herself. Luke stepped back into the house and she knew why. His way of fixing everything was through hot tea. She'd bet he hurried to set up the kettle.

Laura's hand soothed her back. "How are you feeling?"

Moira generally didn't have an attack because she noticed the signs and got ahead of it. Once, at her friends' home, she'd had one, and Luke and Laura had taken steps to educate themselves on how to help her.

With that, Laura had recommended she keep one of her inhalers at her and Luke's place, since she spent so much time there. Thank goodness Laura had recommended it. Otherwise, Moira would be at the hospital that her brother—and Danny—had instructed her to avoid at all costs.

"I'm better." She looked over at Laura, who sat on the stoop beside her. "Thank you. You saved my life."

Laura laughed. "Of course I did. I need my Irish friend to finish teaching me how to speak Irish Gaelic, so I can go back with you and find me a hunk of an Irishman."

Moira laughed. Laura had said that when she'd met her but had yet to start a lesson.

Sadness and determination slid into her body. Would she ever get to go home again?

Laura stood. "How about we go in? I'm sure Luke's almost ready with the tea. Do you need his help to stand?"

Her recently oxygen-deprived body didn't want to cooperate. She worked to get up from where she'd fallen to the ground, shifting on unsteady legs but only made it to her knees.

Laura's arm went around her. "Come on, I'll help you."

Instead of getting a moment to prepare her, the arm Laura had placed around her to help disappeared, and disorientation wrapped itself around her. Moira fought that frustrating panic that lived in her life for the moment. Her immediate thought was she'd suffered something permanent from her attack. When warm arms wrapped one under her knees and the other behind her back, she relaxed into Luke's big arms.

After the steps into their home, Luke settled her on the couch. Then he strode into the kitchen and returned with a cup of hot tea. Either noticing her hands still shook or just out of choice, he placed the cup and saucer on the end table beside her.

Laura sat in the armchair while Luke took an oak chair from the kitchen table and swung it around and sat backward. Both friends looked at her expectantly. Weakness and burning lungs still plagued her, but moment by moment, everything eased.

"Thank you. I felt like I was dying." She scrunched her eyebrows into a V. "Did I wake you two?" It couldn't be more than eleven, but she wasn't sure.

"Noooo," Laura dragged out the word. She looked at Luke and grinned. Luke, on the other hand, looked like he'd just eaten a lemon. "Loverboy over there had a blind date but said no after seeing him."

"Well, you would've too. My men don't need to be as large as I am, but I don't like them looking like a waif."

"Tell all," Moira said.

After knowing them only a couple of months, she felt comfortable with them. "This guy's name was Danny."

Moira stiffened. "Uh—" She stopped because she wasn't sure she wanted to know the truth.

Luke waved a hand as if to ward off a fly. "Not your Danny, although yours is one tantalizing package." He winked and laughed. She couldn't agree more.

"He is hot. Since you're not dating him, would you mind if I do?" Laura's question took Moira by surprise.

Jealously flashed through Moira at the thought of Laura with Danny. Maybe it was because they'd recently kissed. "First, he's not my Danny. He's my brother's friend, who is helping me get set up in America. Second, date who you want. I'm not dating him." If Laura and Danny hooked up, she'd move to Boston with her brother, whether he wanted her there or not.

She caught the glance her friends made at each other. They were up to something or just knew something she didn't. Either way, she wasn't sure she liked it.

"My story is not important," Luke said. "He won't be in my life, and if he applies for me as his personal trainer, I'll work him so hard, he'll leave with his tail between his legs."

They all laughed. She could imagine what that would look like. It might be fun to watch, although she would feel bad for this other Danny.

"So, Sweetheart," Luke said, "what had you so winded? How many blocks did you walk?"

Embarrassed, she held up four fingers. "But," she tried to justify, "I was running, not walking."

Their eyes widened, and Laura took over. "Why were you running? Was someone following you? Do we need to call the—"

Moira held up her hand. "Stop, Laura. It's okay. No police, no emergency."

"Then why?" Luke asked.

How much to tell them? They didn't know why she was in America, so she couldn't bring that into the conversation. "I had two men following me."

"Oh, girl, you have to be careful," Luke advised.

"How'd you give them the slip?" Laura eyed her over her mug.

She hadn't thought this through. Maybe she could skirt around it. "I ran into *Sláinte*, right into Danny's chest, and two of the men he worked with. They hid me."

Luke's brows furrowed. "How?"

Taking a long drink of tea and trying not to show how it burned her throat going down, she looked at them both to gauge how the next words would go over. "Well, he kissed me."

Laughter exploded from both her friends. "I knew it," Laura said with glee.

"I told you first," Luke said, in an attempt to claim the glory.

They sobered at the same time, which made her worry.

Luke looked at her, calm as day. "Let me get this right. Some men chase you and you escape into *Slainté's*. Danny kisses you—which we'll talk about how it was later—and you run again? Was Danny's kiss that bad?"

Safety had foolishly been the last thing on her mind. She'd simply reacted in the moment—albeit badly—and had needed to get out of there. The question, though, dealt with the kiss. She'd been kissed before, but that kiss had blown her mind.

Knowing Luke really wanted an answer to the last question, she blurted, "It was the master of all kisses." Her eyes widened at her disclosure.

"Oh, no," Luke said, "You're going to tell us all that mushy stuff."

After being scared, relieved, feeling heated, almost dying and, finally, free and relaxed with her friends, surely, they could have this conversation. They shared Luke's and Laura's encounters. No rules existed except—nothing too personal or graphic. Although she had an inkling that Luke would have loved all the explicit details.

With a grin, she leaned back, bringing her calves under her, and began. "At first, I didn't realize what he'd planned...."

Chapter Eighteen

Danny wanted to kick his own ass for allowing Moira to give him the slip. He'd waited for hours at his home, and when she hadn't returned, he'd called Stone and felt guilty until he remembered Stone's temporarily single situation. They'd have to get him out with the other agents. He could probably use their support.

When he'd installed the tracker in Moira's purse, Stone had raised a brow but hadn't questioned him. He knew using HIS equipment for personal use had to be cleared through Jesse or Devon, since they followed civilian laws when able. Besides, no one touched or approved the use of Devon's equipment without his okay. Basically, Jesse, if he agreed, would tell you to go to Devon for his approval.

Stone's voice sounded scratchy. Danny hated waking him at two in the morning, but Moira could be in the hands of some violent criminals. "Is this what you dragged me out of bed for?"

"The Underground might have her."

"Shit. Give me time to get there and I'll get it for you."

He'd see where Stone found her and would decide from there. Some would say he was obsessed, but he wasn't. It was only for her safety. Who the hell was he kidding? He wanted her as his friend and lover, and he was ready to say screw his brother's claim.

Danny gritted his teeth as his stomach churned with the force of a tsunami. If the Underground had her—and he hoped they didn't—they could no longer delay locating her. He didn't believe it was the threat from Ireland, but he'd confirm after they found her and find her, they would.

Halting from his trek back and forth across the living room to the kitchen, he slapped his hands on the kitchen bar, dropped his head, and sighed. Fear of failure racked his body, almost paralyzing him from thinking, from doing. Closing his eyes, he felt the wetness behind his eyelids. He didn't want to lose her. That night's kiss meant something. It could be a turning point in their relationship.

Getting lost in his own thoughts, he jumped when his phone rang. *Jackass, it's just the phone.*

Accepting the call, Stone started, "You know if Devon finds out about this, he is going to be pissed."

In his heart, he knew that while he may get shit about it, once Devon heard her story, he'd help him. And why hadn't he told him already? They'd all think Moira was safe based on the trail Justin had created. So, they'd say what he'd done was overkill and probably intrusive. He didn't care. This was Moira. "Can you keep this quiet? You've been able to so far."

"Yeah, but I haven't logged on at this stupid hour for a non-op."

Pinching his nose between his forefinger and thumb, he let any trouble he may be in slide off him. "Did you find her?"

"Um…."

His gut clenched at the way Stone started but didn't finish. Was the address bad? No. Someone had to be there. *Please don't let it be Devon.* He could pull the plug and that wouldn't do.

"Did you really think I wouldn't know when someone logged onto my system?"

It was Devon. Why couldn't he get a break? He just wanted to find Moira.

Ready to take on a bear, if needed to protect her, Danny prepared to battle with Devon. He should've figured nothing slipped by him.

Before Danny could speak, he heard AJ Hamilton barreling into the conversation. "What the fuck is going on here at bumfuck early in the morning? Don't you think I'd get an alert when someone enters this building and who it was. I found it odd that Stone was here. Who the hell is on the phone?"

"It's Franks. AJ, why you? Where are your brothers?

Besides Devon, of course."

"I'm here because it's my rotation for the team support. Now, Franks, you'll tell me what's going on and if we need to bring your team in."

He hesitated, knowing he shouldn't keep her story from them, especially since this potential new threat had emerged. Declan may have asked to keep it quiet, but he trusted these men and women.

"Is this a standing story or should we sit because it'll take long? Remember my brother and I were woken from sleep, so it better be worth it."

He slowly ran a hand down his face. "If Moira's safe, then you should sit down."

"Christ," AJ said in a voice that told him AJ wanted more trouble like a hole in his head. "All right. Stone, I'm guessing you're tracking her with one of our devices?"

That emphasis on the device owner didn't go unnoticed. He might just get more than a palm slap. Fine, as long as he could still watch her. The urgency to do so grew in him. He could be overreacting, but it wasn't worth taking the chance.

"She's at a safe address Franks provided."

He could've fallen to the floor with the level of relief that shot out of him. She was at Laura and Luke's—that was the only other address besides his own that he'd provided. He wanted to kick himself. He should've checked there, even if it meant waking them.

"Good. Get your ass in here, Franks." Someone cut the call before he could ask AJ a question.

At record speed, he changed into his black cargo pants and T-shirt and took his gear to the truck, all the while wanting to rush over to Moira. Considering how little attention he paid to the speed limits, not getting a ticket told him that was a good sign for his cause.

He'd hoped the tremor he had would've subsided, but it hadn't. It probably wouldn't until he held Moira close and knew she was safe.

After arriving, Danny, Devon, and AJ walked into what was called their HQ kitchen. Instead of those little appliances and only a microwave in most places, this had been made into a full kitchen, gas burners and all.

Devon walked to the coffee pot and made sure it had plenty of water for each single brew. After he finished at the sink, AJ leaned over the basin and splashed water on his face.

Danny hoped they wouldn't be too pissed at him for taking and using that tracker, considering it was against agency policy. Plus, he had another he'd recently installed in a pair of her shoes. It'd taken a cobbler to help with that task, but it was done.

After each of them brewed a cup of coffee, they sat at a round table with chairs between them. "Spill," Devon demanded after a sip of coffee and a moan of satisfaction.

Danny's hands around his cup became the focus of his gaze. He shouldn't be nervous, but he was, and that outright pissed him off, giving him what he'd need to fight if necessary.

Looking up, he wasn't sure which brother to look at, so he decided go back and forth between them. Wondering which brother to start with told him he was procrastinating.

"It's my roommate."

He felt a presence behind him, and it took all his will to not turn from the brothers. Maybe the other brothers had awakened?

Danny watched the changing expressions on Devon's and AJ's faces. They went from surprise to a gleam in their eyes. That seemed odd. He had to see who was behind him, even if it meant giving Devon and AJ his back. AJ typing on his phone seemed strange too, but who was he to judge.

He turned and had never seen a better sight. Such appreciation for the support nearly made his eyes water again. This was no time for emotions. Behind him stood the rest of his team, including their leader—Ken Patrick. Danny had been running the team in his boss's absence, but he was a poor substitute. The special ops guys could handle so much more than his DEA ass.

He surged to his feet to greet them. How had they known? *Stone.* He shifted his gaze to the man and saw a sly smile on his lips. He must've put the word out something was off since Danny had been called in with a possible op.

Stone split off and handed Devon a laptop. The man couldn't exist without one. In no time, he had it booted and ready.

"May as well have a seat where you can." The resignation bled into AJ's voice. Danny expected he'd preferred to be snuggled up to his wife, Megan.

Ken stood beside Danny. "Whatever's happened, I ordered it."

The Hamilton brothers rolled their eyes. "Of course you did." Sarcasm laced Devon's voice.

The one bit of advice Ken had given him for leading the team was to always take responsibility, no matter the situation. Oh, and to bring everyone home. Preferably alive.

Cowboy walked to the coffee pot, and while his cup brewed, he waved his hand. "Don't wait for me. Keep this little doggy going."

Some of his team hadn't learned office etiquette and he'd say Cowboy was one, but his friend tended to color outside the lines anywhere he could.

This time Devon's lip quirked at Cowboy, so Danny released a breath that things hadn't started off on the wrong foot. When Ken pulled a chair up beside him and gave a brief nod, Danny sat straighter, knowing his boss really did have his back. Ken had been the rock for the teams. While he liked Grits—Bravo team's leader—he preferred Boss.

Stone had made the right call because having his team learn at the same time kept him from repeating the problem.

"Okay," AJ said, looking like he'd sat taller in his seat with the team here. "Franks, what's going on? You said your roommate. What does she have to do with this besides the fact that you've turned into a stalker?"

Chapter Nineteen

That hadn't been the accusation Danny had expected. He'd thought it'd be about using HIS resources. Stalker? Him? No, they didn't understand yet.

"I put a tracker in the liner of her purse when she arrived from Ireland in case something happened and I needed to locate her."

"That wasn't one of your wisest decisions," Devon added as a small, irrelevant comment.

"It seemed like a good one at the time." He felt like arguing over this because it had, but it was already done, so they needed to talk about what happened to her and why she was here.

Devon shook his head. "Hell. Did you even consider the fact that trackers can be linked back to us?"

No, he hadn't. Panic tapped at his body, but he held it at bay. Mostly. Getting HIS into trouble was the last thing he'd wanted. Surely they'd toss his ass now. "I thought our stuff was untraceable."

"No. Not everything anyway." How had Devon perfected that quirk to hide a smile? "We can discuss it later."

"Can't you—" He waved his hand around toward the computer setup. "—make it disappear?"

"Probably, but I won't. I won't mess with the company's records. View them, but not change, unless completely necessary for the safety of someone. Now, spill. I'm ready for my second cup."

"Moira's the sister of a friend of mine in Ireland. She's not here on vacation to visit friends. Her brother, Declan, called me several months ago, before he feared for their lives. Seems he decided to fall in love with a drug boss's daughter. We had a plan for their extraction, but then he called and said there had been a change and they were headed to America right away."

The atmosphere in the room shifted, as if a collective breath had been held waiting for more details. All movement stopped to include Doc, ready to put a pod in the coffee maker. They protected people. It's what they did, no matter how difficult. They'd give their lives to protect someone. It'd been bred into them, which was why after years of protecting people, they were chosen for HIS.

He'd bet his last dollar Alpha team's new focus became Moira and nothing else. He only hoped he wasn't overreacting. But he'd rather be too heavy-handed than allow her to fall into danger's hands.

No one spoke, so he continued, "Moira's an artist. She did well enough in Ireland to live comfortably. One afternoon her friend asked her to fill in on a cleaning job. It was to help prepare a mansion for a dinner party. She mostly dusted, but the woman in charge didn't give her a break. Moira was frustrated and asked her friend how bad it would be if she quit. Given the green light, she planned her escape from who she called a taskmaster."

Noticing Doc still hadn't put that pod in his hand into the coffee maker, he motioned for him to continue. Doc looked at his hand, shocked as if he hadn't realized he held the pod. Even though the room came alive again, attention remained on him.

"Since my brother covered her and her brother's trail so well in Ireland, I promised I wouldn't share her story unless I had to. Well, I think it's time." He never should've allowed his promise to override his commitment to the agency and protecting the innocent.

He listened to some foul language and knew he'd earned it for keeping this secret from them. They were people to be trusted. Not only as agents of HIS, but as friends.

AJ gritted his teeth and seemed to have a hard time speaking. "I get that you gave a promise to someone, but you should've included us from the beginning. We'd have kept her safe."

He gulped at the ferocity of AJ's voice. There'd been no reason at the beginning, when she first arrived. Sure, he'd given her a tail, but that had been more for his comfort than her safety, because as far as they'd known, she was dead to the threat in Ireland. Besides, Moira would've hated him for it. Now though was the time and she'd have to deal.

Best to avoid arguing with one of his bosses over whether he should have included HIS from the beginning. "Anyway, the dinner was at the home of someone from the *Seanad Éireann*." When he received blank looks, he realized he'd repeated Moira's words. "It's basically the senate. Minister Donnelly."

There were some nods with mumbles of agreement in all forms. He also expected plenty of "get to the point" mumbles in there. He just couldn't seem to spit it out in the brief and concise format that had been ingrained in him since he'd joined the DEA, and then HIS. With Moira involved, brevity didn't exist in his thoughts. This was too personal, and although he needed to share, he didn't want to.

"Did this minister threaten her?" Cowboy asked, all excited. "Because I'll be glad to protect your roommate since you haven't spanked that ass. She's hot."

Rage, no, it was jealousy… no, it was rage covering his jealousy… made his muscles tighten, especially around his shoulders and neck. He wanted to take Cowboy apart, limb by limb, even with that damn twinkle in his eyes. That asshole remembered the trip back from the festival.

He was saved from acting out by his team leader.

"Cowboy, shut the hell up," Boss said. The agent waved his hand as if giving Danny the green light. "Go ahead," he said, before he took a sip of coffee.

Danny's own mug was empty but getting up wasn't possible for him. To his surprise, Doc grabbed his mug to make another cup. Thank God for this team.

"Cowboy, we don't know. While Moira had been there, she'd watched a known drug lord meet with the minister and an assistant commissioner with *gardai*. Police," he added for clarification.

A few whistles rang in the air. Put a drug lord with government officials, and it was a bomb waiting to explode.

Doc handed him the coffee, and Danny took a grateful sip and opened his mouth at the heat of it. No one laughed because they'd all done it at one time or another. The liquid fireball burned its way down his throat to his stomach.

"What's Moira's full name?" Devon asked, never looking up from his computer screen.

His wide eyes sought out Stone, who looked like a kid trying to not be observed. "Aoife Moira Gallagher."

"What's that first name again?" Devon asked.

"Aoife, pronounced like I said it. 'Ee-fah.' It's the Celtic version of Eva or Ava." That last part had been useless information, and Devon's expression agreed.

"How do you spell it?" Devon turned back to his screen, his hands hovering over his keyboard.

He spelled her name and stiffened at Devon's hands flying over his laptop keyboard. "Devon, stop. Your search could trigger an alert."

After rolling his eyes, Devon gave Danny a bored stare. "It won't be from any search of mine."

"Well…" Danny gulped, ready to take more hits today. "My brother set her and her brother up with fake passports and I got a driver's license to match."

Devon and AJ looked at each other, and Danny hated when he couldn't read them.

"You did that?" Devon asked him but looked at Stone.

"No, I helped. Her new name in the system is Moira Lee Wright."

Chuckles went around the room at that.

"I'm not even going to talk about the illegal stuff yet, well, I am on one thing. But she's not a citizen."

He and Stone looked at each other, and Danny mentally shrugged.

AJ waved his arm. "Can you get to the damn point?"

Obviously, he felt the same about Reagan's swear jar disappearing. "As she left the cleaning job, she was caught by someone to take a tray service to the minister and her guests. Only, she waited outside since they were talking. They'd left the door open a crack. In a hurry to leave, she set the tray on the floor and heard someone threaten to kill her brother. So, she ran, knocking over the service tray in the process. As you can imagine, it made noise."

A variety of responses came from the team, but they all had one theme. "Damn."

"Did I mention she recorded them and they spoke about working together?"

The team stood, waiting through the entire story; he

knew they didn't miss a thing.

"When she left, Moira went straight to her cop brother. My brother got the two of them out of the country. Plus, her brother's pregnant girlfriend, who happens to be the daughter of said drug lord. In the air, the drug lord's daughter needed medical attention, so the flight stopped over in Boston. They sent Moira on to me as planned. She lives with me, so I can keep a watch on her in case my brother's plan falls through. She only has one set of friends, and—" He looked at Stone who nodded. "—she's there now."

A few eyes flicked to what they could see of Devon's big screen with a red dot pinpointing Moira's location.

"She didn't actually hear what was on the recording at the mansion, until later at her brother's home. It didn't matter though, because if they knew someone was listening, that person would be in trouble. My brother staged their deaths in Ireland to keep the drug boss off their trail. He's keeping his ear to the ground for trouble."

AJ wiped his forehead before speaking. "If they still think she'd dead, why the problem now, especially if she's just at her friend's house and your brother hasn't told you of a threat?"

Danny took in a calming breath to keep from feeling that urgency and fear lacing like knots through him. "Last night, two men followed her."

AJ's inhaled breath permeated through the room. Alpha team stood stoically. Doc and Cowboy must've updated them before they entered HQ.

Danny continued, "Based on Doc's and Cowboy's visual IDs, we think they're from the Underground. Whether they chose her or Boyle—the drug lord in Ireland—hired them, we don't know."

AJ swore, and Danny wasn't sure which option garnered it, and that set like a lead weight in his stomach, rolling around to keep him from stopping. "How's your brother getting his information?"

"He works for Boyle." As he expected, a stillness raced through the room. All eyes were riveted on him. "That's a story for another day, but it benefits us right now. We can trust him. He got them out."

The brothers seemed to think for a minute. Then they both began snapping orders.

Devon told Stone to get to the computer and keep watching that dot.

"But this is my team, too. I should be by their side," Stone insisted.

"They need you at that console watching that dot. Besides, you need to earn your keep." Stone sullenly left the room, and Devon chuckled.

Since Stone had begun helping Devon with their computer backup—their lifeline—he'd had a hard time making the break with the team. While they'd hoped he could do both, it wasn't possible.

AJ rattled off his instructions. "Saddle up. You'll cover Franks's house and Moira. Ken, you go back home and recuperate. If the team needs help, we'll get it for them."

Ken looked around the group. "Where are the replacements?"

"Oh," AJ said with a sly smile. "They're here."

The twins stepped out of the shadows and almost scared Danny. They were damn spooky. If they'd talk more, they could probably offer a lot to the team. Until then, he'll take backup. They'd saved him on that cliff when the hostiles had closed in on him, before he'd stepped into blackness.

That flight through the sky had been a scary-as-shit move and an exhilarating one. Now he knew why Cowboy pushed for more and more. That rush of power… no, life… could become an addiction. He had heard that from Ken and Jesse while discussing all the services. That had been a conversation that got him thinking as to why, if spec ops were a better fit, had they hired "alphabets?" It made him feel second-hand, but now wasn't the time to ponder that any further.

Ken walked over and shook their hands, and, to the team's astonishment, Jane and John had a conversation with him. The team kept glancing at Ken or each other, not sure what had happened. Maybe their talkativeness would carry over to the rest of them or at least to ops.

Turning back to the brothers, Ken appeared ready to argue, as Danny would've expected. Then AJ held up a hand, stopping their tangent conversation. "Do you want me to call Sugar and tell her I sent you home, but you didn't go? I imagine she'd not be happy with you taking your battered body out of your home."

Boss—as the team called him, even though the brothers were technically the bosses—dropped his head a bit and brought his hand up; using his thumb and forefinger, he pinched the bridge of his nose. He sighed as if it pained him and lifted his head. "All right, but I expect to be kept in the loop." His glare at Danny told him he should make it happen.

AJ nodded. "Done. Now go home."

Before he left, Ken put a hand on Danny's shoulder, gripping tightly. "If you need me, you'd better call me. If any of you get hurt—or Moira—because you didn't want me out there, I'll kick your ass so bad you won't be able to sit down for a month. Then, you'll run drills from dawn to dusk."

There was no chance he'd call Boss. The man had been beat to hell and shot, oh, and held captive. He hadn't fully recuperated, but Danny wouldn't say anything that might keep him from leaving. "You know I will."

After Ken departed, they got back down to business.

"Is there anything you can think of about last night that we haven't discussed?" AJ asked, with his brows raised.

Telling the brother that he'd kissed her and that might've made her run wouldn't happen. He'd come to that possible conclusion because she'd run in for help, then ran out to possible trouble. Then she hadn't stayed where her bed was located. *At least*, he told himself, she hadn't been in a man's bed… as far as he knew. He hadn't worried about Luke, but maybe a friend of her friends?

He wracked his brain to find any little snippets that caught his attention last night but came up with nothing because his back had been turned. "No, but Cowboy and Doc might've seen more."

AJ's face scrunched in confusion. Danny feared it, but he should've known he couldn't avoid this question, no matter how much he wanted to.

"Why didn't you see anything? Were you in the shitter?"

Cowboy laughed, and it only got louder, until he'd bent over, clutching his gut. Danny wanted to shoot him in the ass.

Hoping to head off Cowboy, Danny turned back to AJ and said, "We, uh— We—" He couldn't get it out.

"We played movie star," Cowboy said, with a grin so wide Danny wanted to knock it off his face. He liked Cowboy, but the man sometimes tested his patience.

"Movie star?" AJ asked, looking between the men.

Oh, hell. He'd forgotten that wasn't a HIS standard protection technique. In fact, Cowboy had only come up with it a few days before as a joke.

"It's something we created—more out of fun, than anything else. The way Moira crashed into me and our being about to exit before the confrontation, with limited options, we decided to implement it. It worked great."

"Uhm, so I take it the two of you stood as protection refusing to allow anyone close. What I'm curious about is how you hid her from prying eyes?"

Danny coughed into his fist. He felt like a school

kid trying to find a way around the truth. A truth he'd promised himself he wouldn't share. Well, he had a negative trend on keeping secrets where Moira was concerned. Ready to buck up and tell the truth, he should've known that Cowboy would take this glory or shame, since he'd hidden it until now.

"He kissed her. And I'm not talking about a peck on the lips. They were down and dirty. I expected them to drop on the floor and tear their clothes off," Cowboy said proudly.

Danny groaned. He needed to transfer Cowboy to the other team. He wondered how Cowboy's former Air Force Pararescuemen tolerated him while he'd been on active duty.

AJ looked at him sternly. "Was she willing?" Devon halted and looked at him expectantly.

Anger rushed through Danny's veins at the implied meaning of the question. "What kind of man do you think I am? Of course she was willing." Shocked at first, but she'd easily fallen into their kiss, and there was no way she'd been faking it for the sake of their ruse.

The brothers each crossed their arms over their chests and leaned back. It was eerie how much these two were alike. They surveyed him, looked at each other and both nodded. What the hell? He hated when the brothers did that. It was weird how they could communicate without speaking out loud.

"All right. We'll let you and your team take the lead. If I feel you're not using your head, I'm bringing in

Bravo team."

He surged to his feet and felt the heat creeping up his body, his spine, and his neck. "The fuck you will," he all but shouted. They wouldn't take him away from protecting her.

The brothers both grinned. At least they hadn't given him that sly smirk or twitched on one side of their mouth.

Fired up to get this party on the road, he asked, "Can I get ready now to go pick her up?"

AJ shook his head. "No. We know where she is, so sit down. We have more to discuss."

Were they for real? He needed to be at her friend's place when she woke, or he might lose her again. His heart was too invested. Danny couldn't handle it if someone took her, and he wasn't there to protect her.

"Now," AJ said forcefully.

"Can we at least send someone to sit on the house?"

"Ken sent the twins there before he left."

Holy hell, those two were going to bring their team to a whole new level. He didn't know them, but deep down knew they'd take care of her. So, he sat, ready to negotiate if necessary. Anything for Moira. Even if it meant losing his brother's love in the bargain.

Chapter Twenty

Disoriented, Moira searched for what had woken her. Cuddled deep in the softest mattress she'd ever known, she wished to sleep the day away, unless her mind woke her with inspiration that she needed to get on a canvas right away.

With a sigh, she admitted that she was acting like a big chicken. She and Danny had become friends. So much so that she thought about the pain of losing him when she returned to Ireland. Of losing what they'd built and the emotions behind the two of them.

That included the underlying desire that had simmered all along but took a new turn last night, which brought her back to how she'd act around him. He'd kissed her as part of a ploy to hide her. It hadn't been real to him. Once she'd overcome the shock, the kiss had turned real for her.

Three knocks pounded on the front door and jolted

her to a full sitting position. Rubbing her hand over her face, she knew her time to decide how to act was over.

While most people would worry who knocked at this early hour, she knew who it was. Danny Franks. She imagined that not returning home last night had worried him. She shouldn't have turned off her phone to avoid his calls and texts. It'd been immature.

Climbing out of bed to dress, she heard Luke at the door. Knowing Luke, he wore only his boxers because, while he liked to look at a good-looking man, he also liked to show off his personal-trainer body, hoping he'd get a look that'd excite him. She chuckled as she put her shoes on, then straightened the bed.

She finished in just enough time because Danny walked into her room without permission. She rolled her eyes as he searched the room before his gaze turned softly on her.

Obviously realizing she was safe, he leaned against the door jam, crossing his arms over his chest and moving one booted foot over the other. He half pulled off the cool pose, but the black military type clothing and the weapons ruined it. If he'd been trying to pull off badass, she'd have given it to him. The grin, though, was too flirty for badass.

"Are you okay?" he asked.

The concern ringing in his voice made guilt rise for avoiding him last night. "Yeah. Listen, about last night—"

Standing straight, he held up a hand. "There's nothing to say."

She studied him, trying to decipher if he meant her coming home or them snogging? When a woman shorter than her five-six and looking equally as badass as Danny moved behind him, she decided it'd have to be a discussion for a later day.

"Sorry, Jane. I couldn't wait."

This—Jane, she supposed—looked as if she'd been prepared to enter the room until she saw Danny. Interesting. Had their plan been for the woman to come in first? That would've been nice since she might not have been dressed. In other words, he couldn't wait to either check for her safety or miss her not being dressed. The latter sent a delicious chill skidding up her spine.

Picking up her purse from an armchair in the room, she glanced to make sure she hadn't left anything. She spotted the inhaler beside the bed and wasn't sure she should take it or leave it. She liked that Laura and Luke had one on hand, but could she trust her trip to Danny's? Last time they'd been that close—snogging—she'd had to use one.

Laura appeared in the doorway—not in her usual silk robe but dressed to the nines. How had she put on makeup that fast? Of course, since Moira mostly used a tinted moisturizer, it took her less time than most to put on her face paint. That's what it felt like. A clean canvas with all colors available but some standard rules, like eyeliner goes around the eyes.

Laura nodded to the bedside table. "You can take that one. We have another. Just bring another cylinder next time you're around."

She snapped it up and flew to her friend, tossing her arms around Laura's neck. "Thank you. Thank you so much. You might've saved my life."

"What?" Danny's words came in a bark, and the two women jumped and split apart. "What happened and why didn't you call me?"

Laura stepped up first. "Chill, GI Joe. We didn't have any trouble."

Not wanting a war between the two overprotective ninnies, she walked out of the room. "You coming, Danny?"

A growl emanated from one of them. She couldn't tell which. Too many people were focused on her, and she didn't much like it. The fact they cared warmed her heart, but this was too much.

Before she reached the front door, Jane moved in front of her.

Moira did have a problem that she wanted to discuss with Danny. The more she'd thought through the events of the night—excluding the public make-out session—this didn't have the feel of the troubles she had from Ireland. They could be, which was why she wanted to go through it with Danny. This Underground possibility that Luke had been mentioned also bothered her. In fact, it scared her more than the Irish drug lord since she'd get a heads-up from Justin if he became a problem.

Secretly glad Danny had arrived to collect her, she'd been surprised he'd been wearing his work gear.

Able to sense Danny approaching from behind, she didn't jump at his words. "Moira, this is Jane. She's going outside before you, and you will stay behind her at all times."

"Are you sure all this—"

"Yes," he said curtly.

She shrugged. If that was best, then she'd trust him. She only hoped Jane, or anyone else, didn't plan to watch her paint. She'd call a halt to that quickly.

They exited as he'd instructed. They acted as if bullets could fly at any moment. With it being so early in the morning, the streets were nearly empty.

He spoke in her ear. "Never let your guard down."

She was officially freaked out, especially since she'd gone on her own from the tavern to Laura's. Was this what the security Danny and his teammates did day-to-day?

Danny slid a hand to her lower back to guide her from following Jane. "You're in the back with me."

Things would feel better and make more sense when they got to Danny's house. If she said that enough, she'd eventually believe it. Once belted into her seat, her body went rigid at the armory the agents carried. Were their weapons and carrying them even legal?

Life had been easier when she'd just been a painter in her homeland. She sighed. What was done was done. She'd been in the US long enough—three months—that she'd felt safe, until last night.

In the driver seat was someone she didn't recognize,

but he looked a lot like Jane. "Where are Cowboy and the other guy from last night?"

"Investigating." He didn't sound happy about it.

Thinking on that response, she pulled in her eyebrows and asked, "I thought you said the brothers—these Hamilton men—worked the investigations."

"They do, but it's different. If they were available, they'd help with this."

Noticing they didn't seem to be going directly to Danny's, she looked at him in question.

"Since we don't have Cowboy and Doc, we're checking out the neighborhood before we stop."

"Oh." She turned to stare out the window, keeping her gaze on nothing particular. Would this become her life now? She'd been lucky in having Justin and Danny at her side, and she'd been safe.

When they pulled into a spot on the street right in front of his house, she wondered how they'd been so lucky. These spaces filled up fast and stayed that way. Then, Jane, who'd exited the SUV before they parked, tossed an orange cone in the back of the vehicle.

She spun to Danny. "I thought you couldn't do something like that."

With a one shoulder shrug, he grinned. "You're right. Slide over and exit my side."

She turned to the window, where another guy faced outward from the vehicle, but he also covered her entire door. She just shook her head. There was time to figure out all their *Mission Impossible* stuff. Danny had informed her that wasn't the type of agents they were.

While the two of them moved up the walk to the front door, Jane had already opened it. She turned and looked at them, before walking in the house with her gun like she was on some cop show.

Beside her, Danny stiffened, and she didn't know why.

"Shit," Danny said beside her. "John, get up here."

The man had already been doing that, so she guessed they had those ear things Danny had told her about.

Before Danny dashed off, he reminded John, "Protect her with your life."

She froze, fearing what had Jane and Danny spooked. She jumped at that thought.

They waited for what seemed forever, even though she knew it'd only been around five minutes, before John turned to her and motioned her toward the front door where Danny waited, watching their back. Their six, he'd taught her one night.

When she faced Danny, sympathy swam in his eyes. Why?

"I'm sorry, Moira." His voice had almost cracked at his emotions. She couldn't understand what he was apologizing for.

Glancing behind him, her heart sank. "Nay." Her pulse sped up, beating through her veins. Her hands turned so clammy she wanted to rub them on her pants. Instead, she pushed by him. Her studio had to be secure. Surely, they wanted something downstairs. Drugs or money? After racing up the stairs, she sank to her knees when she reached the top. Everything was in disarray and destroyed.

An arm slid over her shoulder, pulling her into an embrace that allowed her to weep over all she'd lost. It wasn't just the destruction of her studio. It was her only link to who she'd been in her homeland.

A second arm went around her, and she snuggled into Danny's chest, thoroughly dousing his shirt while she cried.

His soft kiss on the top of her head and his tight hold on her brought her sanity back to normal.

"I'll help you restock the place."

His tenderness renewed the tears that'd just slowed. She'd miss him so much when she finally went home.

Chapter Twenty-One

Opening the door to Cowboy and Doc, relief lifted from his chest. Not only did they have more agents protecting Moira, but he also wanted to know what they'd found.

As they walked into the living room, Cowboy blurted, "Dude, your place smells like—"

Danny sighed. "I know."

"Is it your choice or hers?" Cowboy continued on his path to embarrass him, but it wouldn't work.

He stared at the agent, knowing he was bringing levity to the meeting. "Does it matter?" Sure, it smelled like flowers, but he didn't mind because it wasn't overly powerful, and it was Moira's favorite perfume now spilled from a broken bottle.

They sat and updated Danny. They arrived with nothing. If the Underground wanted her, they were being tight-lipped about it.

Danny jumped up and wanted to hit something. Hard.

"Dammit! Someone is fucking with her, and I don't like it. Not one bit."

"How'd they get past your security system?" Doc asked from the couch.

"They busted a window. I don't have window alarms or motion sensors." He dropped in the chair opposite the couch. "Just door alarms."

"How is she?" Doc always worried about people's health—both physical and mental.

"I think she's heartbroken more than anything else."

Cowboy leaned back on the couch and stretched his legs, before crossing one over the other. "Do you think it's the guy in Ireland that she ran from?"

He sighed wearily. "I don't know. She was in one photo before Devon had it taken down off the website we found."

"It was a Celtic site, though. An Irish one."

Cowboy had it right. "I doubt the minister or Boyle check out those sites."

"True," Doc agreed, "but their employees might."

"If he hasn't made the move in the last three months, why now? And why just tearing up her studio? Why not her room, instead of just the broken perfume bottle?"

With his nervous, arguably ready-for-battle energy flying through his nerve endings, he jumped from the chair again and paced. No matter his feelings for Moira, he had to be level-headed.

"If it's him, he's coming now because he found out she's still alive." Danny wiped his hand over his face, trying to clear his head and settle his brain to figure this out. "Here's my gut's guess. He may know she's here, but it's not him. Boyle is a cold-blooded killer and would hire the same. So, the men at the tavern and whoever fucked up her studio aren't in the same class."

His teammates nodded, but their expressions showed a flash of concern. It only lasted briefly, but it told him how they felt about this op. Technically, it wasn't an official op. AJ had given him leeway to use the team—not like he wouldn't have—to collect Moira.

Doc leaned forward, resting his forearms on his thighs. "I think this whole thing stinks to high heaven. There are several options. Someone in the Underground is keeping it secret. The ruined studio doesn't fit with that option. That could be an angry artist who doesn't like the competition or a disgruntled client."

"Yeah," Danny said, but without conviction. "I don't see the last two going to the effort. But there might be something to your thought. This was a message, but I'm not sure what kind."

Cowboy pulled his legs up and straightened in his seat. "Whoever did this has been watching the house and guessed the limitations of your security system. They knew neither of you were here and did it not long after you'd left late last night."

He'd already been racking his brain to see if he remembered someone poking around more often than should be or starting a casual conversation with himself or Moira.

"I know," Cowboy said. "I'm looking into this more. If it's who's chasing her from Ireland, he may've used muscle but not killers. They're taunting her to confirm she's the right person."

"That sounds plausible," Danny said.

"Has she said anything or hinted about trouble?" Doc asked.

Danny gave him a sideways glance. "You saw her. She only asked for help when she couldn't get away. Like us, she knew better than to go out the back door right away, in case someone was waiting. So, if she had problems outside of the reason she's here, I doubt she'd share them unless they got out of control."

"Damn stubborn women," Cowboy muttered.

"Agreed."

"Let me call AJ about it all. My plan is to protect her, keep our ears to the ground for local or international chatter."

Cowboy gestured his thumb to the front door. "What about the scary twins?"

He and Doc chuckled at that. HIS only needed the two of them to confront a perp and they'd be spilling the beans, without so much as a word from either twin. Come to think of it, he'd only heard a few words from Jane and even less from John. "They're with us. They'll be our nighttime secret weapons." He paused, then added, "Let me call AJ. Then we talk to Stone."

"Stone?" Doc's brow furrowed. "Is he back with us?"

Danny shook his head. "I think he's done with his

field days. I'll have him dig up what he can about our potential suspects. When Moira arrived, I had him pull what he could of those at the mansion that day, but I set it aside when I felt she was safe. Stupid of me."

"Don't sweat it. We'll take care of it." Doc stood. "Got anything to drink in the fridge?" Doc loomed over him.

"Help yourselves. There's also snacks in the pantry." He stepped to his office to make the first call.

AJ picked up before the second ring. "What the fuck? You should've reported already."

True, but he'd needed to calm down. Pissing off AJ would doom anything extra he might need or make them pull him. "We had a problem."

"Go ahead."

"We found her easily this morning and brought her home. The problem is that someone has been in my home and destroyed her art studio on my third floor."

"Don't you have a security system? If not, I'll meet your ass in the ring."

He wanted to laugh. AJ, well, he wasn't good in the ring. As if channeling his boss, Danny's finger and thumb rested on the bridge of his nose before he answered, "Of course I have a security system. It just isn't on the windows or inside motion."

"Do you think it's the Irish threat?"

"I couldn't say. There's no chatter of her in the Underground, but I won't write them off completely. The two thugs could've been trying to fill a quota and decided she looked good for it." Danny took a breath and continued. "Whoever did the deed last night knew Moira wasn't there, knew I'd left, and knew my house and security system, or made a damn good calculated guess on it. Plus, they targeted her space."

"Shit. Hang on," AJ said and muted the call.

He hated when the brothers did that, but, sometimes. it was better than hearing them loudly discuss the situation. As he began running down all he had to do, AJ returned.

"Devon will be there tomorrow to replace or upgrade your security system to include the second and third floor. He'll also install some cameras that'll give you full coverage of front and back. Front will cross the street, so you can see anyone hanging out."

That took the first thing off his mental list of to do items. This system would be significantly better than what he'd planned. "We'll be here. About my team—"

"Keeping Moira safe is now an Alpha team op. You'll remain. Make room in your home for them. Have someone come grab what you need. Make sure to remind Cowboy that every situation does not require a flash bang."

Danny smiled at the idea because he knew it to be true. "Thank you, AJ."

"Don't thank me yet. I'm your coordinator, and I get short-tempered when I'm called away from my wife and son for something that can wait. That's not to say don't wake me up before shit happens. Okay, you know the drill. I want Moira covered 24/7. If things get bad, we take her to the safe house. Stone will continue to pull intel for you. No more jumping the gun for you and taking away part of my job."

An "oops" almost slipped out.

"Make sure she is on board or bring her to Jesse's. Kate will convince her."

Damn true on that. "Roger."

AJ hung up.

Knowing his team had approval for this op, versus going rogue, released some of the rope coiling in his stomach. With a nod, he made his way back to the living room, wondering if he had any food left after Doc and Cowboy opened the pantry.

Surprisingly they only had bottled water open. "Did you guys have breakfast?"

Doc nodded. "We did drive-thru. Did you guys eat?"

"We did before Moira went to bed. The twins took turns."

Wide eyed, Cowboy asked, "Did they say anything?"

"Nope," Danny said as he shook his head. "I did get a nod from each of them."

"Damn odd," Cowboy said.

"Didn't we cover this earlier?" Danny asked.

Cowboy shrugged. "Just trying to figure them out."

"Maybe they just need to warm up to us," Doc countered.

"Once they feel comfortable with us, I'm sure things will be different." He held his phone out in front of him.

"Are you ready for us to call Stone?"

"What about the twins?"

Cowboy just wouldn't let that go, but he did need to bring them up to speed. Turning on his microphone, he ordered, "Mission brief. Jane, you need to be in here. John, we'll broadcast the meeting, so just interrupt us if you need to."

"Why Jane?" Danny didn't recognize the voice, but it had to be John. The man did speak and might be protective of his sister.

"She's going to be close to Moira, so I need you to handle things alone. We don't have a sniper to spare, but let me know if you need Jane back. I think it'll be easier to protect her with a woman most of the time."

He counted his heartbeats in wait of whether John would respond.

"Good plan" was all he said.

From a black ops guy, who may not even legally exist, that put confidence back in Danny.

Chapter Twenty-Two

While Devon and crew updated his system with inside cameras, sensors on every window, glass breakage sensors, and motion sensors, Danny took Moira shopping to replace what she'd lost. It wasn't a necessity and, according to Devon, was a risk not worth taking, but with Jane, John, and Cowboy all surrounding her and carrying concealed weapons, Danny felt they could keep her safe.

They still had no idea who destroyed her studio. It made no sense. Sure, she'd been followed, but to follow-up with destruction? It sounded like two separate incidents. It could be the same person and would be better if it was, so they didn't have to keep an eye on more than one front, but still….

They were going to handle things as if Moira had been found. Well, except for today's excursion. Doubt crept in. Maybe he shouldn't have pushed for it. Was he losing his objectivity because he wanted the girl… wanted to please her? Had Boss and the brothers encountered the same issue? Granted, he wasn't in love, but he could see himself falling in love with Moira. If only she wanted to stay in the States.

Once Justin collected the info to bring Boyle to justice, she could live freely. If she'd only stay, he'd help her get her start as an artist in any way he could. Surely Jesse and Kate had a contact that would be of use.

"Danny, can we go home now? I'd like to be there when all of these packages are delivered," Moira said.

His heart warmed when she said "home." It may have been a slip of the tongue, but he'd hoped the three months since she'd been here, she'd begin to consider his home hers. "Sure." With that, the group turned and still maintained a protective circle around Danny and Moira. They were intent on their duty, and while none had liked the risk, they'd stood up to be selected for the detail. Doc had been left behind because Devon said his height would be of benefit during the install.

"Did you get everything you wanted?" he asked.

"*Nay*, but I have enough to get started again."

He had no idea what she planned to do with all the paintings anyway if she was leaving, unless she planned to pack them all up and ship them. "What are you planning to paint next?"

"The streets of Dublin. More specifically one street. It holds memories I like to revisit."

"Anything you want to share?"

He looked at her and caught a blush creeping round her cheeks. "Well, it's silly really."

That made him chuckle because now he wanted to know. "You can tell me."

"Okay. Remember I said it was silly."

He nodded and glanced at her again. God, she was beautiful. In blue jeans and a comfy looking T-shirt, her figure drew him to her, and his blood ran south. Damn, he had it bad for her.

"Well, we were at a bar and it was the first time my parents bought me a pint of Gat."

"Okay," he said slowly. Odd memory.

"I told you it was silly. It's just, that was the first time they acknowledged me as an adult. So, I remember that feeling of gratification and think of them."

That was heavier than he expected. "That is a good memory," he said, because anything else would be wrong in some way. "I have a memory from my father." Now he felt stupid about what he was going to say. "It was when he gave me my aviator pilot watch." He showed her the item on his wrist. "It told me he had faith in me becoming a pilot."

"And you did."

A pilot who was afraid of taking flight. "Yeah, I did. But, like you, I remember that moment every time I look at my watch. So I get your need to recreate the scene so you can revisit it."

"When I go home, I can visit it as often as I want. But, until then, the painting will do."

They were quiet the remainder of the walk back to his home. Once there, he marveled at how much Devon, some of the Hamilton brothers and a few from Bravo team had accomplished.

"The glass has been replaced in your window, and all windows have sensors on them, so no one will sneak in that way again," Devon said, when Danny approached him.

Devon's voice didn't sound it, but Danny felt like he was being chastised for not protecting his home better to begin with. "Thanks. I appreciate it." Anything to make Moira safer.

"I'm still ready to kick your ass for taking her out today," AJ told him.

Bristling, Danny stiffened and straightened, ready for a fight, even if only verbal. "I made sure she was safe."

"She'd have been safer here with all of us," Brad Hamilton said.

Of all the men to tell him about keeping his woman safe, these three took the cake. *His woman*? He wanted her to be, but there was still the matter of his brother. Based on her holding Danny's hand, he didn't think she held any regard for his brother, but he owed it to the man to speak with him first, in case his brother did hold a regard for Moira. Then, there was her wanting to return to Ireland. He guessed he could go with her, but his home was here. That realization let him feel how important it was for her to return home. Home held a special place in your heart. Maybe since she wouldn't have any loved ones still there, she'd then consider staying.

"She'd just been freaked out and you brought men she doesn't know here. Of course she needed to get out. Besides, I'm not certain the three of you, especially you, AJ, are the best for telling me how to protect a lone woman."

"Hey, times with Megan were different," AJ blustered.

"Yeah, sure. You kept her on the run with you instead of handing her over to the safety of your brother's protective arms. At least I'm utilizing all the protection available."

"Megan was still different," AJ hedged.

"Maybe not." Let them take that for what it was worth. He'd just let them know Moira meant more than a friend needing protection. If they tried to take him off lead for the op because she meant something to him, he'd go ballistic. Only Boss could usurp his leadership of the team. Technically, any Hamilton brother could do that, but they didn't. They left the teams to Boss and even followed him when they participated on a mission. Well, mostly. They each took over when the women, they later married, had been in danger.

"So that's how it is." AJ shook his head. "Only a man in too deep would even consider putting a tracker on his woman."

Okay, it sounded wrong, but he knew it wasn't. She'd been free to move around, but between the men he'd hired and the tracker, he'd known where she was in case she'd been in trouble. Well, except for last night, since he'd chosen not to replace the men. He'd become comfortable and somewhat safe. He swallowed at the thought of the danger she'd been in when he'd been drinking beer with the guys.

"Anything on the men who chased her?"

"Underground by association, but no specific IDs on their names."

His gut clenched in fear for Moira. If they had caught her…. He couldn't think it. "So now we need to figure out if she was a target of opportunity or contracted."

"It sounds like they gave up too easily for a targeted pick," Brad said. "Think about it. They let the boys turn them away from checking, not only the woman being kissed, but the women's restroom. Then, they weren't waiting outside the door for when she left. No, I'd go for target of opportunity. Those two were probably trying to impress the bosses. I'm upset to say that since they didn't get Moira, they probably snatched another woman."

Danny nodded. He liked that line of thinking, but not that another woman may have been abducted. They'd keep an eye out for anyone suspicious, potentially from the Underground, but he'd keep that hope she hadn't been targeted. Just in case there was another faction at work, he'd check in with Justin and Declan to see if they knew of any activity.

"But someone still broke in and destroyed her studio," Devon said. "*That* was targeted. It screams petty though. The Underground would've trashed the entire place."

It did seem petty. "Moira doesn't know anyone she's

upset since she's been here. Couldn't it have been the two men who tried to grab her as a revenge for escaping them?"

"Then that changes things and would mean she wasn't a crime of opportunity," Brad said.

"We may have one or two contacts in the Underground. We'll see what we can get from them," said AJ, who'd been an enforcer for a drug lord, albeit undercover FBI. If contacts had been made, he'd have made them when he went through that dark time of his life.

"Well, until we find out, you're all restricted to the house," AJ directed. "No more shopping trips."

He wanted to argue out of principle, but AJ had it right. They needed to stay together and out of sight. Now, if only he could convince Moira that was best, without scaring her to death about the potential threat.

Chapter Twenty-Three

The soothing sound of the storm outside didn't interrupt Moira's mind. She slid her brush across the celestial blue on her pallet for her drybrush stroke, but her mind wandered. Even though she'd painted mostly works of Ireland to keep the memories alive, Moira enjoyed living in America.

With a heavy sigh, she pulled back, and, with a critical eye, she inspected what she'd created so far. She hadn't thought about what she'd been painting since her brush and muse helped bring it together. Another painting of the streets of Dublin. She'd only been to this narrow street, with bars on both sides and friends congregating on the street blocked off for traffic, a few times. Her recollections sometimes surprised her.

Taking the time to thoroughly clean her new brushes, she jumped when the front door slammed. Even with Danny's teammates outside, fear ripped through her, and her body shook as small droplets of water dripped from the brush in her hand. They'd been on house arrest for three weeks now, and neither Danny nor the guards had slammed the door. She could only assume it was someone else—they'd been found. Thunder boomed at that moment, driving the terror home.

Her chest heaved and she couldn't catch her breath. *Not an attack, not now.* With her heart pounding, her gaze raced around the room for a hiding place. She decided on the far corner, yet her legs wouldn't move. Those wobbly legs. Why couldn't she move? Her life might depend on it. She closed her eyes as tears spilled down her cheeks and hoped Danny returned before whoever broke in, either killed her or took her away. *Danny, where are you?*

"Moira, you here?" Danny's voice traveled up the stairs to her third-floor haven and unfroze her mind and body.

As her legs buckled, she fell to the floor with a combination of relief and anger at him for almost giving her a heart attack. Or as she would say to her brother "putting the heart crossways in her." She hoped her voice didn't sound as frightened as she'd been. "Yes, just cleaning up."

"Can I come up and see?"

She squeaked. In no way did she want him to see her like this. Like a scared little girl. "Nay, it's a work in progress." He understood that no one saw her *ealaín* until it was complete.

Slipping inside her bedroom, she freshened up and

waited until her body felt normal again.

The walk down the stairs with her hand gliding on the banister elicited a laugh from Danny. She narrowed her eyes at him but wasn't upset. "What's so funny?"

Sucking in a breath as he tried to calm his laughing enough to speak, he finally won the battle. "You. You looked like royalty gliding down the stairs. Did they teach you that at that prissy boarding school?"

They actually had taught them a great deal of comportment. Ignoring him and his "prissy" comment, she walked past him and peered into the refrigerator and groaned. She shut the door and turned to Danny; his eyebrows rose as if to laugh again. Ignoring the expression and his damp hair needing a comb, she asked, "Are you hungry?"

He gazed at her for a moment with a tight jaw, and she worried what she'd done. Not moving, his serious gaze bothered her. As she looked closer, it wasn't serious—it was heated.

"Did you know you've got a perfect ass?" he asked

Her body tingled in pleasure, but she had no idea how to respond. Instead, she changed the subject. "Who's open this late for takeaway?"

A quirk at the corner of his lips told her he saw through her. After a moment—too long of one—he checked his watch. "For delivery, we have Chinese or pizza."

She wrinkled her nose. "I'd like Chinese. How about you?"

With a shrug, he agreed, "Chinese works. There's a—"

Waving her hand to cut him off, she turned to the counter. "—menu in the drawer."

After ordering enough food for the crew and leftovers galore, they stood, and his gaze continued to bore into her. Walking to the refrigerator, she asked, "What'd you like to drink?"

"Guinness. You've ruined me for American beers." He moved to the shelf where he kept the alcohol.

Sitting, she squirmed a bit. They'd not had this stilted a silence since she'd first arrived. They'd also not spent so much time together since before, he'd worked days or weeks at a time, leaving her alone. Her nerves were getting the better of her when they shouldn't.

Another boom of thunder shook his house before the power blinked and remained off. They remained still, her hoping the lights would return. She wasn't afraid of the dark but preferred to avoid it unless sleeping.

A light appeared in Danny's hand. Moving his cell phone around, he found her. "Candles," he stated firmly. "Do you have your phone?"

She kept it in her pocket or purse, always, in case her brother called. She pulled it from a pocket.

Through the glow of her screen, she caught his nod before she turned on her flashlight app. Touching her arm, he led her to a cabinet she'd never explored.

Her mouth dropped. Was he expecting a zombie apocalypse? Accepting the handful of items, concern climbed up her throat. "What about the security system?" It'd taken days to get everything installed to Devon's satisfaction. With it, she felt safe. When it was turned on, that was.

"Don't sweat it. It's got a battery backup. We'll be fine as long as it isn't off for long. But, remember, we've got Cowboy and John watching over the place. If need be, we can bring Doc and Jane back."

Once they'd set up enough candles to leave no dark corners, she relaxed.

"Come on. Let's sit and chat."

As she settled on the couch, she relaxed. Whatever the scent, the candles did the job.

"First," he started the conversation, "I'm sorry for being late. Tonight, let's just do some good ole Q & A to learn more about each other." He waved his hand as if he'd just called her to the stage. "Ladies first."

Embarrassment flooded her at thinking of how she'd reacted earlier when he'd arrived. The team had said Jane would be her companion indoors when Danny wasn't home. She should've realized Jane would only open the door to Danny or a team member. The agent would've called out had there been trouble. She also would've left when Danny entered. It all made sense in hindsight.

"Are you okay?" he asked with concerned eyes.

Like she'd been taught by her mother, she took a deep breath and counted to ten before releasing it. She didn't know if this was the official fix, but it worked for her. "You can go first."

After a pause he asked, "You've been here nearly four months, what do you think of America? Maybe making it your home?"

How to answer that? She'd been given no incentive to stay. She picked her words to not let her true feelings burst free. "I miss my homeland." She shrugged nonchalantly. "But I might be convinced to stay."

"How?" Lead balls dropped to the pit of her stomach. He didn't act like he wanted her to stay. That kiss must've meant nothing to him.

Thinking quick on her feet, she chuckled. "My turn." She hoped the takeaway would arrive soon because she didn't want to answer that last question. Oh, she thought of a whopper that might give her a clue to his dating. "Cowboy mentioned you'd been dating a lot before I arrived. Do you really want to get married that badly to go on so many blind dates?"

Choking on the swig of Guinness he'd just taken, he coughed and coughed and coughed. She began to think he planned to do that until the food arrived, so he'd not have to answer. Granted he didn't have to answer, but something within her, somewhere she didn't want to yet acknowledge, wanted to know his stance on marriage. Not that she planned to marry him. Still, she wanted to know.

So they'd each hit on tender topics. If he gave her any attention as a woman—more than tonight and the kiss to hide her—she'd spill her guts to him.

"Let's see." He wouldn't look at her, which she

found odd. Did he plan to lie? "No, I'm not in a rush to marry. The children I babysit from time to time for my bosses' families give me plenty of kid time. I used to do it more often before you moved in. I don't want them interrupting you while you work." He took another drink of Guinness and she'd throw something at him if he did that fake choking thing again. "As for the dating, Sugar's decided I needed a woman in my life. She's been pushing to set me up, and I'd given in. Until recently."

Her breath hitched. Dare she hope he stopped seeing other women because of her? "Why?"

A deep, rumbling laugh that had her wanting to do all kinds of things to him reached her. "Now it's my turn."

At the hard knock on the door, she jumped. When her gaze locked with his, Danny smiled. "It's okay. Takeout, remember?"

She must've looked like a frightful rabbit the way his eyes had softened to soothe her.

Danny set his drink on the coffee table, stood, and walked to the door. "Why the hell did I install a doorbell when everybody knocks or just walks right in?" He turned to give her the evil eye when she'd giggled at his question. She caught his smile before he turned back.

While Danny dealt with paying and carting the two bags to the living room coffee table, she collected plates, utensils, and napkins for them, plus a beverage for her. Before they filled plates, Danny called Cowboy in to grab something for him and John, and then take it back to their posts.

Alone, candlelight and a casual dinner created a romantic air. She became downright giddy with the knowledge.

Sliding to the floor at the living room coffee table, her body warmed as his strong thighs settled beside her. Hoping for the "hand almost touching" scene like in movies that brought on snogging, she smiled as she took a sip of beer.

Chapter Twenty-Four

When Danny turned to Moira in the kitchen after dinner, and she bounced off his chest, this time, he caught her. The heat flying between them had been nearing an inferno. They'd talked and laughed like normal people having dinner, but the looks they'd shared had been so hot, the flames engulfed them.

He'd known cleaning up the dishes—few as there were since they'd had takeout—would be a good excuse to get close to her, to touch her hand when handing off dishes to dry. And he knew that bumping into her could also be an option. Case in point.

He held her arms tightly against him. He heard, rather than felt, the hitch in her breathing. It fed his desire to take her to bed. And it was damn time he did that with her.

"If you don't want this," he said in a hoarse voice, "now is the time to speak up."

With her adorable Irish accent, she said, "Aye, I want this."

He pulled her so close that nothing but air could move between them. He lowered his head and tasted her sweet lips. She tasted like Chinese takeout and beer and something unique that he longed to taste more of.

Brushing her lips softly, he took his time playing over the top of them, before prodding her lips open with his tongue. She didn't stop him or hesitate. In no time, the kiss turned fierce, his tongue demanding dominance and his mouth hard and wanting.

Justin's name flitted in and immediately out of his mind. She was his, and he'd fight anyone he needed to for her, including his brother.

With his arms around her, he tightened his hold. Now that he had her, he never wanted to let her go.

Their mouths melded perfectly, and their kisses set his cock to standing strong, ready for her. The thought of being inside her made him groan with need and try again to get her closer, although it was impossible.

"You taste so good," he rasped.

She laughed. "Yeah, like Chinese food."

He grinned down at her. "There's that. Plus, more."

With that, he took her mouth again, rubbing his hand up and down her back, resting on her nicely shaped bottom. He squeezed and pulled her tightly against his groin to let her feel his hard length and his desire for her. When she moaned, he could've come at the sound alone. Making love to her became his number one priority.

She made the first move by tugging his shirt from his jeans and pulling it over his head in one smooth movement. It didn't embarrass him that he'd been too slow to initiate this phase of their making out, but he made sure to reciprocate. After, he stared at her in a white lacy bra and couldn't decide whether to remove it properly or rip it from her body, so he could see her bare breasts. Luscious breasts he'd been eyeing for a while now.

To make it easier for him, she turned with her back toward him and the hooks facing him. He quickly reached up, unfastening the first hook, before he heard, "Friendly, incoming," in his ear.

He dropped his head and worked to hold onto what had once been passion but had turned to anger. Whoever interrupted them had best have a good reason. And he couldn't think of any at the moment.

He refastened the bra and turned her. "You'd best get dressed." He reached for his own polo. "We have company."

Her eyes widened, and he wasn't sure if it was surprise or fear.

To alleviate one possibility, he said, "It's friendly."

Relief washed over her features. So, she was more scared than she let on. He'd remember that.

They'd just finished tucking their shirts into their pants when the knock on the door sounded. He couldn't do anything about the bulge proudly displayed in his pants. It'd go down in no time, but it might be noticeable to their guest, who was apparently someone they knew.

When he answered the door, several emotions ran through him—anger, worry, relief, to name a few. Justin—whose girl he almost took to bed—stood on his doorstep, looking worse for wear.

"Come in," Danny said. As his brother entered, he noticed the sling holding Justin's arm tight to his body. The bruises had purpled but the swelling in his right jaw remained. "Have a seat."

Moira gasped and squeaked when she saw Justin. Before he could ask another question, Moira was lavishing attention on his brother. Technically, her boyfriend, or so he'd assumed. And if that was the case, she'd cheated by kissing him. But he wouldn't say anything. He would ask Justin to step back though. Unless he loved her too.

Whoa, wait a minute, love? Impossible. She hadn't been here that long. Okay, it had almost been four months. However, they hadn't even had sex yet. How could you love someone without having sex? Heck, they'd just kissed for the first time. Okay, the second time if they counted the tavern kiss. Still, maybe he just liked her a lot. He knew he wanted to be with her both in and out of clothes all the time. More than he had any other woman.

"He knows you're alive," Justin said to Moira. "I barely got out of there myself."

"What happened?" Danny dropped in the chair opposite the couch where Justin and Moira sat close together.

"It's the money. Declan pulled funds. Dead men don't pull funds."

Damn. He forgot to talk with Devon about a safe way for them to access their funds. Since Moira hadn't needed any, he'd forgotten about the situation. If only he'd done so at the beginning, maybe they wouldn't have been found. "Does he know where?"

"No. And he tried hard. I had a dislocated shoulder"—he pointed to the shoulder with a sling on his arm—"and some bruises, but luckily, no internal bleeding and nothing broken."

"How'd you get away?" *And did you lead them here?* He wanted to know because, right now, he wasn't sure whether to trust his brother. Danny figured if Boyle had found out about Justin, his brother would probably be dead or close to it.

"Boyle chose the wrong guy to beat the truth out of me. It was too easy to overpower him. Maybe he didn't try hard because everyone loves Diana, and they don't want Boyle to find her."

"Excuse me," Danny said, before standing and walking down the hall to his bedroom. Directly into his comms mic, he said, "Heads up. Stay alert."

"We already are," John answered.

With John and Cowboy on duty tonight, he felt safe. No one would get by those two. He still was glad John hadn't kicked Cowboy's ass yet. Then again, their night partnership was young. "I'll brief you as soon as I have the facts."

"Roger," Cowboy said.

Rejoining Justin and Moira, his stomach lurched as Moira gingerly traced the bruises on his brother's face. Tenderly. With emotion. But was it love? Heck, she didn't love him either, but he hoped she'd come around if they were a couple and had the chances other couples did. It'd be tough with her in protection—especially now—but it wasn't impossible.

"Tell me everything." He regained his seat and focused on his brother's beat-up body, not Moira reacting to it.

"Someone at the bank alerted Boyle. I'm not sure why they didn't tell him where it came from, since they'd surely know. So he came to me first. I almost had him convinced someone had hacked the account, but, in the end, he didn't want to believe that. He wanted to exact his form of punishment."

"Kill them, you mean," Danny said.

"Yeah, including Moira, but not because of Diana and Declan. Boyle figured out she was outside the door during that meeting and won't take the chance that she heard something she shouldn't have. But don't get me wrong, he wants Declan in a fierce way." He took a deep breath and appeared to be in pain doing it. Ribs possibly. Justin was probably right about being allowed to break free. Unless he brought them here. But with the way he looked at Moira—with caring not guilt—Danny began to doubt he'd brought Boyle with him.

"At least he doesn't know where we are. It'd be tough to find us in this country," Moira said.

"That doesn't mean less protection here. If anything, it will be tighter," Danny told her.

"It won't take long," Justin said, "for Boyle to browbeat the banker for a location. Since there'd been no need, no one's protecting Diana and Declan."

"Who do you think is Boyle's priority?"

"Moira. You heard her recording. That's the priority. Diana is—" Justin paused, "—just family business."

Fear clouded Moira's features, and he wished he'd asked that question out of her earshot. "Are you sure you're all right?"

"Yeah. I had to see a doc about the shoulder, and he checked me out. The ribs are bruised with small fractures, nothing to be concerned with."

Danny narrowed his eyes. Except his brother's jaw was still swollen. And there might be more. He hoped not.

"Thank goodness," Moira said.

"Okay. We need to call Declan and update the team. Moira, would you excuse my brother and me for a bit? I'd really appreciate it."

She looked about to argue, but after looking at Justin and his small nod, she exited the room. He watched her head to the stairs and refused to speak until she was out of earshot.

"Tell me."

"I was right. There's definitely someone else pulling the strings. I was so close but then the money issue came to Boyle's attention and I was a goner. Thank God the men love Diana. That means there's someone we don't know about. I'm not sure if they're after her too or if it's just Boyle. All I know is I failed in making our dad's killer pay. After all those years working in the organization, trying to find out who pulled the strings, so I could bring down the man who had our father murdered, it's all gone up in smoke. I have nothing but Boyle. Oh, I can bring him down, but without who's in charge, it's almost a waste, because someone else will just jump in that slot."

After a minute, Justin continued, "After failing our father when he was killed, I wanted so bad to bring down the person behind the attack. To bring closure to us all, especially Mom. To show the agency that I was right about who ordered the hit, because that is what it was. I was there and nothing could convince me otherwise. All these years for nothing. I've wasted this time."

Danny couldn't help but be moved by Justin's journey to find a killer. By his wanting to do this for their family. He'd been angry at his brother for disappearing. Then to hear he worked for Boyle, that anger grew into something deeper. But hearing the story wiped it away. This was his brother who wanted things to be as they should. The right killer to be brought to justice.

"You haven't wasted the time. We bring down Boyle, and if someone steps in, we figure out how to bring them down." Notwithstanding HIS had no jurisdiction anywhere, especially in Ireland. But they'd find a way. They always did. And he still had agency friends he could phone. "We'll find a way. Maybe even work out who the boss is." The anonymous boss worried him. He hated the unknown.

"I'm sorry, I'm not sure who the boss is, as in drug boss. I think he pulls strings and Boyle is just one string of many."

"Strings?"

"Yeah. It's a hunch, but my gut thinks it's right. I just had no proof."

"Mm. We'll figure it out."

Chapter Twenty-Five

"And you're sure he doesn't know where they are?" AJ asked for the hundredth time. Or so it seemed like it. Justin had been updating HIS on what he knew, and it'd been an interrogation like no other. It had been obvious the men didn't trust him, and Danny understood the feeling. He hadn't, at first, but it was his brother, and once he'd given him the benefit of the doubt, trust had come. Except for the slight wavering when he'd shown up the night before.

"I don't think so, but I don't think it'll be long before he figures it out. At least to Boston." Justin had been confident in his answer, every time he'd given it.

AJ and Devon huddled together. It irked Danny that they left everyone else out of the discussion. Yet, he had to remember these were the men taking the risks and who would have to fight any battles that occurred because of their actions.

"Here's what we're going to do," AJ said. "The information on Boyle goes to the DEA. But, you,"—he pointed at Justin— "aren't the one to give it. You burned that bridge. Danny will provide Boyle on a silver platter to them."

"What about who really leads it all?" Justin urged. He'd been fighting that point the entire time. Yet, with no proof, even Danny wouldn't do anything on it. Not with legal channels anyway.

Devon shook his head. "You've got nothing more than speculation. Danny can tell the DEA we think there is someone higher, but that's it."

"I want to be the one to bring down Boyle. He ordered the hit on my father," Justin said.

"You're no longer a law enforcement officer and you can't prove it," AJ insisted.

Justin had one man who'd admitted to overhearing Boyle order their father's death, but the man had soon disappeared.

"Do you really think Boyle would've hired you and let it slip he killed your father?" Devon asked.

Justin deflated. "He hired me because he thought I could be bought. It took a long time to convince him I really could, and that's when I was able to get the evidence on him for drug running. But no, I guess I never really expected him to drop his admission of having my father murdered in my lap. I'd just hoped."

After a bit more rehashing of what Justin knew, Justin and Danny were left alone.

"Why didn't you tell me Mom is getting married?" Justin asked.

"If you were around more, you'd have known. I like Mitch. He's a nice guy and treats her like a queen."

"Until I find work, I'll be around more. This is as good a place as any to lick my wounds."

"You did an excellent job," Danny told him. "Don't forget that."

"And I get none of the credit," Justin bemoaned.

"Oh, the agency will know it all came from you," Danny assured him, knowing his brother meant having his reputation restored.

Justin slapped him on the shoulder. "Thanks, brother."

Danny swallowed. This next part was about to test the brother connection. If he really loved Moira, things were going to get tight. Danny didn't plan on losing this battle.

"I need to ask you something," he said.

"Go ahead."

"It's about Moira."

"What about her?"

What about her? She's beautiful, kind, and a lovable person. And I love her. "Are the two of you serious?"

Justin gave him a blank look. "Serious?"

"Yeah, you know, do you love her?"

It took another moment before Justin reacted, and when he did, it wasn't what Danny expected. He laughed. *Laughed.* "Oh boy."

This was not a funny conversation. There was

nothing funny about it. Danny felt insulted for him and for Moira. "What's so damn funny? Are you serious with her or not?"

"You have feelings for her, don't you?" Justin asked.

At this point he saw no reason to hide that fact. "I do."

"Danny, there's nothing between Moira and me. I'd love it if there were, but she doesn't see me that way."

Elation filled Danny. The one obstacle he'd held in his mind was gone. Vanished in an instant. She was free to be with him. All this time, she'd been free. He wouldn't have traded their getting to know each other before moving to the next step. But now, Moira would be his. He wanted to do a fist pump but restrained himself.

"She's all yours, brother."

At that moment, he was called over to the computer area of the war room, so he only nodded to his brother.

Seated around the computers, Danny waited for AJ to get to the point. He'd never known the Hamilton brother to be so long-winded. So much so that Danny's leg began to bounce. He put a hand on it and that seemed to work. Anxiety riddled him, mixing up his feelings and his warrior mode. He needed to protect Moira, so he waited for AJ to finish.

"I've been weeding through résumés—which I never understand why we have so many because we've never posted a job availability—for a third team."

Why the hell were they talking about this now when his woman needed them? Jane and Doc were watching her, but he wanted to be there. "You're going to put a bunch of newbies all together and send them out without adult supervision?"

"While that might be fun to watch, we don't need a bunch of bodies returning. No, my brothers and I will conduct training here and run them through all we can until we get the land cleared to expand the field."

"Enough of that," Devon interjected. "Tell him."

"All right, all right," AJ said to Devon. He gave Danny a serious expression that knotted his stomach. "Did you get your helicopter license?"

Confused, since Danny had no doubt AJ already knew the answer as it'd been discussed at HQ and the brothers always seemed to know what happened to him, he shrugged. He had, but going up again was another matter. "Yes." With AJ, he had no idea what would come out of his mouth next. "Remember? I almost got my examiner killed." He drew out on a long breath.

Why this question now? He swung his gaze between the brothers and then to Stone, who kept his nose on the keyboard. Shit. What was this about? While unrealistic to jump to such a conclusion, he did. His fear of not being good enough rose up and wanted to choke him. If they wanted to get rid of him for not having special ops or military background like most, that meant the majority of the six brothers and one sister agreed. As he opened his mouth to say something, although he hadn't figured out what to say, Devon interrupted.

"Get to the damn point, AJ," Devon said.

AJ narrowed his eyes at his brother. "You owe Reagan's swear jar some money." Devon snorted his response, and AJ swung his gaze back to him. "Here's the deal."

Those were words that could ruin a man's life. Danny didn't run away from things, but something made him want to get the hell away before AJ finished.

What surprised him was when Devon told AJ to "Beat it" before he turned back to Danny.

AJ didn't leave but crossed his arms over his chest; anyone who didn't know him would assume him to be calm. Members of HIS knew better. They could see what was hidden from outside eyes.

Ignoring AJ, Devon took over. "Have you thought of what you would do now that you're a helicopter pilot?"

Oh. They're worried he'd leave. That released a pressure from his body to know they cared. Much better than firing him. "Actually, I haven't." Why would he when he didn't plan on flying anytime soon?

Devon slapped his hands together. "Perfect. If you'll agree to be our helicopter pilot while employed, we'll reimburse you for what you spent for training."

If he hadn't been sitting, he'd have stumbled back at the gratitude he felt. He'd gone from worrying they'd fire him to them making him an asset to HIS all in one short conversation. AJ may have been an excellent undercover FBI operative, but his business communication skills fell a bit short compared to the other family members.

Before he could share his fear about going back up in a helicopter, AJ startled them all when he snapped his fingers and smiled. "I've got it!"

"Got what?" Danny hesitantly asked.

"I remember where I've seen Moira before and maybe others might've also."

Seen her? Danny's gut clenched and his heart seized. He didn't want or need her public in any forum. He snapped his gaze to AJ. He could throttle the man for keeping something like that out of their pre-op briefing. Angrily, he commanded, "What do you mean you've seen her? Isn't this something you should've shared with us?"

Ignoring Danny, AJ turned to Devon. "Go to this Irish Festival website." He handed Devon a piece of paper Danny had seen him writing on a few moments ago during his "ah-ha" moment. After Devon put the site on his big screen, AJ directed him. "Go to the photos tab."

"Exactly why were you on this site?" Devon asked.

"Once I told Megan someone from Ireland was here, she began researching, which meant I was stuck looking at what she found."

The screen had all of his attention, so AJ's words meant nothing. Nothing else mattered at the moment. He wanted to slap himself on the forehead. That was the trip he and Cowboy had pulled her from. Not soon enough, apparently.

He didn't fight the strange feeling of protectiveness, attraction, or his flat-out need to have her in his bed. Had it been another woman, he'd have laughed at that.

AJ stopped Devon as he scrolled down the screen of

photos. He pointed to a photo on the screen. "There. In the picture with her artwork in the background."

His breath caught at the sight of her. Hell, he saw nothing but the woman whose lips he'd tasted the prior evening. The woman who felt more right in his arms than any other in his life. Just to be certain it wasn't a doppelgänger on the screen, his eyes raced through the names beneath the picture. He didn't need to really read the name. He couldn't mistake her or confuse her with another woman. Damn if she didn't look cute in that Celtic outfit. Now, he just had to keep her safe from all the threats that surrounded them.

AJ and Danny stood. Danny started the conversation, tagging Devon first. "Is it possible, or likely, that someone in Ireland would see this?"

"It's possible," Devon reluctantly said. "How probable, I'm not sure."

Scrunching his brows down, Danny continued his questions, "What'd ya mean?"

"Normally, I'd say a low probability. But, since it's mostly an Irish festival, that might intrigue Irish readers on both sides of the pond."

Something spun hard in Danny's gut and what felt like razor sharp prongs cut him deep. This was the second photo. He'd had thought she'd be careful. Maybe she had been. She hadn't posed for the photo; she just happened to be standing in her booth. Still. He wanted to slap his fist on the desk.

Living in the US, she'd told him of the freedom

she'd felt and how much she loved it. After nearly four months of nothing, he'd bet his last dollar she hadn't felt threatened at all. The men the other night must've scared her since nothing had happened since she'd moved here.

"I can get them to take the pictures down." Devon grinned mischievously. "One way or another." He looked downright gleeful.

"Will you check if she pops up anywhere on the web and get it cleared out?" Danny asked.

"Already started, Ball Park." Devon's grin turned into laughter, and AJ joined it.

Danny's gaze slid to Stone. He shook his head and shrugged. Damn Cowboy for starting that horrible call sign.

Chapter Twenty-Six

It'd been a long day at headquarters and a long night with Justin over for dinner. Thankfully, his brother had decided to stay elsewhere for the night, which gave Danny the perfect opportunity to further his relationship with Moira. Something that had not left his mind even during the deep conversation with HIS about her safety.

He'd returned from HQ with flowers after leaving her with Jane and Doc for the day. They would be there every day from now until Boyle was in custody. Maybe even longer since what Moira overheard was still being investigated. He'd provided the DEA that recording nearly four months ago, and they hadn't seemed to do anything. At least not enough for Danny. The group on that tape could be a serious problem for Moira.

Then the whole helicopter thing had been dropped in his lap. He'd not given an answer because he wasn't sure he could. They'd shown him the helicopter they'd purchased—odd since they didn't have any pilots, unless they were counting on him and scrubbing new recruits for someone qualified to fly. It still hadn't stopped his gut from churning. He and Wayne could've died if he hadn't gotten lucky in landing. He couldn't imagine transporting his teammates and knowing he might kill them.

What was he to say? He wanted to fly. He wanted to be like his father who'd been in the Army Reserves and flown for them. Only, Danny wasn't joining the Army. So, what did he do with that license then? Maybe he should try. Baby steps and all. Right now, though, his focus turned to Moira who'd just returned from her shower all cute in pajamas and no makeup. Adorable. His heart beat deeply for this woman.

"You look cute. And clean," he joked.

"I love the double shower heads in the bathroom. They're amazing."

He'd splurged in the guest bathroom when he'd remodeled the old house. Now he was happy he had. "I'm glad you enjoyed them."

They stood within reach of each other. The electrical pull between them had each of them taking a barely noticeable step closer to the other. Close enough that Danny reached out and cupped her cheek. With a thumb, he caressed the soft skin. Touching her face wasn't enough. He had to have her close.

With his free arm, he snaked it around her back and drew her to him. Tight against his chest, where he felt her breasts. The heat of her body sent pulses of desire snaking through him. He had to kiss her. Feel her lips against his.

It only took a moment to act on that need. He held her face with his palm on her jaw and leaned down to gently touch his lips to hers. He wanted to devour her but forced himself to go slowly. His mouth moved over hers. With his tongue, he traced the fullness of her soft lips, teasing them apart. His tongue entered her mouth, and she welcomed him while he explored with slow seductive strokes.

* * * * *

Moira was in a haze. A sexually induced haze. Danny's lips on hers almost knocked her to her knees they were so tantalizing. And being so close…. She reached up to slide her arms around his neck and rubbed her body against his while he made love to her mouth.

When he lifted his head, she gazed in his eyes, watching the hues shift in his whiskey-colored eyes with the darkness of desire overtaking them.

Groaning, Danny smothered her lips with his, kissing with a ferociousness she couldn't define. Nor did she care to. This kiss fired every nerve in her body, and she didn't want it to stop. While demanding, it was also loving and gentle. One wouldn't think the three could be combined, but Danny Franks had mastered that feat.

Maybe tonight they'd make love. With the fever he lit in her body, she hoped so. He'd moved the slowest of anyone she'd ever dated. Granted, they hadn't actually been dating, but they were something. Something that pulled at her heart strings. Tugged hard at them. But she couldn't get tied down with someone here when she could go home soon. Danny said they had the goods on Boyle. That meant he'd be arrested and she'd be safe.

Then she thought about the tape she'd recorded. The conversation she hadn't been able to make out until Justin played it back. Maybe it'd be longer, but she'd get to go home and that was the point of it all.

It meant she could have fun with Danny, but she couldn't do something stupid like fall in love.

He'd pulled back from their kiss and watched her. "My room or yours?" he asked in a low voice that danced through her.

Without hesitation, she responded, "Yours."

That seemed to please him, and he turned her around and led them to the stairs for the second floor, where the bedrooms were located. It occurred to her that it was odd that Justin hadn't stayed the night like before, but now she was glad he hadn't. She might not have been this free around Danny with him nearby. Not this early in what they had.

When they arrived at his room, she stood for a moment and took it all in, before she turned to him and pulled her pajama top off. She dropped the Scooby-Doo embellished item to the floor and reached for her PJ bottoms.

His hand stopped her. "There's no hurry," he said in an almost hoarse voice. Lust had gotten to him like it had her. How could he not want to jump in bed and get to it? Her body was an inferno for him. She didn't need all the foreplay. There'd been plenty of that over the last couple days when they'd been around each other.

She gasped when one of his hands cupped her breast. In reaction, she moved forward, pushing it closer in his grasp.

With his other hand, he ran it up her arm, before sliding back down again, then moving it around her back and drawing her close, her breast still caught in his hand. Being this tight against him made her want it all even faster. She'd never learned to slow down lovemaking. Most men preferred to avoid the foreplay and do the deed. She'd always taken her cues from them.

Now, this man was loving her, and she couldn't wait for what else he planned. Any ideas of rushing evaporated when his lips crushed against hers in a hard kiss, a continuation of the one they'd shared downstairs. This one demanded her response, demanded she give over to him all that she was… at least for the night. Willingly, she kissed him back with her silent agreement to acquiesce and enjoy the loving but not rush to the finish.

They broke apart, and he stepped back a half step, giving himself room for the hand with her breast. His other hand slid up and they both molded the breasts to his hands. With each thumb mimicking the other, he flicked her taut nipples. He dipped his head and took one nipple in his mouth, sending ripples of pleasure through her.

Her moan slipped out and she closed her eyes to the excitement in her body. Her hands reached for the hem of his shirt to draw it off him. He lifted his mouth for a brief moment, allowing her to remove his shirt.

She reached up and ran her hands up and down his naked chest through the light brown curls. He had a magnificent physique. She knew he hit the gym daily, mostly to be in shape for his job. She enjoyed the benefit of it. Hard muscles, sleek lines, and no fat defined his torso.

Lifting his head, he gazed at her with a longing that squeezed her heart.

Impatiently, she reached for his jeans, ready to get them off. So much for the slow and steady.

He chuckled and pulled her hands back. "I've got it."

While he divested himself of his pants and underwear, she did the same. Now they stood facing each other naked. She looked him up and down and wanted to whistle at the whole package. Feeling it would probably be inappropriate, she stuck with "You're handsome."

Once again, he chuckled. "I was about to tell you how beautiful you are and how much I've looked forward to this."

He had? She wondered for how long though. She wouldn't tell him that before the kiss she'd already started wanting him. That might get too weird.

Ready to move forward, she walked to the bed and crawled up to the middle. Watching him devour her with his eyes, she crooked her finger in invitation.

He smiled and stepped toward the bed, then grabbed a wrapper from his nightstand. He sheathed his length before putting that first knee on the bed.

With him at her side, his mouth captured hers as their hands explored each other's bodies.

After a few minutes of enjoyment, he whispered, "I want you so badly."

"Take me." She was ready. Her body had enough foreplay. The man could kiss and that alone sent heat throughout her body, especially at her core.

He levered himself above her and gently nudged her trembling thighs apart. Not quivering from nerves but from a deep-seated need.

Slowly, his hands found her heat and his fingers slid in her folds, gliding over her wetness.

The next feeling was his cock seeking entry. His eyes latched on hers as he slid through her slick passage, filling her comfortably. Their locked gaze as he pushed in had been erotic, increasing her need for him.

When he began moving, she wrapped her legs around his thighs. The pressure and depth added to his surging in and out of her heat. He leaned down and touched her lips briefly, then kissed her breast, clamping on her nipple lightly.

Her fingers dug into his shoulder blades as his strokes became more demanding, more powerful.

Each stroke brought her closer to completion, and she whimpered at how much she wanted to get there and how much she wanted this to last forever. Not all the men she had been with had cared about her pleasure during sex, but with Danny's attention to her needs, she knew he would.

That thought was brought to reality when he reached down and ignited the climb to ecstasy by rubbing her clit.

Responding to his touch and his kiss, the world swirled around her with all the colors that typically ended up in her paintings. Several Gaelic words came to mind to describe this wonderful place but none in English. Actually, she wasn't sure she could speak at all.

Higher and higher she rose. "I'm gonna come," she announced.

"Fly, Baby," he whispered.

And she did, flying through a world of pleasure where wave after wave of bliss rushed through her. After it was done, she was near boneless, but felt every inch of him as he pumped a couple more times and came himself.

Now this was something she'd repeat every night until she left.

A flicker of a question came to life in her mind, taking her by surprise. *Is this worth staying for?*

Chapter Twenty-Seven

Danny woke with a start at the knock on his bedroom door. Who the hell was in his home? Moira was next to him, and he had no other guests. Then he remembered. The men—and woman—who watched the house.

He grumbled, "I'll be right there." Looking out the window, he saw it was early morning, likely around shift change time. Whichever agent it was had best have a good reason for entering the house and waking him. He also hoped whoever knocked didn't remain at the door, so Moira could slip out when she woke.

"What's the matter?" Her low, sleepy voice tugged at him. He could wake to that every day of his life.

"I don't know. I'll go find out. Sleep." He kissed her softly on the forehead, angry at getting roused from bed and leaving her. He'd planned to spend the morning making love to her again. And then again.

Silently he dressed in the jeans and shirt he'd discarded

the night before. To hell with wrinkles. With his current mood, he dared anyone to comment on them.

Instead of opening the door wide, he slid through a crack to hide Moira in his bed.

Cowboy raised his eyebrow at the gesture, then sported a cocky grin. "It's about time. You two have been dancing around each other for way too long."

Ignoring his comment, he asked, "What's the matter?"

"Oh, we've caught a stalker. She's in the living room."

"She?" With all the trouble that could possibly come down on them, a female threat never entered his mind, even though the Ireland Minister was female.

"She was trying to find a way inside the house at dawn. The Russian and I watched her for a while, but when it looked like she was about to break a window, we stepped in."

Ignoring how Cowboy had already dubbed John as The Russian, not knowing how that would go over, he asked, "Anyone we know?"

"Oh yeah." Cowboy chuckled and Danny wanted to punch him.

Not caring he was barefoot, they stalked down the stairs to the living room and Danny stopped short. Barbara. No, Barbie. Trying to break into his house while he and Moira slept. Had the woman lost her damn mind?

"Jane and I saw her walk by the house yesterday," Doc said, as they approached. So both shifts had stayed to protect them. He loved his teammates.

Barbie jumped up. "Danny, what is the matter with

these two Neanderthals? I was just walking and minding my own business and they stopped me and brought me here like a common criminal."

This chick's mind was seriously warped. What had he ever seen in her? Granted, it'd only taken a couple dates to figure her out, yet years to get rid of her. Damn that blind date and him not being prepared to head it off before it happened.

"Sit," he demanded. He waited until she finally gave up her stance and flounced down on the couch. "What were you doing around my house this early in the morning?"

"As I said, I was just walking around."

"Yeah, around the window casements," Cowboy added with a snort.

"You can't seriously believe these men that I was doing something wrong."

While he'd never expected something like this from Barbie, he believed his men. "Actually, I do believe them. They have no reason to lie. You, on the other hand, do."

"Well, I never."

"Give it up, you're not Southern," Danny said.

"Okay, so I looked around your place. It's a nice one, and I missed our time together. I hoped to get a glimpse of you."

"In legal terms, they call that stalker behavior," Doc added.

"I did nothing wrong," she insisted.

Moira made an appearance, dressed for the day.

"What are you still doing here?" Barbie asked Moira.

"I'm a guest. You, on the other hand, appear to be a criminal. Is that what woke us?"

Danny cringed inside. Not that he planned to hide his relationship, but he did not want to hash it in front of Barbie.

"Us? Us?" Her voice rose with each word.

"That's none of your concern. Now what were you planning to do with that rock?" Cowboy asked.

"I don't know what you're talking about." She kept her gaze on Danny. "I can't believe you're sleeping with the Irish slut."

Moira flew across the room and slapped Barbie. Lightning fast, he grabbed Moira and pulled her back, and the men grabbed Barbie before she jumped up. A cat fight was the last thing he wanted to see this early in the morning.

"That's it. I'm pressing charges," Barbie screeched.

"Go ahead. We'll let them know how you came to be here," Moira taunted back.

"That's enough. What to do with you?" he directed to Barbie.

"Well," Barbie said seductively, "you could kick the bitch to the curb and invite me back to your bed."

"First, I'm not kicking Moira anywhere. Second, you were never in my bed."

"It'd only have been a matter of time."

The woman was batshit crazy. Then a thought hit him. "Have you broken in here before?" The destruction of Moira's studio had been personal. That sounded like something Barbie would do. Well, after her potentially breaking in today, he'd say that. Before today, he'd just thought her full of vile words.

"No." Barbie looked away as she said it.

"Son of a bitch," Danny said.

"Looks like we've got your vandal," Cowboy said.

"I didn't destroy her studio. You've got the wrong person."

Danny stiffened. "We never said studio. We just said vandal."

"Well," Barbie blustered, "it's the word on the street about it."

"No," Danny said, "we never spoke of it so it couldn't be on the street." He was glad he still held Moira because she was blistering for a fight. "Calm down," he whispered to her.

"I'm going to kill her," she whispered back.

"No. She'll get hers." His voice held strength in that conviction.

"Why'd you do it, Barbie? Why destroy something in my house?"

She pointed to Moira. "It's her. We had a date, and if it wasn't for her, we'd be dating again."

They wouldn't, but he thought to keep that to himself for the moment. "But this was my house you vandalized."

"But it was her stuff, not yours. I took special care of that."

The thoughts of a crazy mind always baffled him. Still holding Moira back, he whispered to her, "Please go in the kitchen. Maybe make some coffee." She stiffened, then with a jerky nod, swept out of the room.

He sat on the couch, keeping his distance from Barbie, and nodded to Cowboy who left the room, phone in hand. When she made to slide closer, Doc's big hands grabbed her shoulders. "Stay," the medic said.

"You broke the law and destroyed stuff I cared about."

"But it was hers," she spat.

"Yeah, and I care about her. A whole lot."

"But you can care about me again."

"No. That ship sailed. Now, you're going to be arrested for breaking and entering, along with vandalism."

"What? You can't do that to me." Desperation laced her voice.

"I can and I am. Cowboy is calling BPD to come pick you up. Until then, you'll remain right here under Doc's watchful eye." He stood and walked to the kitchen, ignoring Barbie's screeches of protest and love.

Moira's tense posture told him she was still pissed. Whether at him or Barbie, he wasn't sure, but he had to test the water. "Cowboy's calling the cops. She'll pay for what she did."

"You should've just let me beat her arse."

A smile tugged at the corners of his mouth. His little spitfire minx. "While I would've loved to see two women go at it, ripping off shirts and all, it's best to let the law take care of it."

He opened his arms, and Moira went into them with

her head on his chest.

"I'm not sure whether to be happy or worried that she did this and not Boyle. Having one more person after me doesn't feel good."

"Honey, she's some wacko I made the mistake of dating. She's not a major threat like those from Ireland." If he meant to soothe her, those words probably didn't, but it was too late to take them back.

"I want to call my best friend back home. She's got to be worried sick about me."

He didn't like it but had a feeling this event called for a BFF to talk to about it. "I'll see what we can do. Now, we can't go back to bed since the police are on their way, but how about we make the group some pancakes?"

"Sounds great."

She didn't pull away from his chest, seeming content in his arms a while longer. That was fine by him. But he needed to make sure that call happened for her. He'd do anything to make her happy.

Chapter Twenty-Eight

After seeing Barbie led out by the police, Danny and Moira enjoyed a lazy morning cuddled up on the couch watching the news. They'd discussed the outrageousness of several celebrities she'd seen in the news and laughed at others. Easy conversation flowed. So when she asked a question outside what was on television, Danny startled for a moment.

"I know I asked before, but can I call my best friend, Cassie, back home? She's got to be worried, especially if she heard I died. I can't let her keep thinking that." She leaned away from where she'd been lying on his chest. "I won't tell her where I am. Promise."

That was a risky call. He didn't know this Cassie. She could be a blabbermouth. He had to check out the risk first. Justin or Declan would know if it would be safe. And he would try to make this happen because it meant so much to her.

"I'll think about it." That was the best he could give her at the moment.

She studied him, and it made him a bit nervous for no reason whatsoever. His feelings for her were strong, and he didn't want them to show and scare her away. Heck, she may push to go to her brother in Boston, even though Declan had already told her no. Danny had already learned she was persistent.

With a sly smile, she leaned her head down to his and kissed him. Her mouth was sweet seduction. She tasted of the orange juice she'd had to drink with breakfast where they'd shared plenty of touches, kisses, and a bit of playful groping. Oh, and they'd cooked food between it all without burning the bacon.

A knock on the door interrupted what he'd hoped had been a christening of the couch. Thankfully they were dressed, but still, they'd been having a ravenous make-out session.

After untangling from each other, Danny stood, reached for the earpiece he'd refused to wear that morning, since he had plenty of protection, and put it in his ear. Heading to the door, he looked back at Moira, who'd assumed a guilty look on the couch. He wanted to laugh at her expression, but he also wanted to soothe it.

Opening the door, as he had no need to check who it was first, since the men wouldn't allow just anyone to knock on his door, he smiled at his brother. Just the person he wanted to speak with, only he'd rather it hadn't been at this particular moment.

"Hey, come on in," he said to Justin.

His brother did, and they moved to the living room. Danny lounged on the couch next to Moira, and Justin sat in a chair across from them.

Danny reached over and opened his hand to Moira, hoping she wouldn't leave him embarrassed by not taking it in front of his brother. This was a test to see how deep her feelings might run. Sure, it was an easy one, but it was what he had right now.

Without hesitation, she placed her hand in his, and he tightened their grip, then dropped them in her lap, holding them together with strong emotions.

Justin smiled but didn't comment on their joined hands or how close they sat on the couch. "I came to tell you I'm going to visit Mom."

That he hadn't expected. Not with everything going on. Surely Justin would want to be in on catching Boyle after everything he'd gone through. "How can you just walk away?" he asked belligerently. Moira gently squeezed his hand and he took note of her meaning. He'd been too tough. But still….

"The DEA has everything. They're handling the case right now. Even the investigation HIS has going doesn't involve me. My work is done. I'm not part of any inner circle, so I can't do anything else. Boyle will try to kill me on sight, so I won't be able to bring him in alive."

"But you didn't trust the DEA. They treated you horribly. How can you just leave it to them?" Danny stared at his brother, finding it hard to believe the change in him from years ago.

"There's new leadership since I was there. I think they'll actually do something about this. Based on what you said from your meeting with them, it sounded like Boyle was already on their high priority list."

Maybe realizing how badly Danny was taking the news, Moira offered to make coffee for them. After she stood and left, Danny watched her backside as she walked then he asked Justin about her friend.

"Moira wants to call Cassie and tell her that she's okay. What do you think? Can we trust her?"

Turning back, he saw Justin thinking it through. "They were best friends and very tight. Cassie went nuts when she heard Moira had supposedly died. It was all I could do not to tell her the truth. As far as trusting her, I believe she'll keep the secret if she knows it would put Moira in danger if she talked. But I wouldn't make it a regular thing because you never know if phones are being monitored."

They chatted a bit about their mother, and Justin announced he planned to go home. Their mom would be happy to have him there after so long of an absence. Visiting their mom and providing her protection, instead of being embroiled in everything, was probably the best thing for his brother's mental state. Having someone watching over their mom was also a good thing for Danny's piece of mind.

Moira returned with three mugs of coffee on a plate, since he didn't own a serving tray, and her hands were too small to manage three mugs. After she retook her seat, he told her the good news.

"You can call Cassie—"

Her excited move cut him off as she spilled coffee on her jeans. She jumped up, sloshing the dark liquid on the floor, then handed Danny her cup before she rushed off to the kitchen, mumbling the entire time.

"I'd say you just earned a bunch of brownie points," Justin said with a laugh.

If she got this excited about talking to her friend, he could expect many more displays as he planned to do everything in his power to make her happy for the rest of her life.

Rest of her life? Yes, he was ready to admit he loved her and would do what he could to convince her to remain with him forever.

Chapter Twenty-Nine

"The girl is in the States. Baltimore, Maryland, to be exact. We haven't located the brother yet," Quinn Murphy said from behind his large walnut desk. "But we will."

"How did you find her?" Boyle asked, sitting as if he owned the place, which pissed Quinn off all the more.

"She made a call to a phone we've been tracking ever since we heard she was alive." Quinn knew sooner or later she'd contact his fiancée and felt no guilt tracking her phone calls. Yet she'd waited until they found out Justin Franks lied about killing her, her brother, and Diana.

Boyle raised his voice. "But I want Declan Gallagher. I want his balls in a grinder. I just need to lean on the banker more."

Quinn knew Boyle believed Declan led his daughter astray, but he'd learned Declan had tried to avoid his relationship with Diana. For the simple reason he was *gardai* and Boyle was a criminal, albeit a smart one. That was the reason Boyle had been chosen to partner with Quinn.

As a puppet master, Quinn controlled many aspects of government and the criminal element. Boyle was one and Donnelly was another. The officials he couldn't control, Quinn blackmailed. And people just thought Quinn came from old money. Yeah, that money had dried up before he hit puberty. Nay, other people made him rich. And he wouldn't allow some woman to ruin it. His fiancée's friend or not.

Now, he needed to control the situation. Because of that, he decided he should be there face-to-face with the potential threats to his empire. It was a risk, but some risks were meant to be taken. He'd still use Boyle, even though he knew the US DEA was after the drug lord. If he lost Boyle, there was someone else ready to take his place. And be under Quinn's thumb.

"We go to the US and find Moira. She'll lead us to her brother."

He wanted Moira so he could find out how much she'd overheard while snooping outside Donnelly's office that day. He'd received no backlash, but that wasn't always a positive sign. His well-placed snitches in both the UK and the US—granted he had few across the pond—were quiet. He didn't like it.

"We?" Boyle asked stupidly.

"Yes, we. I need to be there when the girl is questioned. She may've overheard us. And that's a problem."

"No one would believe her. Not with you and Donnelly involved."

"I won't take that chance." To keep under the radar, he'd been working for a minister instead of taking a lead role.

He'd have to trust Boyle enough to get some answers. He looked at the man. Quinn had never trusted him, and many times, he'd thought of offing him because he was more trouble than he was worth. But he had no other sacrificial lamb to take with him on this trip.

Trusting Boyle was his only safe option. Unless.... An idea began to form that required he find Moira's brother before they traveled. He might be able to pull this off and his secrets would remain safe.

Chapter Thirty

"Alone again," Danny said to Moira as she walked down the stairs in her cute cat pajamas—pajamas he intended to take off her very soon. His imagination went wild with what she wore beneath. Would it be no bra and lacy panties as before or a bra and panties? He hoped the former. He salivated for that option. Nothing tempted him more than naked breasts. Okay, plenty tempted him, but they were high up there as one of his favorite things.

"Unless you don't count Cowboy and John watching over us from outside." She plopped down on the couch next to him.

He didn't forget his teammates were there, but he didn't count them as part of what was happening inside his home. He'd ensured privacy unless he needed to be contacted for an intruder or situation. It was only because they were home that he could relax enough to be intimate with Moira. He felt safe, even with trouble on the horizon.

He had no doubt Boyle would arrive soon. He expected the man would find her and her brother. But he also had no doubt HIS would stop Boyle before he got anywhere near Moira. Danny would bank his life on them all being able to protect her. He'd never allow something to happen to her.

"Let's just pretend they aren't there."

Moira snorted. "Easy for you to say. Not so easy for me to remember. I'm a prisoner."

He recoiled at the sting that statement wielded. On some level, he'd worried she'd think that, but he'd never meant her to feel that way. "Don't think of it as being a prisoner. Think of it as having your own safety force. Besides, we've been out."

"That was before Justin came back with the news. Now I'm stuck. I'm not asking to go anywhere. That'd be stupid. It's just being told I can't."

Although he'd like to change that, he wouldn't. Her safety came before her happiness. This, she'd recover from. A bullet, she wouldn't. "It's only temporary. We'll be back out again soon and then we won't need the tail." He smiled, hoping to bring one to her face, but failed. Now appeared to be a great time to change the subject.

"When will you paint my portrait? I'm sure my mom would love it." *Get her talking about something she loved.* That had to work to elevate her mood.

"I haven't painted portraits."

"Oh." That didn't work.

"But I'm willing to try." Her excitement shined on her face with her bright eyes and the smile she wore when talking about her hobby. No, her livelihood. "Tomorrow," she decided.

That settled, he reached for her. "Now, let's discuss tonight." With his arm around her shoulders, he turned her to meet him chest to chest. His heartbeat ratcheted up a notch at her nearness.

"What's there to discuss?" she asked.

"This," he said, before he smothered her lips with his. He launched a near brutal assault on her mouth… tempting… tormenting… challenging… punishing. All his emotions on keeping her safe yet not willing to give her up when the threat ended came out in his kiss. Realizing he might bruise her lips, he backed off, and while his tongue continued its assault, his lips softened and the kiss gently deepened.

Kissing her… the taste of her was an aphrodisiac. Just being near her, his dick would get hard and his heart would expand, tossing blood flow to both, making him lightheaded.

When his breath hitched, he lifted his head a fraction. He looked down at her beauty when she was in the prelude to passion. The darkness of her eyes, her flushed cheeks, and ragged breaths, all made her sexier than ever.

He couldn't resist her swollen lips. He brushed them once, then twice, before covering her mouth with a soft, gentle kiss. This kiss contained his emotions… his caring… his desire… his love.

With a bit of maneuvering, his hand covered her naked breast under her pajama top. Naked. His mind briefly wondered if that was normal for women and pajamas, but it whisked out of his brain faster than his mind fully processed it. His focus was on the woman in his arms, the lips he kissed, and the soft breast in his hand.

"Mm," he murmured, when he lifted his lips a fraction, "you taste so good."

"You too," she said in a hoarse voice.

Good. She felt the need also. It was more with them. Suddenly urgency filled him. He had to have her right here, right now. He reached down and pulled her top over her head. "I have to have you."

"I'm yours," she purred.

The woman was temptation personified and didn't even realize it.

Then they got into a frenzy of removing clothes. Him, his. Her, hers. They needed to get naked and fast. And forget the bed. That required travel—albeit not far—and steps. No time.

With a throw pillow behind her head, Moira laid on the carpeted floor. Thank heavens he'd added the extra cushioning when he'd had the carpet installed. It'd remained soft enough.

Dropping his head, he sighed, then jumped up. After a mad dash to his room for a condom, he nearly sheathed himself on the run. Lying beside her, he took her lips in his while he checked if she was ready for him. He wanted her now but wouldn't hurt her. The demanding kiss had been the extent of any potential cruelty he'd impose.

Reaching between her legs, he was relieved to feel the wetness. Yes, she was ready and wanted him. That made his heart flip.

He leveraged himself over her and settled between her thighs. Keeping eye contact with her, he reached down and maneuvered his dick at her opening. With one agonizingly slow push, he entered her completely.

As euphoria flitted through his nerve endings—from his toes to the top of his head—he began to move inside her.

He kissed his way down her silky throat, nipping and kissing until a low moan escaped her. He could barely wait until the next time—which would be soon after this time—so they could take it slower and he could enjoy her body as his playground.

He should tell her he loved her. Okay, maybe now wasn't the perfect time, but after. Was that the right time? No matter. He would.

When her fingertips dug into his shoulders, he knew she was close, and he concentrated on his strokes, even though he wanted to go hard and heavy.

"Faster," she whispered.

Who was he to argue, especially when he wanted it that way? He didn't respond orally; he just did as she asked and found himself coming close to his own orgasm.

He felt it move along his spine and his balls drew tight. He focused on pleasuring her, and when she finally cried out his name, a groan erupted from deep within his chest as he let go as well.

After a moment to catch his breath, he rolled off Moira and pulled her close. They remained on the floor and he had no intention of moving anytime soon. Their rushed, frenzied love making took a toll on his ability to coordinate his limbs.

Yet, he had to move to dispose of the condom. He made the quick trip and returned to the spot he'd held before he'd left her arms.

His gut churned, but he knew now was the right time to tell her how he felt. She might not say anything back, but he was pretty sure she wouldn't get up and leave either. At least he hoped she wouldn't.

He took a deep breath for fortitude and went for it. "I love you, Moira. Please say you'll stay and give us a shot."

Silence met his admission and request. With it, a strong feeling of loss hit him. He didn't want them to be over. Not when they'd just gotten started. In fact, she hadn't even opened her eyes to acknowledge him. Silence that told him everything, until he realized why.

Moira was sound asleep. He hoped he had the guts to say those words to her again.

Chapter Thirty-One

Moira giggled as Danny, once again, moved from the spot she'd placed him. Although she wasn't complaining much about the kisses or nips at her neck. At this rate, she'd never get his portrait painted. Each time he moved, she had to reposition him, while fighting off groping hands.

After last night, something had changed between them, and she couldn't lay her finger on what it was. They seemed more in tune with each other. More a couple than just sexual partners. It was hard to explain, but she felt the difference in Danny and in herself. They'd crossed a milestone she'd never crossed with a lover. They cared for each other and deeply.

Had she fallen in love? Surely not. Granted, they'd been dancing around each other from the time she'd arrived, but they'd only been lovers a short time. Surely it wasn't possible to fall in love so quickly. Or had it been quickly?

She mentally shook her head and focused on her art. She couldn't fall in love because she was going home. A place she missed with all her heart. Yet, lately, being with Danny had meant more to her.

Enough. She had to focus or his mother would never get a portrait of her son.

"So, how long does this take?" Danny asked, his voice laced with impatience.

She sighed. He'd continued to ask that question since they began. She had him sitting for hours, only taking short breaks. She felt that it wouldn't be long before all was over and she'd be free to return to Ireland. She wanted to finish this before then.

"Another hour and you can go. I'll finish it from memory or have you come up for a short while." She had remembered every feature of his strikingly handsome face, whiskey-colored eyes, dirty-blond hair, and strong, sculpted physique. She could've painted the entire portrait without him sitting for her. Having him with her had been fun, though. Including his lack of discipline in sitting still.

"You really like this? Sitting for hours, painting?"

It was her life, but how to explain that? Non-artists didn't understand the need to hold the pencil or brush and create something using every emotion the artist carried. Each piece was an extension of her creative mind. "I love it. I can't imagine not holding a paintbrush in my hand."

"Better you than me. I couldn't stand doing the same thing for hours at a time."

She stopped herself, before adding a brush stroke to canvas. "Don't you sit for long periods of time when you're out there doing your protection thing?" Because of her earwigging—she reminded herself it was eavesdropping in America—she'd heard some of their stories, and she thought they'd discussed sitting and waiting for hours at a time.

He rubbed his jaw and she wanted to swat at him to be still but said nothing. He'd been pretty good most of the day—when he did sit still—so she'd give him that one without saying anything. Throughout the day, she'd said plenty. "Yeah, I guess so. Sure," he sounded more confident in his answer, "we do sit and wait a lot." He laughed. "It's not the same, yet it is. I'm no artist, but I get doing what you love, no matter the time commitment."

"How did you come to work for HIS?"

He shifted a bit and smiled. The smile she wished he'd worn for the portrait. His mother would've loved it. "Easy. I met Brad Hamilton in a bar. We were each drinking in solitude, commiserating about women." His grin turned shy, and she could've sworn he blushed. "He got into an argument with someone and it led to a fistfight." He looked at her, before shaking his head. "He didn't provoke it. The men came after him."

"Men?" Really, the men in HIS didn't seem to do things halfway.

Danny chuckled. "Yeah, three of them. Now, being

my new drinking buddy and all, plus I'd had a few beers, I jumped in to help him. After that, we met up at the bar a few times, and he asked me all kinds of questions about myself and my career. Then one day, he invited me for an interview with HIS. The rest is history."

It was Moira's turn to chuckle. "That's a unique way into a job. I can't imagine many consider getting into a bar fight a quality behavior they'd choose."

With a shrug, he said, "No big deal. They unfairly targeted him anyway."

"And you just had to jump in?"

"It seemed like a good idea at the time."

Moira rolled her eyes. Men. She'd never understand their logic.

"Are we done for the day?"

She distinctly remembered telling him another hour, but she caved. Truth was, she also needed a break. "Okay, for today. Tomorrow you owe me an hour."

With lightning speed, he jumped from the chair and approached her.

"Oh, nay," she said. "You can't see the artwork in progress."

He shrugged. "I'm not after it. I'm after the artist."

"Give me a few minutes to clean out my brushes. Then I'm all yours."

Leaning over but using a hand to shield his eyes from seeing her work, he kissed her gently and lightly. "I'll be down in the kitchen getting supper together."

"What are you thinking?"

"I'll do a stir-fry with plenty for the team. They could use some vegetables. Or so my boss's wife tells me." This time he rolled his eyes.

"I've never cooked stir-fry. I'll be glad to learn."

"It's easy." He glanced at his watch. "But lots of vegetables to cut so let me get moving."

He kissed her once more before departing.

She sighed with contentment. Her world rocked. Playing house with Danny was more fun than she'd ever imagined such a position would be like. Would she ever find something like this when she returned home? Being comfortable around each other? Feeling cherished by another? Treated as precious cargo yet with faith in her strength? Feeling loved?

Nay, scratch the last one, but feeling close to it. And that almost sent her into a panic attack. What if he fell in love with her? She was moving back across the ocean. That was a bit too far for a long-distance relationship.

Slowly, she brought her erratic breathing under control. The whole mess would be wrapped up shortly and Danny wasn't in love with her. And she wasn't in love with him. *Liar*, a little voice said.

Moira shook her head and rinsed out her brushes. Sometime later, she ventured downstairs to Danny watching TV from the kitchen with a large knife in his hand, half-raised, ready to chop something. He probably was, but the frozen stance made her giggle.

"What do I need to do?"

He turned and smiled. Placing the knife on a cutting

board loaded with broccoli, he said, "You can cut the zucchini. Here." He placed a cutting board in front of her then handed her the vegetables and knife. "Cut it like this."

She didn't let on that she knew how to julienne a vegetable. It was more fun watching him show her. Since she knew how to cut, she watched the breadth of his shoulders and the muscles in his arm as he moved. The man had a fabulous body.

"Got it?" He stepped back and placed the knife on the cutting board.

Nodding, she added, "Aw, sure look it."

He shook his head at her Irish slang. He wasn't sure what that phrase meant, so he just smiled. "Good." He returned to his spot on the opposite counter—their backs to each other. Pity. She'd appreciate ogling her man-candy.

After vigorous chopping of a mountain of vegetables, Danny confused her for a moment when he asked, "Are you sure?"

It took her a moment to remember he also spoke to the team through his earpiece. She thought she'd mastered holding two conversations at once. That was until she met Danny. He could manage three. One in front of him, one on the phone, and one in his ear.

"We have company." He didn't sound happy. After answering the door, he returned with her brother.

"Declan." She rushed up and hugged her brother. Her heart felt so full with him here. She looked behind him. "Where's Diana?"

"She's safe in Boston."

Confused, she asked, "Then what are you doing here? Not that I'm not glad to see you, but Diana?"

"I'm here for you."

Her happiness plummeted. She had no idea if he meant to go to Boston with him or if it was finally safe to go home. While she planned to one day go back to Ireland, she hadn't planned on leaving Danny, just yet.

In her ear, Declan whispered, "There's plenty I need to say to you. Privately. We'll speak after everyone goes to bed."

Unnerved by his request, she said the only thing she dared. "Okay." The beautiful world she'd enjoyed earlier began to crumble, and she didn't like it one bit.

Chapter Thirty-Two

After a loud, fun dinner with the team, Danny, Declan, and Moira sat down to chat. Worried about what her brother wanted to speak privately with her about, Moira allowed the two men to speak about her like she wasn't present. It didn't matter. Tonight had sealed how close she and Danny were. Yet Declan wasn't happy—if his facial expressions and tension were any indicators. And why was he being so secretive? It set her on edge.

"Boyle has learned where Moira is, so I'm taking her out of here." Declan waved his hand to stave off any argument. "I know you do a great job, but if she's not here when he comes, she's safe."

"He'll find her and then you and Diana. Remember your banking records. It's just a matter of time."

"I've hired a security team, so there's nothing to worry about."

Danny looked around. "Where's this team?"

Her brother looked pained. Or something similar. "They're with Diana. Just driving back and forth isn't a problem."

Based upon Danny's stupefied expression, he didn't agree. "What about the others who were in the room whose conversation she overheard? That's got to be trouble just waiting to happen."

"I have it on good authority no one suspects a thing."

"Just who is this good authority?"

Declan seemed reluctant to say, but she wanted to know also—especially if her safety was being put into jeopardy.

"It's Quinn Murphy, assistant to the Minister. If Donnelly knew anything, Quinn would've known."

Moira watched her brother and Danny go at it as if they were on different sides of her safety. If HIS hadn't been doing the job pro bono, she'd think he was just trying to hang onto business. She hated to leave the safety she knew, but what her brother said made sense. HIS would take out Boyle when he showed up here looking for her. Best if she wasn't even near the place when that happened. Less chance of getting caught up in it if the mission went— What did Cowboy call it? Right, FUBAR. She wanted to giggle at the story he'd told in which he'd used the word, but the conversation at hand was too serious and important.

With Quinn confirming everything, her churning gut was put at ease. Cassie's fiancé would know what happened in that office. Heck, he all but ran the minister in thought and process.

Once HIS took care of Boyle—and she had no doubt they would—and since no one suspected her of earwigging, she was free to resume her life in Ireland. Somehow that didn't excite her like it once had.

If Danny asked her to stay, would she? She dug deep into her heart and soul for the answer because staying with him wasn't like staying the night with a guy back home. It'd be serious. And the more serious it became—and it probably would—the less likely she was to see her homeland again. To have drinks with her best friend. To stroll the streets with memories of her parents.

Well, thank goodness she didn't have to make the choice. He hadn't asked, and surely, he wouldn't ask now. They'd just say goodbye, like adults who had a relationship that had run its course. Only theirs hadn't run its course. Heat still flowed between them.

"Moira?" Declan asked.

As she refocused her attention on the men, she noticed they were staring at her. "What?"

"I called you three times."

"Oh." Oops. "What's wrong?"

"Danny says you have to choose to leave with me. He's wrong, but tell him you're coming with me, and once they take care of Boyle, you're going home."

Home. It warmed her heart to think of it. But to choose? Normally, she liked being in charge of her destiny, but in this case, she didn't mind Declan making the decision. Yet they were going to force her to voice it.

She looked at Declan then Danny. The latter looked angry and wounded. She didn't want to leave what they had, but she couldn't stay, not when he hadn't asked her to. Well, he was asking her, but he was asking her for her safety, not for a relationship.

She just went with what Declan expected. Her brother's feelings, she knew. Danny's, it was too late to discuss them. "What Declan says makes sense. Boyle will come here. I'd rather be far away when he does. You'll take care of him and we'll all be safe."

"Moira, you're making a mistake. What if Boyle doesn't come straight here?"

She wet her lips to stall while she thought. "Well, Declan's employed some security. Haven't you?" she directed at her brother.

"Yes."

The men went back and forth on the topic a bit more, then moved on to others. Declan was now into American sports and the animosity seemed to ease. After a couple hours, she became tired. When the two men didn't seem to want to break up their chatter anytime soon, she slipped off to bed. Her bed. For two reasons. One, because Declan wanted to speak with her. Two, because she was chicken and didn't want to say goodbye to Danny.

It wasn't long before her brother visited her. He slipped in her room and closed the door behind him.

"We have to leave now," he whispered.

"What? Why?" That made no sense. They were

leaving tomorrow.

"My contact says Danny is working with Justin who's still working with Boyle."

She shook her head. "Nay, Justin isn't working with Boyle any longer. The man wants him dead."

"It was all a ruse to get Danny's help. They're just keeping you safe until Boyle can get here, without being stopped by US authorities. And he's on his way."

The other made no sense. Danny and Justin were good people. They'd never sell her out. Something wasn't right. "How do you know this?"

"I told you. Quinn. He knows everything that happens, and Boyle is so far up Donnelly's ass, he knows even more. Like that your call to Cassie was traced. Not that they really needed to locate you since Danny was sitting on you."

Traced? Shocked, she shook her head. This couldn't be. Danny, whose hands had touched her everywhere with loving tenderness, could not be holding her for Boyle. Nay. That had to be wrong.

Again, she shook her head. "You're wrong."

"Boyle still wants me, and I never told Danny where Diana and I were staying. They planned to use you to get to me. Has Danny or Justin asked about me?"

Her back stiffened. They had. Casually. Including if she'd received Declan's address. This couldn't be right. Danny couldn't do this to her after loving her so gently. Had it all been an act?

"Just pack an overnight bag. Quinn has a place for us

to stay along the route. He's driving Diana up to meet us. Like I said, we're moving. Too many people know Diana was in the hospital."

"Wait, Quinn's here?"

"I called him to check on things. I didn't like there never being any information. That's when I began to think something had happened. You were fine with just Danny. Then Justin showed up and things began to change." He waved a hand. "Pack and be quiet."

She didn't pay attention to what she tossed in the small bag. As she zipped it closed, she hoped she'd grabbed clean knickers.

They exited through the back door and were swiftly met by Cowboy who was speaking, but not to them. Another communication thing, which meant Danny knew they were leaving.

"Look," Declan said, "we're leaving. Now, get out of the way."

Moira didn't like him being rude to someone she called a friend, albeit loosely, since Danny wouldn't let Cowboy hang out around her much. If at all.

"No" was all he said in response. When he looked behind them, Moira hesitated to turn. She knew who'd be there and how angry he'd be for them slipping out. But he'd agreed she could leave. Now that she thought about it, he never had. He just stopped arguing after she'd agreed to leave with Declan.

"Going somewhere?" Danny asked. She looked over at him. He stood wearing a pair of sweatpants and a much-worn T-shirt. At least he wasn't carrying his weapon. She took that as a plus.

"We're leaving," Declan told Danny.

"Now? Christ, you drove eight hours to get here and now you want to turn around and drive eight more? That's dangerous."

"I appreciate the concern, but we need to leave as soon as possible."

"What the fuck for?"

Moira volleyed back and forth between the two men. This seemed deeper than them leaving. However, if Danny was truly in with Justin and Boyle, then he wouldn't want her to leave. Not even a few hours earlier than agreed upon. Suddenly, she felt the need to leave. She didn't know whether she could trust Danny or not, but she didn't want to risk it.

"I'm helping him drive," she piped up to keep Declan from outright accusing Danny of being in league with Boyle.

Danny looked at her. "Your license isn't even valid."

"I'll chance it." She hoped it never came to that.

"I still think you should get a good night's sleep before you depart."

"Like Declan said, we're gonna head on." Her heart was ripping apart now that the break was actually happening. She had no idea it would hurt so much to leave him.

His gaze searched hers with an intensity that made her want to crawl all over him to get as close as she could.

"Well, I guess this is goodbye." His eyes never left hers when he spoke. Hurt flared in them, but what else could she do? Boyle was on his way. Whether Danny helped Justin or not.

This was not how she'd envisioned them saying goodbye. She'd expected lots of time in bed exploring each other's bodies to remember every fine detail, like the scar on his ribs from a knife, or the fine hairs on his chest. Good grief, this sucked. "I guess it is." She hoped the sorrow she felt was there for him to read.

After a few more terse words between Danny and Declan, she and her brother were on their way. It hurt her that at no time since Declan arrived with his news had Danny asked to speak with her. To ensure she didn't want to stay. To ensure she was okay with the discussion. To ensure they had a proper goodbye.

A tear slipped down her cheek, and she quickly wiped it away. She wanted to go home. Whether she left Danny's or not, she'd be going home soon anyway. She may as well get used to the idea that she'd never see Danny again.

Moira dozed as her brother drove from Baltimore to wherever he planned to stop for the night. When she woke to his slowing, she noticed on her watch that she'd slept for nearly three hours. So much for helping Declan drive.

She frowned at the cabinlike structure they'd pulled up to. Maybe it was one of those Airbnb places. It was plenty isolated. She saw clear land and woods surrounding it. It would be a great place to hide out until Boyle was apprehended.

When they entered the lodging, Declan turned around and looked at her with sorrow in his gaze. Confusion slammed into her.

"I'm sorry, Moira. I really am, but he bribed our guards and got in. He said he'd kill the baby, then Diana."

Shock hit her at such a deadly scene and belatedly at what he'd said. "What do you mean, you're sorry?"

"He means"—a tall, thin man approached from the back of the cabin— "in order to get his girlfriend back, he brings us you."

Declan stepped in front of her. But it seemed kind of late to show a protective gesture as far as she was concerned. "Who are you? Where's Quinn and where's Diana?"

"I'm the man who will take you to her."

Moira didn't like this one bit. And what did Quinn have to do with Diana being captured? He was supposed to bring her—

Oh nay, she just got it. Quinn wasn't a good guy at all. Did Cassie know? Of course she didn't. She'd not have agreed to marry him.

"You, girl," the man said, "come here. You get tied up until Quinn arrives."

"Nay," Declan asserted. "This isn't how it's supposed to go. Bring Diana here and we'll exchange, but until then—"

When Declan's stance changed, she peeked around

him to see what was happening. Her eyes widened. Her mind honed in on two things. Her brother planned to exchange her with someone for Diana. And the man held a weapon on her brother.

Chapter Thirty-Three

"Are you just gonna let her go?" Cowboy asked.

Danny sat on the couch, leaned forward, elbows on knees, head in his hands. She'd left. She hadn't even said goodbye or given him a chance to ask her to stay. He'd hoped she'd have come to his room after Declan made the announcement. Once again, he'd planned to tell her he loved her and ask her to stay.

No, he hadn't wanted her to leave and he'd thought she'd wanted to stay. She would want to visit Ireland regularly. But he didn't think she'd leave, especially like she did.

Not even a goodbye. His heart hurt. She had snuck away with her brother.

He kept racking his brain. What had he done wrong that she'd just slip away? Things had been great until her brother arrived. Until he'd started talking about them being free to return home. That had been assuming

Boyle was in custody.

Luckily, he was. Danny had just learned that DEA agents had met Boyle when he'd arrived in the States. The teams were displeased. Not that Boyle was in custody, but because they'd had nothing to do with it. Of course, no one was more disappointed than Danny. He'd hoped they'd make the murder charge stick. His dad had been an agent—one of them—so he imagined they would work hard to get that result.

"Are you?"

Danny had forgotten Cowboy's question. "I don't have much of a choice. She made it clear she wanted to leave."

"Bullshit. Her brother said something to her to make her leave. She wouldn't have left you without an explanation, if at all. That woman is in love with you. She just hasn't admitted it."

That statement gave him a glimmer of hope. Did she really? She couldn't. Otherwise, she wouldn't have left.

"I'm telling you that her brother is the reason she left."

"What could he have said?" What would make her leave? It had been almost as if she was wary of him. Would Declan turn her away from him? But why? She was secure here. So what if Boyle had actually found her? Danny wouldn't have let him get to her.

"I don't know, but it would've been all lies."

His phone rang, and he looked at the time. Ten thirty p.m. Who'd be calling at this time of night? A nervousness at the unknown number settled in his gut. "Hello."

"Danny, it's Diana," the weak voice said.

Fear lodged itself in his heart. Moira and Declan couldn't have arrived this quickly. "What's wrong? Are you okay?"

"Quinn didn't know I had this phone hidden."

Danny had heard Quinn mentioned again. The hairs on the back of his neck stood on end. "What's wrong?"

"He just left to meet Declan and Moira."

Why was this important? "Start at the beginning and tell me what's going on."

"It's Quinn. He held me hostage while Declan got Moira for him. Declan didn't want to do it, but Quinn threatened me and the baby. He left me locked up in our flat and took my mobile. He didn't know we had several burners hidden."

Danny hadn't listened to much after *Declan got Moira for him*. "Are you okay?" He had to think with a logical mind when his was spinning with revenge and getting his woman.

"I'm fine. The baby is restless, though. Then again, at this stage of my pregnancy, that's pretty much a norm."

One thing settled. "Tell me who this Quinn is?"

While Diana told him about Quinn Murphy, he jotted the name down on a piece of scrap paper before him and added *Moira in trouble*, then handed it to Cowboy. His teammate never asked; he just picked up his phone and dialed. Danny knew it was to HQ.

"What happened to your security detail? Why did he

leave you and where was he going?"

At this point, Danny was moving through the house, getting his gear together. Since they'd been protecting Moira, it was all handy.

"All I know is that Declan was to bring Moira someplace, and Quinn would meet him and do the exchange. Quinn told me there was a change in plans and he was leaving me to meet them. Declan would be free to drive back for me. Do you think he lied?"

Quite possibly, but he'd worry about Moira's brother later. Moira was his priority. "I don't know. We're going to go after Moira. If Declan's not with her, we'll find him. Okay?" He needed to get off the phone so he could call HQ.

"But how will you find her?"

Danny grinned and didn't care if he was called a stalker. It worked to his benefit tonight. Unless she'd changed clothes, her shoes had a tracker. "Oh, we've got ways. I'm going to go for now. Keep this phone and we'll call you. Let us know if Declan returns."

"Thank you."

"You're welcome." He ended the call and reached for Cowboy's phone since he was on with HQ.

"Are you ready?"

"Hello to you too, Franks," AJ said. "Devon is already researching Quinn Murphy. Go ahead with the rest."

"Quinn held Diana captive and threatened her baby unless Declan brought Moira to a specific place."

"Where?"

"I don't know."

"Why wasn't she there with you and the team?"

"We think her brother told her something to turn her against us. It's the only reason that makes sense."

"Okay. How long have they been gone?"

"An hour and a half."

"She could be anywhere."

"Actually, we can locate her."

"Good God, Franks, don't tell me she's wearing another tracker. Didn't you learn when we made you get rid of the other one?"

"Sorry, I have to tell you."

Danny heard conversation in the background and knew AJ and Devon were discussing him and the tracker. At the same time, he and Cowboy were locking up his house for their trek to headquarters.

Devon came on the call. "Is it one of ours?"

"Yes. From the same lot as the other one." He waited an excruciating five minutes before Devon spoke again.

"Okay, best I can get is she's on I-95. But if they're headed to Boston, they'll be turning real soon."

They'd never catch up to them. All he could hope for was that nothing happened to her. They'd be about two hours behind, once they'd had time for the team to regroup at HQ and get their gear. Plus, if they were going into Boston, Old Man surely had to make some calls, so they weren't arrested for carrying their weapons. And not just handguns.

"Has the team been recalled?" John had followed

them, so it was just Jane and Doc unless Stone came in for support. They'd be angry something happened to Moira after she'd walked away. Granted, he didn't know what was happening to her or what would happen, but if this Quinn threatened to kill an unborn baby, then he was someone to fear.

"Of course. Boss is also coming in."

Having Boss back for this meant a lot. It wasn't just that he didn't have to be in charge, it was because of Moira and his feelings for her. "Good."

Cowboy blew every speed limit to get to headquarters and the entire team was already there—they'd also have to had blown through the limits. The fact they'd rushed spoke volumes about their commitment, the knowledge giving Danny a weird warm and settled feeling.

Boss approached him and held out his hand. "How you holding up?"

Boss would understand the craziness in his system, his gut, and his heart at the woman he loved being in trouble. Boss had been previously captured with Sugar, and he hadn't been able to rescue her. "I'm good."

His team leader assessed him and must've felt good about keeping Danny on the op because he just nodded and went back to his locker.

"You'll never catch them," AJ said from the doorway to the locker room.

He didn't have to be reminded they'd be behind them by two hours. He'd never be able to live with himself knowing he could have stopped her from going. He could have told her then that he loved her and wanted her to stay.

"There is one way," AJ offered.

The helo. They'd make great time if they had the bird to fly. But could he do it? Danny still had a fear of crashing. Was he good enough to keep them in the air? No matter the level of fear he had for going back up, he needed to do it to save his Moira. They couldn't afford to be two hours behind.

"You just have to—"

Danny interrupted AJ. "I accept." There, he was now the official pilot for HIS. He was solely responsible for getting the troops from point A to point B safely. It was a burden he'd accept to save his woman.

"Good." AJ handed him his flight checklist. "Get out there for preflight. It's already fueled."

The last of AJ's words tapered off as he bolted from the locker room out to the landing pad that had been recently added.

Danny didn't rush his preflight. Experiencing how a component could quickly fail, becoming life threatening to the passengers, the task was too important to think of the need to fly to Moira's safety.

He'd wondered how he'd balance the safety of his teammates and the necessity to speed to a rescue. That need to prioritize both the agents who were his friends and the woman he loved, wrapped him in knots. All depended upon him. All could die because of a single failure on his part. His worst fear could come to life.

The reality of the situation nearly paralyzed him. In his heart, he knew Moira counted on him to save her. In his teammates' faces, he saw how they needed him to get them to Moira. Everyone trusted him.

"You doing okay," Cowboy asked, as he approached the open cockpit door.

Sitting in the pilot seat, Danny looked away from the preflight checklist he knew from heart and hadn't been focusing on. He'd rather been staring at it while his thoughts swirled in his fear-clogged mind. To prevent Cowboy from seeing the truth in his eyes, Danny quickly refocused on his checklist and went back to inspecting the instrument panel.

"I'm fine," he responded tersely.

"Ya know," Cowboy nearly drawled, "I remember when you were in pilot training and you wanted HIS to get their own helo, so we could move faster."

He had spoken with Cowboy about that. A fantasy of sorts since he'd never expected the Hamilton brothers to actually purchase a helicopter. He'd wanted it for all the reasons his nerves were on edge today. With a helicopter, the teams could improve response times.

Before, Danny relished that he could be the one to get the teams into action, speeding up their chance for rescue or op success. It hadn't been a power trip. It'd been that he finally offered something valuable to HIS.

He'd never considered something like the situation on his flight evaluation could happen. Sure, he studied and trained on potential emergencies, but he could've gotten the two of them killed. If they hadn't had the clear space, he wouldn't be here to allow his anxiety to eat at his gut.

Danny didn't respond, but that didn't stop his vocal friend.

"You've gotta know we trust you." Cowboy sighed loudly and continued, "What happened to the confident pilot I knew?"

Blood boiling, Danny snapped his gaze to Cowboy's. "He almost died and took someone else's life with him. Now I've got an entire team depending on me not to kill them. If I do, there's no telling what'll happen to Moira."

"Well, hell, that's all?"

Danny couldn't believe he was wasting valuable time with this discussion. He turned away to finish. Just a few more checks before he got the rotors going. Then a few more items on the checklist and they'd be ready to hit the sky.

That thought tightened the coil within his body.

"You survived. So did the FAA guy."

"But we almost didn't," Danny spat out. Didn't Cowboy get it? And the fact the team trusted him bothered the heck out of him. They didn't seem to grasp shit could go wrong while in the air and the ground tends to be a long way down.

"Danny, stop for a second and talk to me."

He automatically stopped. He couldn't remember Cowboy ever calling him by his first name. Looking down to the landing pad at his friend, Danny nodded. "Go ahead."

"Let me ask you this. If an airplane pilot had an emergency and successfully landed the plane, would you fly with him or her?"

He nodded. "Sure. It shows they can handle themselves under pressure." Something began to turn in his mind, but he couldn't, or wouldn't, grasp it.

"Okay. If someone had been in a car accident and survived, would you ride with them again?"

"That depends on if they were drunk driving."

"Good point, but not where I'm going," Cowboy said.

Danny had a good idea where his friend was going, and he wasn't sure he could get there.

"Your accident was a mechanical failure. It happens. But you saved both lives on board and even the aircraft. That's an impressive feat." Cowboy put his hands in his front pockets. "Look, I know you have an uncle who crashed with your cousin aboard."

Danny started at that. It wasn't something he'd ever shared. In fact, he hadn't been thinking about it. He stiffened his back. Or had he subconsciously been thinking about how his uncle's helicopter had stalled and there had been no chance of recovery? Now that he considered it, the situation had been eerily similar, except Danny had been closer to the ground and kept the engine from stalling.

"I also know," Cowboy continued, "that your father flew a lot of hours with no mishap. His memory pushed you to become a pilot. He believed in the pilot he knew you'd become. Be that pilot for us today." With that, his friend walked away.

Time was ticking, so Danny shelved those words and turned back and began turning on switches to get them in the air.

With everyone onboard, Danny tried not to hurl at the pressure he'd imposed upon himself. After a quick comms check, he took a deep breath and allowed practiced movements to take control. Unexpected exhilaration filled him as the helicopter lifted from the landing pad.

In the air, he pushed the throttle to keep them safe but pushed the line to make up time with cautious speed. Being airborne cleared his head. Not necessarily clear, but it gave him time to think about all Cowboy had said to him. While he understood where his friend's statements came from, he couldn't just turn from fear to confidence. Maybe he could find somewhere in between the two.

He'd completed a thorough preflight. He was prepared to react if something occurred in flight. Knowing those two things did restore his confidence somewhat. He shuddered at the thought of a stall. The chance of that system failure occurring was small—tiny—so he couldn't allow that fear to drive him.

The feeling when he took off reminded him of how much he loved flying. Not just flying, but being in control. That was the reason he decided to become a pilot and not a passenger.

Allowing some knots to ease within him, Danny decided he'd had enough of his self-loathing on his evaluation flight. He may be a newer pilot, but he knew his job. He couldn't control the machinery on a bird, but he could prepare for equipment failures through practice in a simulator.

While he couldn't see himself not worrying about the potential to kill his crew—his uncle had done it as had other nameless pilots—he could be the pilot they needed for each and every op. He straightened his shoulders. Yes, he found the right balance between the confidence in his abilities and the fear of failure.

He'd spent enough of the flight time reckoning his mind with reality. As much as he'd hate to admit it—what guy did?—he'd have to thank Cowboy for getting his mind pointed in the right direction. That would be later. While he focused on flying, HQ kept an eye on the woman he loved.

According to Moira's tracker, she had stopped moving. Devon had her location uploaded. They were going with the assumption the tracker was still on her. Correlating the distance from Boston and when Quinn had left, the man hadn't arrived yet. He should arrive around midnight. That gave the team time to get in there and whisk Moira away. They'd grab Declan if he was there, but after Danny gave him a good punch in the nose for putting Moira in danger.

He'd had more than enough opportunity to ask him or even Cowboy for help.

Google Earth was a wonderful tool. They found a large clearing near their target. When Danny said near, he meant half an hour away if they used the road, which they wouldn't because Quinn would be driving that route. So, the woods it was. Knowing his ability to get lost in the woods, Danny didn't fight Boss for the lead. He'd hate for the team to get lost and something happen to Moira because they weren't there in time.

Finally, they landed and hoofed it double time through the woods. As they were within minutes of the cabin, Danny couldn't believe what he saw through his night-vision goggles.

Chapter Thirty-Four

S*on of a bitch.* Moira fumed at her circumstance. Her hands and feet were bound with zip ties while she sat in a chair. At least they hadn't tied her to the chair. With her hands tied in front, she almost wanted to cheer for that little slip from her captor. Bracing herself the little that she could, she fell over sideways, knocking the breath out of her.

She could not believe her brother. How could he give her to a kidnapper? They didn't even produce Diana. The man who'd met them took Declan with him after tying her up. Was Declan even alive?

She pulled herself in the near fetal position, ignoring that idea, and untied a shoe.

On one hand, she could understand her brother's move. He loved Diana and he loved her. Yet he had to give up one to save the other. She imagined his innocent unborn child made the difference. On the other hand, she was his sister. His flesh and blood. And he just left her to be tortured and possibly murdered. Since it became clear to her that Danny wasn't involved, she could only hope Declan called him for help. The people he worked with had protected her once. Surely, they'd help her now.

Tightening the shoestring between her knees and teeth, she began to saw at the restraints on her wrist. She had no idea if this actually worked, but her brother had talked about it once. She continued the movements, hoping she'd be successful.

All she knew was Quinn ordered the whole thing—holding Diana and threatening Declan to get Moira away from her bodyguards. For all she knew, Boyle may not even be coming. Quinn was bigger than she imagined. In her eavesdropping, she'd heard Danny and Justin say something about a bigger player.

Moira had a hard time accepting Quinn had threatened her family. She believed her brother, but it was all so wrong. They'd been friends for years. But for Quinn to be a bigger player? She couldn't fathom that. Of course, nothing else would surprise her at this point.

And why her? She didn't know Boyle, yet he was intertwined somehow. If only her brother had said something before they arrived, they could've figured things out that didn't involve her getting tied up.

It still came back to why her? Her only time to see Boyle was…. Her pulse jumped as it hit her. The recording. The one she allowed her curiosity to tape. That recording had already been turned over to the authorities. She thought back to when Justin had amplified the voices and played it for her. There'd been the minister, someone she'd later learned was Boyle, then a third—

Her breath caught. *Shit. Shit. Shit.* She was in serious trouble. Quinn had been the third voice. How had she not recognized it? She could only guess that she'd never have expected him to be a participant in that meeting, so his voice wouldn't have stood out. Worse, Quinn had sounded like the boss.

If he knew she'd made the recording, he most likely knew she'd turned it over to the authorities. Her heart pounded. This could be about revenge. Maybe her mind had gone melodramatic, but what else could it be? Based on her being tied up, she didn't expect a friendly chat.

She continued sawing at the restraints. Her pulse raced. The shoestring actually worked, but it took a long time. She had to leave before Quinn arrived. She'd never seen him as a killer, but she had to expect that could be his endgame. If he'd become this big boss Danny has spoken of, he'd most likely done many terrible things. She shuddered at the thought. She was in an isolated location where her only hope was for her brother to get help. Her heart caught in her throat. If Quinn wanted her isolated, he'd never allow Declan time to call for help. It'd defeat the entire purpose of the location. He'd also been alone with Diana, threatening her life. Suddenly she was very afraid of him.

"You can do this," she assured herself. Hearing it made a big difference and she'd say it over and over again, as if it would help.

With Quinn and the whole tied up thing to deal with, she pushed the thoughts of what her brother had done aside. Oh, he told her Quinn had promised he wouldn't hurt her. He only wanted to talk with her. Maybe that made him feel better, until the jerk had tied her. Declan had gone a bit ballistic at that. She couldn't think of that right now. She'd sort it all out later.

Her heart leapt. Success. She'd broken through the wrist restraints. It took a few moments of shaking her hands to regain the blood flow. Once done, she went to task on the ankle restraints. That process went faster as she had the strength of both hands in the sawing motion.

While the feeling returned to her feet, she laced her shoe, then checked her watch. With a rapidly beating pulse, she nodded. "A midnight escape then." As she stood, that second of bravado left. Fear clawed at her with adrenaline rushing through her veins. She needed a way out. She'd heard a deadbolt on the front door being locked, but she frantically checked it anyway.

Her luck didn't hold out. It needed a key. She pushed on the door anyway, just in case, but was disappointed.

Not dwelling on that setback, she went to the first window she could find and unlocked it. It didn't budge. She tried the other three and had no luck. Not to be deterred, she frantically looked around the cabin for something to break one of these blasted windows. Her only option was furniture. The chair it was.

She hefted the kitchen table chair she'd been sitting

on and brought it to the window. It was awkward, and she had to set it down and resettle her grip to get the chair leg up high enough. Once there, she hit the window hard. To her utter dismay, it only cracked. So, she hit it again and again until, on the third try, it broke, and large pieces of glass slipped down the wall, shattering as they hit the floor.

It took more work and the muscles in her arms were burning, but she had to get all of the glass out of the window. She didn't relish a cut deep enough for stitches, and she couldn't get to a hospital before she bled to death.

Her adrenaline screamed, but she knew her time was limited, so she decided she'd made it safe enough. She took off her sandal and used it to wipe the glass from the frame to spare her hands from being shredded.

The window wasn't large, so she either had to go head or leg first. Not far from the ground, she went leg first. Not that she would have chosen headfirst if it had been higher off the ground. Legs first was the smart choice.

Then she halted and her heart throbbed in her chest. This was too easy. Maybe he wanted her to escape just to catch her again and pay her back by torturing her in some way. She had to mentally flip a coin—heads, it was safe and tails, danger awaited. She almost laughed. Danger awaited either way because, at some point, Quinn would be coming. With that thought, she decided to screw the coin and take a chance.

So, out the window she went, and she fell back on her

rear when she landed. She didn't have time to soothe her wounded pride at such an ungraceful landing. She had to get moving.

Panic hit her once she realized she had no idea where she was or how to find help. It made sense to follow the road at the end of the driveway. Glancing back and forth, she had no idea which way to use as her escape.

Moira could end up going in the wrong direction. One way remained open field while the other started with open field that turned to woods. The perfect place for her to hide if someone like Quinn drove that way. She wished Danny was here.

She legged it across the open field, dreading going into the woods, even though she knew it was a smart idea. Almost to the cover, the beam of a car's headlights broke through the darkness. Her heart leapt in fright. Quinn. Who else would be coming to this place at midnight? She picked up the speed to a run over the uneven field. She stumbled but caught herself and kept going.

The car came into view as she slipped into cover. Frantic to escape, she plunged in the near darkness, forgetting the need to continue following the road. It briefly occurred to her she could get lost, but needing to get away overrode common sense.

Bushes scratched her legs where her capris didn't cover them as she moved through the woods. When she heard her name yelled, she stopped for a moment, fear freezing her limbs. She couldn't see behind her, but she'd bet Quinn was there. Every now and then, Quinn yelled her name, and she could swear it was closer.

Now she rushed, unseen limbs swatting her in the head. She tripped over a bush and fell, her hands catching her before she smacked her face on the ground. When she stood, she moved forward again, and ran into something solid.

She opened her mouth to scream, but a hand covered it, and she was spun around and pulled up against a body. Her mind screamed, *He was waiting.*

Chapter Thirty-Five

Danny had purposefully put himself in Moira's path. He hadn't accounted for her not being able to see him. Since he doubted she'd been released, it appeared she'd freed herself. He had no idea how, but pride for her swam through his system. Traveling here, his fear of being too late had reached a level he almost thought unmanageable. Now, he held her safe in his arms. His heart swelled with love. In an effort to remove her panic, he leaned down and whispered in her ear, "I'm here. Don't cry out."

Her body relaxed against him, and he took that to mean she trusted him. Well, rescued more than she'd already accomplished. He and the agents had planned an all-out assault on the cabin to free her. With photos to study, their new sniper was ready to take out Quinn if needed to save Moira.

She nodded. When he removed his hand, it was wet from her tears. That hurt or fear from her nearly broke his heart.

Tears burned the edge of his eyelids, so grateful that he'd found her safe and unharmed. Or she appeared unharmed. He'd kill the bastard Quinn if he'd injured her.

He should release her, but she felt so good in his arms that he couldn't bring himself to do so. He hadn't been there to protect her, but he could hold her while she needed the connection. He loved this woman and would hold her whenever she wished. He'd be there to chase her demons away. First, they had to catch this demon. Yet, he wouldn't release her a moment before he absolutely had to do so.

Boss came close and leaned in. "Tell us what you can," he whispered. "Quietly."

When she didn't pull away but appeared to sway toward Danny, he decided to keep holding her. Like the need to breathe, Danny had to touch her. Had to feel she was safe.

"Quinn is chasing me."

"Only him?" Boss asked.

She nodded, but he doubted Boss could see since he'd lifted his NVGs. But the going bet was Boss was superhuman.

"Wait," she said, "there was a guy earlier. He left with Declan, but I only heard Quinn calling for me."

"Okay. Danny's going to take you to safety."

Danny bristled. He wanted a piece of Quinn, yet he didn't want to leave Moira. During the flight, all the ways he'd make the man pay had worked through his mind. Now, he was left with only one focus. Moira. His heart swelled. She was more important than chasing Quinn. The team would take care of him. So he followed his boss's orders and leaned down to Moira while the twins moved forward, followed by Cowboy and Doc.

"Let's go. I want you to hold my hand and follow in my footsteps." Luckily, he had night vision gear, but she didn't. He hoped she could follow him safely. "Until we hear different, we're still moving through the woods." Meaning Quinn had been captured and everyone was assured no other threat existed. "Are you okay to travel?" He should've asked that first. But she'd made it this far, and something told him she'd make it to safety. His little artist made him proud. She was now an escape artist, finding her way out of whatever situation confined her.

She nodded again.

He wanted to tell her he loved her, but since it'd be the first time she heard it, now didn't seem the right time. "Let's go." He finally let go of her but immediately took her hand.

They eventually left the woods for the road; it took longer to return to the bird since the pace had been adjusted for Moira. What would she say once she found out about the trackers? He grew more apprehensive about telling her. He had no idea how she'd react. They had saved her. Well, she might've made it to civilization on her own. She was at least headed in the right direction. But the team wouldn't have been there to clean up the scene by taking Quinn into custody. Still, he had to tell her. Like a chicken, now was not the time.

At the bird, Boss took up a protective position but informed Danny to see to Moira. Here they could use a light, and he cringed when he saw the lower half of her calves. They were a bloody mess. At first, he wanted to rail at the man she'd told him had tied her up, but he realized it was from her trek through the woods. With that knowledge, he felt partly responsible for some of the wounds.

Quietly, she cried, and her breathing became difficult. Danny didn't acknowledge the tears as he figured she needed the time to decompress. It hurt him, though. He listened to her breathing in case she had an attack.

She worked hard to keep silent, but the sniffing of a stuffed-up nose gave her away. He didn't look up but offered a tissue pack and her inhaler from his kit, thankful he'd snatched an inhaler his home before heading to HQ.

After she blew her nose and took a puff from her inhaler, she informed him, "Declan told me you and Justin were just keeping me safe until Boyle could slip into the country."

How she planned to treat Declan after this deceit, he didn't know. Being the recipient of his actions would be a heavy weight to carry, for anyone. Even more so since the siblings were close. Danny finally looked up to her bright eyes cast in the shadows of the flashlight positioned by her legs. "And do you still believe it?"

She shook her head. "I'm not sure I truly believed it

then. I just couldn't take the chance since Boyle was on his way." She straightened like a thought just occurred to her. "Boyle. Has he been captured?"

Danny gently reached up and touched her thigh to calm down the near hysteria that accompanied her last statement. "Calm down. He's in custody. All the stuff Justin provided will help keep him there."

"I'm sorry."

Danny smiled. He could forgive her anything. It burned that she hadn't trusted him—well, maybe she still trusted him—but she was put in an unusual situation where she trusted the wrong person. "It's okay."

Then he noticed her lips tremble and a tear leak down her cheek. "He traded me."

He stilled one hand hovering over her calf with an antiseptic wipe. "I'm sure he hates that he had to."

"But he didn't have to. He could've chosen to save me."

Unable to imagine the war going on inside her, he remained quiet and went back to tending to her wounds.

"That's wrong and selfish of me," she said.

He looked up and gave her a small smile. "To me it sounds about right."

"Have you heard from him? Did he call you and tell you about me?"

There was so much hope in her voice that he didn't want to disappoint her. "Diana freed herself first and called us. We've since learned your brother overcame his captor and made it safely back to Boston."

Before they could chat more, the team arrived in a car he guessed was Quinn's, since no other had been in the area. Of course, with the twins, he was learning to expect the unexpected. The team itself was a resourceful lot. Quinn seemed to be talking nonstop. When the agents and Quinn got close, Danny heard "You have no right to hold me. I've come to rescue Moira and take her back to Ireland."

"The authorities might disagree with whether we can detain you," Doc said. "They'll hold you for kidnapping, first of all. But give us time. We'll figure out more."

It was time to get home. The team would—if they hadn't already—find out if Quinn had a partner. The last thing they needed was to accept things were done when they weren't. Danny needed Moira safe and able to make her own decisions, without danger hanging over her head. Danny wanted her like she was when she first arrived before they stifled her freedom.

As the rotor blades began to turn, Danny heard Cowboy. "Moira, you're the first hot chick to hitch a ride with us."

Danny closed his eyes. Cowboy was enjoying playing Russian roulette too much. Before Danny could open his eyes, he heard what he'd expected.

"Man down," several agents said with laughter in their voices.

Chapter Thirty-Six

They couldn't get their clothes off fast enough. Moira was so happy AJ had released her and Danny, while the others dealt with the authorities. Tomorrow, she'd have to talk with someone, but tonight, she wanted Danny. It was technically tomorrow already, but that wouldn't stop them. She wanted his arms around her and his cock inside her.

Her nerves were still wired from the events of the night. Thank goodness Danny and his team had shown up. She'd been having trouble navigating and hadn't had a big enough head start. Her fright had nearly weighed her down. But she'd been lucky with her hands being tied in front, shoes with laces, and her capturer underestimating her. She might not be a karate-chopping heroine, but she could hold her own. Especially when her life was on the line.

Quinn swore he only wanted to talk. If that had been

the case, he could've stopped by Danny's, not threatened Diana's life.

She dropped her capris and stepped out of them. They'd almost made it to the stairs and she had already lost her shirt and pants. Well, and shoes, since she'd never have gotten her capris off. Danny was down to his underwear, and he was dropping them now.

She giggled at how furiously they were disrobing. She'd read about it, seen it on TV, but never felt this urgency to have sex. Not just sex. She expected mind-blowing sex. Honestly, sex with Danny was what was called for.

Reaching around her back for her bra clasp, she gave him a saucy smile. She wasn't sure if she pulled it off, but Danny growled before pulling her close and kissing her nearly breathless. His mouth moved over hers with the care of an expert lover before his tongue dipped into her mouth. She loved kissing him.

Sexual awareness zinged through her body and settled between her thighs. Oh yeah, she planned to fuck the hell out of this man.

"Bed or floor?" he asked in a raspy voice, his lips still touching hers. Before she could answer, he lifted his forehead to hers. "Bed, of course. Your injuries."

She wanted it bad, cuts, scrapes, and bruises be damned. She planned to enjoy every moment of their naked tumble in the sheets.

He broke away, looked down at her lace panties and smiled. Grabbing her hand, he led her up the stairs and to his room.

"Get them off now," he said, as they entered his room.

He wouldn't have to ask twice. She quickly dropped her panties and stepped out of them.

Next thing she knew, her back was to the door he'd just shut and his arms imprisoned her. It was erotic as hell. She knew a tiger lived in this man. He played the alpha male well outside the bedroom. Not that he hadn't been an excellent and attentive lover, but he'd never been like this.

"This is for you leaving without a goodbye." He lowered his head and gave her a hard, bruising kiss. One meant as punishment. One that made her knees weak.

He pulled back. "This one is for rescuing yourself." She knew he struggled with not getting there in time to rescue her, but he'd shown up in time to bring her home. She could've gotten lost.

This kiss was soft and sensual. This kiss went to her core. As he nibbled on her lips, every nerve ending was on fire. She needed this man.

Barely managing to get a hand between them, she pushed back. He didn't really move, but he seemed to get the point. Then he did something romantic. He leaned down and put his arms behind her knees, his other behind her back, and picked her up. He brought her to the bed and placed her there with raw lust in his eyes.

Standing beside the bed, Danny took the opportunity to study her before he knelt on the floor and kissed the side of her breast. Then he wrapped his hand around it and suckled her nipple. Lightning shot to her already wired core. He licked, nipped, and sucked until she thought she'd go mad.

When he stopped and stood, she thought it was time. But nay, he knelt between her thighs. That particular part of oral sex was always amazing, but she wanted him inside her. Now. "I want you. Now."

He just grinned at her. She wanted to swat his head. At least he didn't laugh.

"I want you good and ready for me. I want your every thought, feeling, and breath pleading for me to be deep inside you. Make no mistake, I will be deep inside you. Only now, your every thought, feeling, and breath are not for me."

Even though she melted a little at his words, she didn't think she could handle that kind of loving. But she just smiled back as he laid down between her thighs. His breath tickled and excited her. He used his hands to separate her lips, before giving her pussy one long, slow lick as if savoring her taste.

Then he found her nub and her core sizzled. Once he began licking and sucking it, she knew his plan was for her to orgasm before they had sex. It was selfish, but she wouldn't argue with him. She was close enough already.

He alternated with sensual strokes between her lips and torturing her nub. Torturing her in general was more like it. Then she felt it. The boulder that started the fall. It built and built until she shouted, "Danny!" Moira flew, floating down on a cloud soft, weightless, and euphoric. He'd accomplished his goal. Her every thought, feeling, and breath screamed for him to be inside her.

While she lay there like a limp noodle, he reached into his bedside stand, took out a condom, opened the package, and sheathed himself. Then, as if he hadn't left her, he inched his way up her body, trailing kisses along the way. After he loved on one breast then the other, he looked at her and tossed her a cocky grin. And she loved that expression on him.

"Now's the time." His raspy voice started that fire again.

To her satisfaction, he positioned himself at her entrance.

"You're good and wet," he murmured.

"I wonder why that is." She bet she was after that incredible orgasm. But it wasn't enough. There was another fire growing, and he needed to put it out.

Danny entered her slowly, and it drove her nuts. She knew he could enter fast; he'd done it before. He wanted to torture her more.

When he was fully seated, Moira moaned in pleasure. Finally.

"You feel so good," he said in a raspy voice, as he remained still above her.

"So do you." Danny felt good all right. She could stay like this forever. Forever? No. Even with all that had happened to her by men from her home country, Ireland was in her heart.

Before she considered the topic further, he moved inside her. With each slow thrust, the fire in her core strengthened. She wasn't sure there was enough water to put it out. Or bring it to a head.

She shifted her leg to change positions, but he halted her move. "Let me love you," he said. Then he lowered his head to her breast. He knew just how to increase her pleasure by loving on her breasts.

Taking his time, his even thrusts in and out drove her to the brink. With her legs wrapped around his hips, sweat glistened on their bodies, making them slick to the touch.

"You make it hard to hold back," he said.

This was a no-brainer. "Then don't hold back."

"You first."

He didn't have to ask twice on that score. Moira focused on his thrusting and shifted a bit for more stimulation. Within a minute, her fire became a brushfire and she headed for release, ready for the relief from the heat inside her. She climbed a mountain and then she fell. It took longer for the fire to die than she expected. It had a lot to do with Danny and his climax, which was on the heels of hers, and he pulsed inside her.

After a moment, he rolled off her and went to dispose of the condom. Returning to the bed, he pulled her into his arms and kissed the top of her head.

"I love you."

Moira stiffened at the admission. Shocked. Did he really mean it? What did that mean for them? She wasn't in love with him, was she? Okay, she liked him more than any guy she'd dated, but love? Nay.

Unsure what to say, she said nothing.

Chapter Thirty-Seven

After telling Moira he loved her and getting nothing in return, Danny was fit to be tied. The two of them had to report back to HIS where Moira would meet with a DEA agent to discuss what she'd overheard—or had recorded—plus her kidnapping. While she was tied up with the agent, Danny sought his team leader.

Sitting alone with Boss, and maybe being in such a sour mood, he voiced his fear. "Sometimes I don't feel like I'm good enough."

Boss eyed him before speaking. "Is this in reference to HIS or a young lady?"

Danny snorted at that. Both, but that wasn't what he wanted to discuss with his boss. "No, when I led the team, sometimes I felt inferior to the spec ops guys. I know the brothers put me through an intensive training, but I need more. My background is DEA."

"There'll always be someone better at some things.

That's their specialty. We count on the team to do things we can't and shouldn't. Like Doc—specialized. Cowboy—crazy but specialized. The twins—specialized. Do you think you can be all those and lead a mission?"

"No. But—" Boss broke in before he could say that Boss could do all that. Danny knew that now that he was their helicopter pilot, he was valuable to the teams, but he wanted to be even better on the ground.

"Would it make you feel better if Cowboy, Doc, and I teach you deeper skills? Ones that we've used, even though we're from different branches of the military?"

He brightened. "Yes. Definitely yes."

"Understand, no matter how much you learn, your skillset needs to be leadership. Never lose that focus."

He and Boss fist bumped before his team leader left. The easy thing would've been asking the men directly. Easy didn't come into play when someone's pride held strong.

Danny wasn't alone long because Justin arrived to meet with the DEA agent Moira was currently with.

"What's wrong?" Justin asked, as he took a seat in a chair in the lounge.

"Is it that obvious?"

"Yeah."

"Well, it's personal."

"I won't judge." A grin spread across Justin's face.

"It's nothing like that, pervert." Danny laughed, glad to know his brother could bring him back from a mood. "It's just— I mean— Well, I told Moira I loved her, and she didn't say anything."

Justin looked serious. "Was she awake?"

"Yeah." She'd been plenty worn out, but she'd been awake.

"Did you read her wrong thinking she would say the same thing to you?"

Had he? He knew she was a free spirit, but he could've sworn she felt more for him than a fling. "I guess I did." And that put him back in a mood. He didn't want to lose her. He'd planned to agree to several trips to Ireland a year. He'd find a way to pay for them. He just wanted her happy, and he knew leaving her homeland forever would not do that.

"Cheer up. You've still got time. They can't go home until I straighten out their fake deaths." Justin grinned, and Danny laughed. His brother had his back.

Getting serious, Danny asked, "Did you go see Mom?"

Justin exhaled loudly. "Yes. She chastised me so much I had to leave."

Danny burst out laughing. "She is good at that."

"It was like she built it all up during these years."

"Yeah, but I bet she also spoiled you."

A sheepish grin escaped his brother. "Yeah, she made my favorite cookies, did my laundry. She even ironed my jeans."

"They've got him." Danny didn't need to explain to his brother the change of topic. He'd know the meaning. The authorities had their father's killer. Well, the man who'd ordered it. They already had the actual killer.

Justin gave a slight nod of understanding. His "Yeah" left Danny wondering why he didn't sound happy.

"It's about time."

"Sorry I couldn't move faster," Justin said.

"You did what you had to do."

"You know, all this time I worried you blamed me for Dad's death."

An unsettling feeling dropped into his gut. "At first I did. Then I got the facts." He'd kept that anger for too long.

"I heard about the kidnapping and all. You've been a busy boy."

Yeah, he'd been busy. In more ways than one. "Did you hear she rescued herself?" Pride infused his voice.

"I heard you flew. Just like Dad."

In the past, when he was taking courses or training, Danny would bristle when Justin said that. But Justin hadn't been the problem; Danny's disappointment was because he should've finished his flight training before his father had died. He wanted his dad to have seen him as a pilot.

"Yeah." That was all there was to say about it.

Moira approached them, and Justin got up for his turn with the DEA agent.

"All done?" Danny asked, knowing she was unless the agent had asked for more.

"Yes. I'm hungry. Can we get something to eat on the way home?"

"Sure." He loved this woman so deeply it almost hurt. He had to find a way into her heart. He couldn't bear the thought of her leaving.

Realizing they had plenty of privacy, Danny decided to push his point. "Come here." Before he fully opened his arms, she'd launched herself at him. He inhaled her scent and knew she'd ruined him for other women.

Taking the biggest leap of his life, he gave her body a tight squeeze and lowered his voice near her ear. "We've been good together, haven't we?"

A rub on his chest was her response.

Moving his hand up and down her back to help relax her, he put his chin on the top of her head. "I know it's only been a few months, but I want to spend more time with you. I want you to stay here. With me." He needed her with him. He had to find a way for them. Otherwise, his heart would never recover.

Pulling her head back, she looked at him. "As lovers?"

He cleared his throat, hoping to wipe away his nervousness. "I see us getting married in about six months. I'd like it sooner, but I hear women need time to prepare."

She searched his eyes. "My home?"

His forefinger traced her cheekbone with a featherlight touch. "We'll take care of your Visa after you marry me."

With a tremulous smile, she said, "I know, but—"

Her argument shoved a jagged knife in his heart, tearing it to shreds and leaving him sick to his stomach.

Chapter Thirty-Eight

As Moira climbed the stairs to the studio, she silently asked herself, *how do I come to terms with what my brother did? He handed me over to the bad guy.* Then she thoughtfully added, *to save the life of his lover and unborn child.*

She remembered growing up with Declan as her hero. He'd saved her from monsters under her bed, had kissed her wounds like her *mam*. He'd snuck her cookies when she'd broken her ankle, and he'd pulled Donovan O'Leary off her when his advances went too far. He was always there to love and protect her.

In her heart, he could do no wrong. And until recently, he never had. As far as she knew. Although he had already planned for her to leave Ireland with him and Diana, without informing her.

What a dilemma he must've faced then. Stop loving Diana or leave all he knew and uproot all he loved for their safety?

He'd never have stopped loving Diana. Just like she'd never stop loving him. They had no choice.

Although she wished she hadn't had to leave, she'd eventually understood when she'd overhead Justin describing to Danny the torture Boyle had inflicted in an effort to find them.

Which meant she wasn't angry with her brother about the move. For not telling her before they left, aye.

That brought her to his second big dilemma. Diana and his unborn baby versus her. She closed her eyes to think of how hard that must've been for him. One person he loved versus the other. And to be given the added reality of watching Diana die.

Danny had given her the basics to include Declan's plan to call Danny immediately and keep Quinn occupied long enough for he and his team to rescue her.

Only Declan hadn't called. The henchman had taken Declan's phone. Even if he'd stopped, her brother couldn't have called. He hadn't memorized Danny's cell number. It was programmed into his lost phone. No, his only hope was to call as soon as he arrived and Quinn left, hoping it was enough time for the team.

In a fit of bad luck, Quinn had already departed. Once he'd been notified she was at the cabin, he'd left Diana, thinking he'd taken her only cell phone. Her first call had been to Danny. Thank the Saints.

How did she feel about her brother after that? She was hurt and wasn't sure she could forgive him. Was she being selfish when part of her wished he'd chosen her?

She realized he had no choice unless he wanted to lose his child and the woman he'd given up everything for.

It was an impossible situation.

Moira closed her eyes again at the visual of how Quinn had described killing their unborn child. She hated Quinn with every fiber of her being. How could they have been so wrong about him? Poor Cassie, when she found out.... Moira wished she could be there for her.

After the confirmation of Quinn's voice on the recording, Danny said he was probably responsible for more illegal dealings. He assured her that Devon, Stone, and Emily would find out.

She really didn't care what else he'd done. He had put her brother in an unthinkable situation.

A knock sounded on the studio door, and Danny peeked his head in the room. He was so handsome and caring and gentle yet strong. And his touch made her feel more alive than she thought possible. How could she not love him?

"Your brother's here to see you. Do you want to see him? If not, I'll gladly toss him out on his ass."

A smile blossomed on her face at his protectiveness. She loved that about him. Loved? Declan was here, so she should push her brother away until she figured out all her crazy emotions, but she needed to see him.

"It's okay. I'll see him." It appeared Declan had followed Danny, so Danny had said those things so her brother would know he wasn't welcome in his home.

Declan entered, rushed forward, then stopped, obviously unsure if he was welcome.

"Moira, thank God you're safe. I'm sorry. He didn't give me a choice. He had a gun to Diana's temple and a wicked-looking blade at her belly. I'm sorry. I know you can probably never forgive me, but I'd planned to get Danny to rescue you, but Diana beat me to it. I'm sorry," he said for the third time.

When she'd thought to rail at him, his words doused her anger.

"Declan, you're right, I may never forgive you."

He dropped his head, and his posture screamed defeat.

"But you're my brother, my only living family. Well, except for Aunt Margaret and all her cats."

He looked up and smiled at her words.

"I know the terrible position you were in with Quinn. It's just going to take time for me to come to terms with you delivering me to him, even after how he threatened Diana."

"Again, I'm sorry. I don't know what else to say to make it right between us."

"Let's start with giving me time." To get off the sore subject, she asked a question. "Now that Boyle is in custody, will you and Diana go back to Ireland?" It quickly occurred to her she hadn't added "with me." That had nothing to do with what her brother had done.

"As soon as Minister Donnelly is arrested, yeah.

Our lives are there, and I don't want to start a new one here. We're hoping our baby will be born in Ireland." It occurred to her if they'd planned to stay, there'd be the whole passport issue. "Are you coming or are you staying?"

She bristled. "Why would I stay?"

"I don't know, a tall—I can say this because I'm safe in my masculinity—handsome agent who's in love with you."

She wanted to be flippant and say, "Oh him," but the idea of staying was too serious. "I'm going home." That's what she'd wanted these past few months.

As if sensing her need to think, her brother said goodbye and left her alone.

She loved Ireland. Her home. But she'd come to love Baltimore also. She wanted to go home; she just wasn't ready. She wanted more time with Danny.

When she and Declan left Danny's home a couple of nights prior, all she'd thought about was whether Danny worked for Boyle and how he'd reacted to her leaving. He'd been hurt, and that somehow made her feel her brother's information had been wrong. But her thoughts hadn't been because of love.

When she was in the cabin, all she thought about was Danny. But that was because she knew he could rescue her. Not because of love. And when she thought Quinn might kill her after he talked to her, all she thought of was Danny. Not because he could rescue her, but because—

She straightened. Being the last person she was

thinking of before death—unless it's the killer—must mean something. Dare she say love? She couldn't live without him and not because of her situation. She couldn't leave because she couldn't leave Danny.

It boiled down to her being in love. Her body lightened as if a heavy weight had been lifted. It must've been denial.

"I love him," she acknowledged out loud. Then excitedly, she said, "Oh, I have to tell him."

"Tell who what? Do I need to get Declan back? Please say no."

Dumbfounded, she stared.

Danny shifted his feet like a schoolboy. "I just came to check on you. I don't know how things ended with your brother, but I wanted to be here for you."

How sweet and thoughtful. This man was perfect. "Yes," she blurted.

"Yes, you need me to get Declan?"

She shook her head and settled the butterflies in her stomach. "I love you, and aye, I'll stay, assuming you can make me legal in the US."

He walked forward, wrapped his arms around her, picked her up and spun her around.

Giggling, she enjoyed the ride.

Once he stopped, he held her until she caught her balance. He pulled back and placed his hands on her cheeks. "You've made me the happiest man."

He leaned in and their lips barely touched, and she wanted to cry out, but he did it several times, as if kissing every inch of her lips. Then, his kiss deepened until he coaxed her lips to open her mouth. Complying, she accepted his tongue as the two sealed their future together.

Epilogue

When Justin arrived, Danny wasn't surprised. They'd learned the DEA didn't have enough to charge Boyle with conspiracy to commit murder. But Boyle had traded product with the US. So the DEA had plenty other charges they felt were strong enough to send Boyle away for a long time.

"You heard?" Justin asked, as he entered Danny's home. The bruising had faded.

"Yeah," Danny said, following his brother to the living room. Once seated, he asked, "What are you going to do now?"

Justin sighed and leaned forward, forearms on thighs, hands clasped tight. "I don't know. I mean, my résumé does not inspire potential employers."

He'd been waiting for his brother to settle and look forward. Sometimes patience won. "HIS is interviewing for a third team and for open spots on the other teams."

The hopeful look on Justin's face clenched his heart. His brother had suffered trying to bring down Boyle. "Don't think they'll give you any special treatment for being my brother. You have to earn the position."

"Do you think they'll even look at me after working for Boyle?"

"Explain why. It can't hurt. I think you're worthy of a spot on the team. Besides," he smiled, "It'll be nice not to be the only former DEA agent."

"All right. I'll do it. I mean, the worse they can do is turn me down. Right?"

"Right. Did you hear about Quinn?"

He shook his head. "Nothing after the kidnapping."

"AJ informed me Quinn had been in deeper than everyone had expected. Emily found his Swiss bank account with an outrageous sum. How she found it, I don't know and, like AJ, I didn't ask."

"What the fuck?" Justin asked.

"He was a puppet master blackmailing a good bit of parliament and high levels in the *garda* for favors." When Justin nodded, he continued, "He all but ran Donnelly—his boss—who easily gave Quinn up. He had millions squirreled away."

Justin whistled. "I never expected that. No wonder he wanted to know what Moira heard. It would've jeopardized everything if she'd known something incriminating. I'm glad we handed off the tape."

"Ireland wants Quinn, and since the US only had him on kidnapping charges, they plan to send him back across the pond." With more ministers coming forward about the blackmailing, Danny doubted Quinn would fare well in court.

"You need to go see Mom," Justin said.

"Moira and I are planning to do it next month.

"Oh, so she's staying?"

Danny grinned. "She is."

Justin chuckled. "Good for you. She's definitely a keeper."

"That she is." In the week since it'd all gone wrong, he and Moira had been nearly inseparable. Except for when he worked, and, like now, when she painted. She planned to become independent again with her art and save the money from her parents for the future.

Soon, she'd be down. Declan and Diana were stopping by to say goodbye. Moira was torn about their leaving and about the situation they had all endured.

"Speak of the devil," Justin said, standing.

Danny stood and turned to view the staircase. With her hair in that messy bun thing, wearing strappy sandals, yellow capris, and a floral-print shirt, Moira was a vision. His heart did a little flip every time he saw her.

She came right to him and pressed her lips to his. It was a brief, modest kiss, but it still sent heat to his *coileach*. Yeah, he'd learned a few Irish words from her. He'd had to ask when she'd called his dick that.

Their sex life had become very inventive, and he loved every minute of the love and joy she brought into his life.

He looked forward to the future they'd been planning, which included a large family.

A Note From Sheila

Thank you for reading *Midnight Escape*! If you enjoyed reading Danny and Moira's story, I would appreciate it if you would help others enjoy this book, too. You can do that by recommending it to friends, readers' groups, and discussion boards. It would mean a great deal to me if you'd take a moment to write a review and share how you feel about my story so others may find my work. Honest reviews help bring my books to the attention of other readers. Best news, only a few words are needed. Here's a quick link to this book on Amazon: Midnight Escape

About The Author

Sheila Kell writes about the romantic men who leave women's hearts pounding with a happily ever after built on memorable, adrenaline-pumping stories. Or, (since her editor tries to cut down on her long-windedness) simply "Smokin' Hot Romance & Intrigue." Her debut novel, *His Desire* (HIS Series #1), launched as an Amazon #1 romantic suspense bestseller and Top 100 overall, later winning the Readers' Favorite award for best romantic suspense novel.

As a Southern girl who has left behind her days with the United States Air Force and as a University Vice President, she can usually be found nestled in the Mississippi woods, where she lives with her cats and all the strays that magically find her front door. When she isn't writing, you can find Sheila with her nose in a good book, dealing with the woodland critters who enjoy her back porch, or wishing she had a genie to do her bidding.

Sheila is a proud member of Romance Writers of America.

For more information, visit Sheila's website and subscribe to her newsletter: WWW.SHEILAKELLBOOKS.COM

You may also find and follow Sheila on:

FACEBOOK: @SHEILAKELLBOOKS

INSTAGRAM: @SHEILAKELLBOOKS

GOODREADS: @SHEILAKELLBOOKS

BOOKBUB: /AUTHORS/SHEILA-KELL

AMAZON: /AUTHOR/SHEILAKELL

Join Sheila's Facebook Reader Group:
Sheila's Smokin' Hot Heroines

Contact Sheila for information on her advance teams and other ways to follow: sheila@sheilakell.com

Books by Sheila Kell

Hamilton Investigation & Security: H I S Series

HIS DESIRE

He's stubborn. She's independent. Together, desire will determine their future.

Will his stubbornness prevent him from trusting the woman he desires? In Sheila Kell's provocative novel of suspicion and need, a handsome security specialist and a feisty FBI agent are tied by grief and attraction… and the fervor of the unknown.

HIS CHOICE

Every choice requires a decision, but some choices are determined by the heart.

Will his choice mean certain death to the woman he promised to protect? In Sheila Kell's passionate novel of deception and desire, a smoking-hot enforcer and a determined reporter are destined to make choices that will change everything.

HIS RETURN

Only his return can determine her future.

Will the actions of his past prevent him from returning to the woman in his heart? In Sheila Kell's sensual novel of secrets and unrequited love, a wounded operative, and a strong-willed accountant have to decide if the future can only be determined by the past.

HIS CHANCE

One steamy night in Vegas will change everything.

What happens when one hot night in Vegas irrevocably changes his future? In Sheila Kell's sexy novel of second chances and risks, a red-hot computer nerd and a stubborn ex-FBI agent are drawn together by an undeniable attraction and the chance to save lives.

HIS DESTINY

Despite their secrets, he'll discover she's always been his destiny.

What happens when his destiny leads him into the arms of the woman he doesn't think he deserves? In Sheila Kell's passionate novel of distrust and desire, a damaged man and a broken woman are connected by heartbreak and danger… and the heat of possibility.

HIS FAMILY

When family stands together anything is possible.

What happens when a man used to being in control has to call in his family to rescue the woman he loves? In Sheila Kell's novella of danger and desire, a charismatic U.S. Senator and an assertive CEO are connected by the love they share. A love about to be ripped out from beneath them.

HIS HEART

His heart is hers.

What happens when a man is called to protect the woman who captured then crushed his heart? In Sheila Kell's story of danger and second chances, two people are connected by a painful past and a love that is threatened.

HIS FANTASY

Fantasies can come true.

Can one man capture the heart of the one woman who walked away from him? In Sheila Kell's novel of conspiracies and desire, a fierce protector refuses to let go of the one complicated woman whose life he feels is threatened.

A HAMILTON CHRISTMAS

While some may try, no one ruins a Hamilton family Christmas.

What happens when a family comes together for Christmas but upon arrival their vacation takes a deadly turn? In Sheila Kell's novel of intrigue and the love of one family, three generations of Hamiltons work to solve a mystery that impacts one of their own.

Agents of H I S Series

EVENING SHADOWS

When deception leads to vengeance, it's only your heart you can trust.

When his life depends on the woman who holds secrets, can he trust their love will be enough for her to seek the truth? In Sheila Kell's thrilling novel of deception and second chances, two operatives embark on a dangerous journey that will test them as agents, friends, and lovers.

MIDNIGHT ESCAPE

When danger hides in plain sight.

What happens when danger is where one least expects it? In Sheila Kell's thrilling novel of desire and betrayal, a fierce protector and an artist are tied together by a potential threat from thousands of miles away.

Made in the USA
Columbia, SC
08 October 2024

43296104R00221